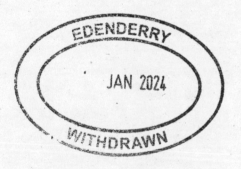

Phantom Limbs

Phantom Limbs

Paula Garner

WALKER
BOOKS

First published in Great Britain 2017 by Walker Books Ltd
87 Vauxhall Walk, London SE11 5HJ

2 4 6 8 10 9 7 5 3

Text © 2017 Paula Garner

This book has been typeset in Dante MT

Printed and bound in Great Britain by Clays Ltd, St Ives plc

British Library Cataloguing in Publication Data:
a catalogue record for this book is available from the British Library

ISBN 978-1-4063-7321-9

www.walker.co.uk

For Zach

When to the sessions of sweet silent thought

I summon up remembrance of things past,

I sigh the lack of many a thing I sought,

And with old woes new wail my dear time's waste:

Then can I drown an eye, unused to flow,

For precious friends hid in death's dateless night,

And weep afresh love's long since cancelled woe,

And moan the expense of many a vanished sight:

Then can I grieve at grievances foregone,

And heavily from woe to woe tell o'er

The sad account of fore-bemoanèd moan,

Which I new pay as if not paid before.

But if the while I think on thee, dear friend,

All losses are restored and sorrows end.

WILLIAM SHAKESPEARE, "SONNET 30"

1

WHEN I FINALLY HEARD FROM MEG, IT WAS
May, historically her month of choice for upending my
universe. It was the ungodly hour of swim o'clock – I was
checking my messages in the dark with one eye half open,
synapses barely firing, when the sight of Meg's name in my
inbox jolted me awake. But with Dara due at any moment to
lasso me for another morning of abuse in the pool, there was
no time to process Meg's brief message, let alone respond.
I grabbed a pack of blueberry Pop-Tarts from the kitchen
cabinet and headed out.

The morning was a hazy purple, chilly enough to make
my breath mist. I guided the screen door closed so it wouldn't
bang and wake my parents – a pointless gesture, since Dara's
style of arrival in her ancient, souped-up Corolla could jar
the fillings right out of your teeth. I tossed my backpack

and my swim bag under the magnolia and sat down to wait for her. I reread Meg's message, then turned my eyes to the house next door that I still thought of as hers.

It was the first time I'd heard from her since we said goodbye in her bedroom, just us and the dust bunnies that had been hiding under the furniture, her parents waiting outside with the moving truck. I clung to her in that empty, echoing room as if the last thing that mattered to me in all the world was being taken away. Which, after the cluster-fuck of the preceding year, it basically was. And there wasn't enough thirteen-year-old swagger in the known universe to keep me from bawling.

Minutes later they pulled away, Meg gazing out the win-dow at me through teary eyes. She might as well have driven right off the face of the earth, because I never heard from her again. Until now, that is. A mere three years and four months later, not that I was keeping track.

Moving on was never my strong suit.

I opened my Pop-Tarts and gazed at the horizon's pink glow, breathing in the smell of rain and earth. On the branches above me, I could just make out the fat magnolia buds. Any day now they would explode into a fucking car-nival of white and pink flowers – a spectacle that had kicked me in the nuts for the last three years. But now? Now I didn't know how to feel about it.

Four springs before, the most amazing thing happened

under this tree. My best friend and I were moving out of childhood and into uncharted territory. Our bodies were catching up with us – Meg's more overtly than mine, but what I lacked in physical maturity I made up for with a Herculean imagination. I was thinking less and less about whatever used to occupy my preadolescent mind and more and more about stuff that would have made Meg blush if she knew. Like how she'd look in a bikini that coming summer. And the way she smelled, all warm sun and green apples and something heady, like a secret I wanted in on. And – mostly – what it would feel like to kiss her. I could not tame this preoccupation no matter how hard I tried. It was like shoveling smoke.

On a warm night in May, right under this magnolia, it happened. The memory of that kiss still made my stomach flip over. What would it be like to see her now? What was she like? It figured that just when I started to face the fact that maybe I'd never see her again, she was coming back to town.

The squeal of tires in the distance signaled Dara's imminent arrival. I got up, tossing the remains of my Pop-Tarts into the bushes and brushing the crumbs off my jacket. She screeched around the street corner, then barreled into my driveway with an eleventh-hour turn, nearly running me over. I leaped out of the way as she skidded to a stop.

"Jesus!" I yelled. "You almost killed me." I glanced up at

the house. If my mom had seen that, my days of riding with Dara would be over.

Dara poked her head out the window. "You shouldn't stand in the driveway," she said.

"I was on the grass." I pointed to the tire tracks in the yard, just visible in the first light of day.

She gestured me toward the car with the stump that remained of her left arm. "Come on, get in. I need doughnuts."

I tugged on the rusted door and climbed in, buckling my seat belt as tight as it would go – the wisdom of experience. "How come *you* get to have doughnuts?" She never let *me* eat crap before practice. Knowingly, anyway. I considered my Pop-Tart indiscretions to be my own personal business.

I reached over and turned down the stereo, which was blasting the Rolling Stones. In Dara's car, I was never in the right decade. Jagger was crooning "Miss You," which wasn't going to help me stop thinking about Meg. Haunted? Dreaming? Waiting? I could have written the lyrics myself.

"*I* get to have doughnuts," Dara explained in a prickly tone, "because it doesn't matter what *I* eat."

Arguing was as pointless as it was tempting. In Dara's view, I was a career swimmer whereas she was a has-been – an aspiring Olympic hopeful whose career was tragically cut short. So while my body was to be regarded as a temple, hers was more like a motel for transients.

She jammed the gearshift into reverse and glanced at me

as she turned to back out of the driveway. "Dude. You look like shit," she said. "Did you just get up?"

Did I just get up? What the hell time did *she* get up? I'd stumbled out of bed about four minutes before she showed up. Oh, for just one freaking morning off … But Dara would have dragged me to the pool by the nipple if she had to. Like an Olympic swimmer, Otis Mueller didn't take days off. Unlike an Olympic swimmer, Otis Mueller would never make it to the Olympics. But try telling Dara Svetcova that.

She blinked at me, all round blue eyes and milky-pale skin, as she backed into the street.

"It's barely morning, Dara. Of course I just got up."

She peered over at my lap, an impish smile on her face. "Do you still have morning log?"

I cringed. "God, Dara, it's morning *wood*. And no," I said, shoving her head back to her side of the car. "Eyes on the road, pervert."

She shifted into first and set us in motion with a burn-out loud enough to wake the dead – as if I didn't have a hard enough time convincing my parents that, contrary to appearances, Dara was a safe driver. She enjoyed few things more than making noise with her car. She navigated our little town like it was the Indy 500, revving the engine and tearing around corners and dumping the clutch. There was no mistaking the one-armed tyrant and her unlikely choice of transmission: the stick shift.

"So how long does it last?" she asked, blowing through the stop sign at the corner. "Do you have to jack off every morning to get it to go back down?"

I ignored her. Was nothing sacred? Apparently not, and I only had myself to blame. Dara had no brothers, she'd never had a boyfriend, and she had no patience for reading. I was the source of her knowledge about "morning wood" – and pretty much everything else about the male body.

In the pursuit of the kind of education you don't get in school, Dara and I played a game that went like this: she'd ask me something, and then I got to ask her something back, or the other way around. It was understood that the purpose of this game was to procure information of a sexual nature, but given our collective lack of experience having sex with other people, all that was left to discuss was our experience having sex with ourselves. As a result, we'd learned a lot about the workings of the opposite gender's body – although in truth, I wasn't convinced it was the male physique that interested her most. Her eyes often seemed to gravitate toward the same places on other girls that I was always trying my damnedest not to look at.

Dara turned into the Dunkin' Donuts lot and parked diagonally across the perpendicular lines. "Come in with me," she said, climbing out of the car and slamming the door. She was wearing her "Kiss My Splash" T-shirt with no jacket, even though it couldn't have been fifty degrees out.

I followed her inside, lured by the sweet, yeasty aromas. The cases overflowed with fresh, tender doughnuts; my eyes lingered longingly over the chocolate ones with their crackled glaze before I spotted the Bavarian Kreme – Meg's favorite. She would put away two of them with a large caramel iced coffee and then insist that her eyeballs were vibrating in the sockets. She'd press my fingertips to her closed eyes and say, "See? Can you feel it?" I smiled, remembering. Dork. Of course I couldn't feel it. But when I was that close to her, vibrating eyeballs – real or imagined – were the last things on my mind.

Dara ordered two jelly doughnuts and a multigrain bagel. Not hard to guess which was for me.

The counter guy tried not to stare, but it's a fact that stumps where limbs are supposed to be are riveting – a reality that didn't escape Dara.

She waved her stump at him. "You wanna touch it?"

I would have laughed at his horrified expression if I didn't feel so bad for him. He was a small guy, Pakistani, maybe, and he barely looked old enough to have a job. He backed up so fast, it was a miracle he didn't end up in the doughnuts with his ass all coated in custard.

When he handed Dara her change, he said timidly, "What happened to your arm?"

Oh boy.

She met his eyes for a long moment, then said, "It just

fell off. I woke up to this thud in the middle of the night. It had fallen right onto the floor." She nodded. "Doctor said it was probably from eating too much sugar. Too many doughnuts." She shoved the change – more than five bucks – into the tip jar. His bewildered expression as he registered her response made me want to punch her in the head.

You'd never guess by looking at her how merciless she was – she had a face as sweet as a rose, until she opened her mouth and let the knives fly out.

I followed her out to the car. "You know, you could cut people a little slack."

"What the hell does he need slack for?" She stuck the doughnut bag under her stump and opened her door. "He has two arms and his whole idiot life ahead of him. The world's his fucking oyster."

"People don't see stumps every day, Dara."

Dara's arm ended just above the elbow. It wasn't horrendous, as stumps go; it was round and fairly smooth save for some scars. And it was useful, too: she could carry things with it, hold beer bottles for opening, help with steering when she needed to shift while turning – things she wouldn't be able to do if the amputation had been higher. The problem was one of visibility. I, like most people, carried my damage on the inside. But Dara wore hers on her sleeve. Literally.

She took her doughnuts out of the bag and bit into one.

"You know," I said, staring as she licked jelly from the corner of her mouth, "it's not like one doughnut would kill me."

"Baby," she said, turning the ignition and revving the engine, "you get your hundred breast cut, and I'll buy you all the doughnuts you want. Shift."

I reached over and did the shifting, which was my job whenever Dara multitasked with her one good arm. "I have until next February to qualify for state," I pointed out, eye-balling her other doughnut nestled on the white bag near the gearshift. Its sugary surface sparkled and winked – I swear it was flirting with me. My bagel tasted like a damp dog biscuit.

"State? State's the least of my worries." She glanced over at me. "Oh, Christ," she said, rolling her eyes. "Here." She held out the doughnut, using her stump to steady the wheel.

I snapped up the doughnut before she changed her mind. "Why?"

"Because you're killing me with those fucking puppy eyes."

"No," I said, chomping into the doughnut, "I meant, why is state the least of your worries?"

"You'll have no trouble qualifying for state if you get to where you need to be by the end of the summer."

"Which is?" I was confused; I had already qualified for the summer championship meet.

"Well, you'll have to drop about four seconds this summer

to stay on track to qualify for Junior Nationals by next summer. After J-Nats, all we need is to drop three more seconds to qualify you for Olympic Trials."

I managed to not laugh out loud. Dara was asking me to drop ten seconds in a race that took just over a minute. I just wanted to cut the two seconds that would get me to the high school state meet. And maybe make finals my senior year. But Trials? Ever? Pure delusion.

Somehow it seemed to escape Dara that this whole Olympics thing was ridiculous – I'd never be that good. She was the real talent. I'd just needed something to do after Meg left, something to get me out of the house, which had become an unbearable place, and to get me out of my head, which was even worse. Swimming kept me from drowning. I liked it. Sometimes I even loved it. And yes, I wanted to kick ass in high school swimming – maybe even college swimming if I was good enough. But that's about as far as my swimming aspirations went. Unfortunately, I'd let myself be Dara's pet project for three years, and she was looking for the payoff, which to her meant only one thing: the Olympics. She didn't care if it was in one year or five or nine; it was the pot of gold at the end of her rainbow, her raison d'fucking être. And I was the leprechaun who was supposed to take her there.

So until I rustled up the cojones to kill Dara's dream and face the consequences, I'd be getting up before the freakin' roosters.

"Hand me my bag," Dara said, gesturing toward the backseat. When I gave it to her, she leaned forward and stuck her stump into the wheel to steer and dug into the purse with her right hand. As the car veered perilously out of the lane lines, she pulled out a piece of paper and handed it to me. It was a schedule, mapped out day by day to the smallest detail. "We'll do dryland three times a week and work on technique between morning and evening practice. If we don't cut corners and don't skip Sundays, we can do it – I know we can."

The girl was certifiable. The Senior Championship meet was two months away!

I stared at the paper. My whole summer, sunrise to sunset, right before my eyes.

It's not like Dara had never done this before – pushed me to my limits, taken over my every waking hour. And I'd always let her. Even during summer, when everyone else sort of takes it easy. But Meg's message had changed everything. If she was coming back for three weeks, there was no way I'd be spending all my time with Dara. Not if I had anything to say about it.

"You're not gonna be here to train me next year," I pointed out. "What happens then?" It was going to take a hell of a lot more than just a summer's worth of hard work to get me to Junior Nationals – and an absolute miracle for me to qualify for Olympic Trials. And Grinnell would be waiting for Dara in August, which actually kind of surprised me because I didn't think she had the grades. But I was relieved they wanted her. Sometimes to me Dara going to college sounded like the beginning of a long, relaxing vacation.

"Don't worry about that."

"Why not?" It seemed like a fair question. Why push myself to chase the impossible if she wasn't going to be around to see this through?

"Because, don't worry about it!"

Dara logic.

As she blathered on about my summer in her POW camp, my thoughts lingered on Meg. *What happened to her?* We'd been practically inseparable for nearly three years. Did she really just forget me? If I was supposed to give up on her at some point, I never got the memo. I guess a guy with half a brain would consider the long silence "the memo." If not that, then the football player might have driven the point home.

Since last year, when she finally appeared on Facebook, Meg had been posting pictures of herself with some padded Neanderthal. That they weren't just friends was agonizingly clear. I, on the other hand, had been a lone wolf this whole time, unless you count the companionship of an eighteen-year-old dictator of frankly indeterminate sexual orientation.

"... and between practices we can grab lunch at that

pizza buffet a few blocks from the pool – they have a salad bar..."

We were almost at the high school. The sun rose over the horizon, streaking orange and yellow through the remaining purple. It was a new day, in all sorts of ways. And as much as I was loath to bring up Meg to Dara, I knew that Dara, with all her grand plans for me this summer, would need to know sometime.

"So guess what?" I said, shifting into second as Dara slowed to turn into the parking lot. "Meg's coming back to Willow Grove." It felt weird to say it, like I was making it up. "For three weeks. Apparently."

"You know what that means?" Dara asked, tires squealing as she rounded the edge of the lot and sped into a parking space, stopping so suddenly that the seat belt nearly sliced me in half. She thrust the gear into first and yanked up the parking brake.

"It means," she continued, grabbing her stuff from the backseat, "you need to knock off more than two seconds in the next three months. Do you realize how much work that's going to take? Your turns still suck, and your starts aren't great, either. Sometimes your breakout is sort of fucked up."

She wasn't even listening to me.

She got out of the car, slammed the door, and strode toward the school, her muscular little ass doing its famous *swish-swish*. I grabbed my bags and ran after her.

"Did you hear what I said?" I asked. "Meg's coming back. So I might be kind of busy while she's here." I hoped that wasn't just wishful thinking.

"Meg who?" She yanked open the door to the athletic entrance.

Man, she really knew how to piss me off. Dara knew perfectly well Meg who. She'd heard plenty about Meg, although it hadn't taken long before she lost patience and told me that love was for chumps and to get over it already.

"*Meg* Meg," I answered.

"You mean the girl who landed you in therapy?" she said without looking back. "The girl you write all the froofy poetry for?"

I followed her down the hallway toward the pool, gritting my teeth. Calling my poetry "froofy" was one of Dara's cheap go-to's for emasculating me. And I was in therapy before Meg even left.

"Yes," I said, catching up with her. "And it's kind of a big deal. If you were my friend, you'd be happy for me."

She whirled around and faced me. "You know what? Fuck you. I've been here for you every fucking day since that girl left you in the dust. So don't give me that *if you were my friend* shit – don't talk to me about who your friends are. *I'm* your fucking friend. Which is more than you can say about her."

She started walking again. When she reached the locker

22

room, she turned back to me. "God, Mueller." She shook her head at me like I was pathetic, tragic. "She never even looked back."

2

IN THE POOL, WE WORKED ON SPRINTS. TO my eternal amazement, there were people who voluntarily showed up to practice before school in the off-season. Most of them did it because they wanted to stay in shape, but they had actual lives and couldn't make the evening practice.

There were six girls and eight other guys at the pool, despite the ridiculous hour, including – always – my medley relay team, because we were determined to set a school record, if a strong enough backstroker emerged to replace D'Amico, who was graduating. And of course there was Coach Brian, who oversaw the entire swim club, head-coached us senior swimmers, and who, I was pretty sure, never slept.

If Dara hadn't been there, I could have spent the whole time thinking about Meg as I put in my yards, lost in the blue blur and muffled echo of water. But even while she was swimming, Dara managed to keep an eye on me, occasionally even alerting me with her shrill two-finger whistle, which confused all the swimmers. That morning she paused on her way to the fountain to holler, "More rotation, Mueller! And quit breathing so much, you pussy! It's a twenty-five, for Christ's sake!" Everyone – including Coach – found this hysterically funny. I wasn't laughing, though. I was wishing she'd go fuck herself.

It's not that I was ungrateful. Dara had transformed me, both physically and mentally – I knew that. When I met her, not long after Meg left, my daily calendar was divided into a triad of moping, writing depressing poems, and shoving my face full of the pies my mom kept making. If baking pies was my mom's coping mechanism during those dark days, eating them was mine. If my therapist hadn't pushed her to get me out of the house that summer, my mom, lost in a dark vortex of her own, probably never would have hauled me to the pool for some fresh air and exercise, and I probably never would have met Dara and ended up her unlikely protégé. She could spot a sucker a mile away, even as she swam laps with her sort of mesmerizing one-armed technique. I had walked to the end of the diving board in my billowy board shorts, held my nose, and jumped. When I surfaced, I flailed my way to the side – to call it "swimming" would have been generous. Enter Dara Svetcova, who flattered me with her attention. She was almost sixteen, which felt a lifetime older than my thirteen and a half years, and it didn't take me long to realize she was the subject of the tragic news story I'd seen a couple of years earlier. Even with one arm, the girl was epic; I couldn't imagine what she'd been like with two. She gave me some swimming tips and encouraged me, and the rest was history.

Looking back, I could see that she was the human equivalent of a Venus flytrap. Hindsight is indeed twenty-twenty.

I was approaching the wall for a turn when Coach stopped me with a kickboard. When I came up, he pointed toward the deck, his expression grim.

Dara huddled near the pool, clutching her stump, rocking.

Phantom limb pains. The sensation that the amputated limb is there, hurting, itching – sometimes even that it's moving or picking things up. The drugs only helped so much. The most reliable relief came from her mirror box: a rectangular wooden crate divided by a mirror. When she put her right hand in, what she saw was a pair of hands, which somehow caused the phantom pains to subside. But if she wasn't at home with her box, sometimes watching two hands rubbing together could help. And to see two hands, she needed someone. And in Dara's world, "someone" was me.

I climbed out of the pool and moved toward her, pulling off my goggles. Abby Stewart knelt beside Dara, rubbing her back, her forehead folding into lines of concern.

Dara looked at me, grimacing. "I need the box."

Abby stood, rising almost to my height. She had to be close to six feet tall. Her long hair, balled up under her cap, looked like a giant tumor on the back of her head. "Box?" Abby asked me.

"I've got it," I told her. "Thanks, though." I couldn't explain the box, especially not then. Abby was easily the most thoughtful, good-hearted person on the entire swim team, and I felt bad pushing her away, but even if anyone other than me *could* help Dara, they'd first have to penetrate her field of barbed wire.

"You don't need the box," I told Dara, sitting down across from her. "I'm here."

"It was swimming," she said into her knees. "It was stroking. I hate it when it does that. It fucks up my timing." Her stump twitched and jerked. "Jumpy stump" she called this phenomenon, and there was no controlling it: it was a ghost limb seemingly controlled by a ghost brain. "God, make it stop!" she said through clenched teeth, trying to wrestle it down.

"Come on." I tapped her knee to get her to look up. "Watch."

She opened her eyes and I rubbed my hands together.

"Good, just stay focused," I said, hoping to distract her not just from the pain, but from the silence in the pool and the eyes, all the eyes. The last thing we needed was for her to be aware that everyone was staring. There was nothing she hated more.

She focused on my hands, her stump occasionally jerking.

I glanced around, and when I did, everyone quickly resumed swimming, pretended they weren't watching. My eye caught Kiera Shayman's, and she gave me kind of a sympathetic smile. I looked away, heat creeping to my face. Kiera was a total siren – an hourglass-shaped breaststroker (which led to the predictable locker-room remarks) who, according to Dara, was into me. And even though Dara was at least as clueless as me on these matters, I still blushed redder than a tomato any time Kiera so much as looked my way.

I patted Dara's shoulder. "Better?" Her stump seemed to be settling down.

"What's gonna happen when you're not with me?" she asked in a small voice.

Honestly, I worried about the same thing when she went off to college. Making friends didn't exactly top her skill set. "You'll be fine," I said, with more confidence than I felt. I stood and pulled her up. "Now go swim."

She handed me her goggles. Dara manages pretty well on her own, but getting goggles on with one hand? Forget it. I helped her get them on, then put on my own. She stared at me for a minute, then flicked my goggles – a gesture I interpreted as some approximation of "thank you."

She turned and went back to swim. *Swish-swish*. Her suit crept slightly up her butt. I fought the odd urge to yank it out for her. I could never quite figure out if I needed to rescue Dara or be rescued from her.

This conflicted feeling was nothing new. Last year at the winter sports awards banquet, Dara sat next to me, and out of the corner of my eye, I saw her trying to cut into a chicken breast with the side of her fork. She pressed so hard, her hand shook with the effort, but the chicken just wouldn't cut. Then she tried her knife, which didn't do much better one-handed – it just slid the chicken back and forth on the plate. I didn't know what to do. Dara would rather starve than ask for help eating, I'm pretty sure. But I was ravenous from practice, and I thought she must be, too. So I cut up my whole piece of chicken and, as smoothly and discreetly as I could, swapped plates with her. No words were exchanged, no eye contact made. I knew I might be in for it later. I could just hear her: *Did I ask for help, asshole? Do I look helpless to you?*

But she never said a word about it. You just never knew with her. There were parts of her that were a total mystery to me.

I got back into the pool and finished my sets. Dara didn't yell at me any more that morning. There was nothing like a phantom limb incident to turn her spunk dial down to zero.

"Hey, Shakespeare, is Dara okay?" Shafer asked me in the

locker room as he rubbed an Axe stick into his pits.

Shakespeare. More than once I'd regretted letting some of my poems be published in the school literary magazine. Another page from the "hindsight" file.

"Yup." I hated talking about Dara. For one thing, she wasn't very open with people, so I didn't feel like I should be open on her behalf – especially with Shafer, the freestyler on my medley relay team, who was a part-time asshole and a full-time pervert. For another thing, people always had questions about our relationship, and I didn't always have answers. No, we weren't going out. No, I wasn't paying her to be my coach. Were we best friends? Hell if I knew. We were together all the time, and we didn't really have many other friends. So maybe we were best friends by default. It didn't really jibe with *my* definition of best friends, which required one part me and one part Meg. I'd never really had a true best friend before or since.

Shafer sat in front of me on the bench. "What're you two gonna do without each other when she graduates? You're, like, fused at the hip."

"I'm sure we'll manage," I mumbled, pulling my T-shirt over my head.

I wasn't actually so sure. As much as I was looking forward to my freedom, life without Dara was pretty hard to imagine. But I supposed I'd manage. It wouldn't be the first time a girl had left me behind.

*   *   *

After school I headed upstairs to my room, but I stopped in my tracks in the hallway. Where Mason's racing car bed had stood this morning, there was now a desk. My mom knelt, wiping the baseboards, her back to me.

After all this time, she was finally de-shrining the room? She'd talked about it for years – turning the room into a craft-slash-gift-wrapping area or an office-slash-guest room – but she had never acted on it. I guess I never thought she would.

And then it hit me: she must have found out the Brandts were coming back. She couldn't leave Mason's room the way it was when they left. Couldn't let them know just how miserably we'd failed to move on.

The room looked so different; the canary-yellow walls seemed to jump out at me with the bed gone. A white scrape arched across the paint where the "spoiler" used to hit the wall – probably the result of Mason's love of jumping on the bed.

"Where is it?"

Mom startled and turned around. She had on Dad's Wildcats sweatpants, and her dark hair was in a ponytail. She was in "project" mode.

"Hey, Otie." She came over and gave me a hug that smelled like lemon Pledge and cinnamon gum. "How was your day?"

"Where is it?" I repeated.

The smile fell off her face, and that's when I noticed her eyes were red and puffy. "I donated it to charity."

I knew I should have cheered her on for this step forward, but what came out was: "Why didn't you tell me first?"

"We still have the crib, Otis. I kept that."

When Mason got his big boy bed, Dad moved his crib into the damp storage room in the basement. At some point someone had covered it in a light blue sheet so that no one would have to actually look at it when we went in search of extra dining-room chairs or winter coats.

Her eyes pleaded with me. "Do you know how happy that bed is going to make some kid? Better to do something good with it, don't you think?"

I averted my eyes, as unable as ever to meet head-on the intersection of her pain and mine.

"Hey, there's something I need to tell you." She hesitated. "It's about Meg and her dad."

"I already know. She emailed me." I slipped my backpack off my perpetually sore shoulders and turned to go, but then I turned back. "Wait, what? Meg and her dad? Her mom's not coming?"

She glanced away. "They're separated."

"Separated? Like, divorcing?"

"I don't know. I just know Jay is transferring back to Chicago and Meg is staying with him for a few weeks."

Transferring back. "Wait. He's moving back? Alone?"

"I really don't know, Otis." She took some pens from a box on the desk and put them in one of the drawers. "I haven't talked to them in…"

I stepped closer, leaning a hand on the desk. "How did you even find out—"

"Apparently your father is Facebook friends with Jay." She shoved the drawer closed, making the boxes on top of the desk jump. "You should probably also know … I guess Meg has a boyfriend, Otis."

"I know."

She glanced up. "You knew?"

"Saw their pictures on Facebook," I mumbled. I thought about explaining that Meg and I weren't actually friends on Facebook, but then I'd be admitting I basically stalked Meg, which probably wouldn't put Mom's mind at ease.

Her forehead creased with sympathy. I looked away, hating how pathetic I must look in her eyes. My gaze landed on a framed photo on the wall, glinting in the afternoon sun. It was one of Mason and me, sitting in the rocking chair on the night of his first birthday. I was reading him *Goodnight Moon* – my birthday gift to him, purchased with my own money, which felt like a big deal to nine-year-old me. He sat in my lap in his green-and-blue zip-up pajamas, sucking his pacifier, leaning sideways to look up at me, wide-eyed.

That picture never got easier to look at. Mason adored

me. No one would ever feel exactly that way about me again. I used to have a brother, and now I did not. People who knew me now thought I was an only child. But I was not an only child. My brother was always there. In a fleeting shadow, a muffled giggle, the smell of toast and jam... In dreams that seemed so real, for a cruel moment. In the permanent sadness in my mother's eyes. In my father's rare brooding silences. In the gnawing hole in me that couldn't be filled. He was right there.

I escaped to my room, where I sat at my desk and logged on to Facebook. Meg was so late arriving to the Facebook scene, I'd had paranoid thoughts that it was part of a strategy to keep me away from her. I'd signed up for Facebook as soon as she left, hoping it would keep us connected. But no. She didn't appear until last fall, not long after my sixteenth birthday (which I admit I'd held out hope of her acknowledging), and then she was posting pictures of herself with that macho asshole.

He was so good-looking, it was only reasonable to despise him on sight. Plus, he was obviously a land animal, which I am not. I was the kid who always struck out. The kid who ducked. The kid who, ironically, didn't like getting splashed in the pool. I guess "sissy" is a fair description. Once in sixth-grade PE I got nailed in the side of the head with a football, and Meg saw it happen. She watched as I stumbled off the field to the nurse's office, clutching my throbbing ear as I attempted – unsuccessfully – not to cry. She held her hand over her mouth, looking like she might cry, too, and somehow that made the whole thing about a hundred times worse.

Later I'd tried to make a joke about my lack of athletic ability. But she shrugged and said, "Who cares about sports?" Which filled me with happiness and hope.

Of course, the punch line was that she ended up with a football player.

Here it was, the picture that stopped me cold: He was in his football uniform, all pads and grass stains and ego, his arm draped so carelessly around Meg that the proprietary sentiment was unmistakable. And there was Meg, honey-colored hair coming loose from a ponytail, bright turquoise eyes turned upward at him. She'd posted other pictures of him over the last year, other pictures of *them*. But somehow, until I saw that picture – saw that heartbreakingly familiar look on Meg's face – it hadn't fully occurred to me that she might ever feel that way about anyone else.

When I first found her online, I wanted so badly to connect with her, to talk with her, but where to even start? *What the hell happened to you?* was probably not the smoothest strategy. The last thing I wanted to do was scare her off before we'd even reconnected. I couldn't tell her I had never really stopped loving her. And I didn't want to be in competition with her boyfriend. To me, that seemed ridiculous – offensive, even. He wasn't there when her dog got hit by a car; I was. He didn't hold her hair back when she threw up at the Wisconsin State Fair after three cream puffs and a Tilt-A-Whirl; I did. He hadn't been her best friend, her first kiss, her first love; I had.

But he was something to her; the picture made that pretty damn clear. Whatever it was, though, it couldn't erase everything that had been between us.

Could it?

I logged out of Facebook and opened my email. I ignored the spam and clicked on Meg's message. It was kind of crazy how a few little sentences had turned my whole world upside down:

> Hi, Otis. It's been a long time, I know, but I wanted to tell you that I'm coming back to Willow Grove next month. It'll be a short trip – just three weeks. But I thought you should know.
>
> Hope you're well!
>
> Meg

Despite obsessing over her message all day, I still had no idea how to respond. Why was she coming? Did she want to see me? She wouldn't have made a point of telling me she was coming if she *didn't* want to see me, right? Unless she was trying to avert an awkward situation if we accidentally ran into each other? Should I ask her if I could see her? What was I supposed to say?

Over an hour ticked by. I'd have to eat soon, before Dara picked me up for evening practice. And I didn't want to wait any longer to respond; it already felt weird to have waited most of a day. Should I ask her how she'd been? Should I ask about her parents? I didn't fucking *know* her well enough now to ask personal questions.

It didn't leave much.

After half a dozen failed attempts, I messaged:

> *Wow, okay – that is news! Yes, it has been a long time. Let me know if you need someone to show you around town.*

I hoped she still had a sense of humor. Meg famously had no sense of direction. In fact, she'd gotten lost on the first day of school in fifth grade, three months after she moved in next door. I was taking the attendance to the front office when I heard someone sniffling in the hallway. Meg had gone to the bathroom and couldn't find her way back to the classroom. I don't think anyone was ever so glad to see me in my entire life. Tears shimmered in her eyes, and I almost couldn't take it. I wanted to put my arms around her, but we had never hugged before. So I just took her to the classroom, quietly pointing out the landmarks along the way: straight past the music room, left after the water fountain… When we got there, she looked into my eyes for a long moment before turning to go into the classroom. I still don't know exactly what was behind that look, but it stirred up feelings in me I'd never had before.

Meg's fear of navigating new territory stuck with her. For good reason, too: that girl could leave Chicago heading for Wisconsin and end up in Kentucky. It made me smile. Thank God for GPS. Without it, she'd be a lost cause behind the wheel when she turned sixteen this July.

I also hoped Meg had another kind of GPS. One that would navigate her back to me.

3

I BARELY LEFT MY VIGIL AT THE COMPUTER
except to scarf down dinner – spaghetti with a garlicky
tomato sauce, fried eggplant cubes, green olives, and fresh
basil. I covered mine with grated Romano cheese and spicy
red pepper flakes and thought, *Meg would like this.* She'd
been one of those kids who liked everything – anchovies,
blue cheese, sushi, you name it. She single-handedly
broadened my palate to span nearly everything – I wanted
to like everything she liked. I bit into an olive and recalled
our parents' martini phase – Meg and I liked to nick the
gin-soaked olives from their cocktail glasses. Did Meg drink
now? Or was she a total square like me?

Over dinner my mom and dad treated the subject of Meg
and her dad's return like a land mine to be tiptoed around.
Before everything fell apart, our parents had been almost as

close as Meg and I were. In the summers, we all had dinner together more nights than not, and we often planned our weekends together, too. Our parents referred to us as "the kids," as if we were siblings. But I didn't really know exactly how much our parents stayed in touch after Mason died and the Brandts moved away. The geographical distance was probably the least of their challenges. And the subject of the Brandts in general was one all three of us tended to shy away from.

"You know," my mom said, swirling the wine in her glass and glancing up at me, "it's possible they won't even stay in Willow Grove. They could stay in the city. Jay might want to be close to work."

"They're staying up here," my dad said quietly. "Could you pass the chili flakes?"

"They are?" My mom's eyes flicked to him, sharp, accusing. She didn't hand him the chili flakes, which were right in front of her, so I reached across and slid them toward my dad. "How do you know?" she asked him. "How much are you talking to him?"

"I'm not! He mentioned it in his message, that's all." My dad picked up the chili flakes and sprinkled them over his pasta so carefully that I was pretty sure he was more worried about setting my mom off than over-spicing his spaghetti. His defensiveness made me wonder if he missed Jay. He must. But my mom was the primary force in his life and we all knew it. He would probably do anything to keep her happy – even giving up a good friend. That didn't seem fair to me.

"Well," my mom said, reaching for the salad bowl, "I don't see why Meg would want to be up here. She obviously left it all behind when they moved."

You could cut the subtext with a knife.

Something out the dining-room window caught my eye and I glanced up. The kid next door was running after a soccer ball that had rolled into our yard. He dribbled the ball back toward his yard, but his dad rushed in and tried to steal it. Their legs tangled and the boy tumbled to the ground, flinging his arms out dramatically and playing dead. Laughing, his dad pulled him up.

My dad used to laugh.

I watched him twirling pasta onto his fork. "Dad? How long have Jay and Karen been separated? Do you know?"

He shook his head. My mom watched him for a long moment, then stabbed some salad onto her fork. It was so quiet after that I could hear the chewing.

After practice I had a message from Meg. I read it in the locker room, which did nothing to slow down my post-workout heart rate. Then I endured an interminable six-minute drive home with Dara before I could tear up to my room and open it on my computer:

I know, it's kind of crazy. I can't believe my dad's really moving back.

*FYI, I'll be back June 11. We're staying in that Extended Stay hotel at 43rd and Sanders. You know the one.
We used to pass it on our bikes. I'm there for three weeks, and then I have to be back after the Fourth.*

I will wisely take you up on that tour, if you were serious. ☺

For a casual message, it pretty much knocked the wind out of me. I was still reeling from the fact that after three years of silence, here she was, talking to me. And she wanted to see me – I reread that last line about the tour until it was seared on my brain, smiley face and all. And she had referenced Mason, sort of: those bike rides were our unauthorized visits to the cemetery.

One month. She'd be back in town in one month. It seemed unreal. I wrote:

I definitely was serious about the tour. June 11, OK. I have a swim meet on the 25th. You're welcome to come to it, if you want to.

I considered deleting that. It seemed stupid. Why would she want to come to my fucking swim meet? But I wanted to make it clear that I wanted to see her, and the joke about the tour seemed too easy for her to dismiss.

I stared at my message, then finally hit Send.

I tried to study for my calc test while I waited for a response. Finally, at eleven, it came:

I'd love to come to the swim meet, if I can. So hard to imagine you swimming! In a Speedo and everything? I can't picture it.

Just the word "Speedo," coming from her, sent an electric jolt through me. Did she realize I wasn't exactly the same skinny little weakling I was when she last saw me? Still, the idea of her thinking about me almost naked gave me palpitations. I *had* to look better naked than Football Guy. A swimmer and a football player? Please. Bring it on.

Oh God – had she seen him naked?

Must. Stop. Thinking.

I couldn't come up with a single safe thing to say. Ultimately I just wrote:

I'm looking forward to seeing you. It's been a long time.

Saturday morning after practice, I showered and dressed, then waited in the hall for Dara to come out of the locker room. Kiera emerged, combing her wet hair. "Hey, Otis. You know Dara left, right?"

"She did?" I checked my phone for a message. Nothing.

"You need a ride home?" Kiera smiled at me and tipped her head. It reminded me of Meg, who had this way of tilting her head when she asked me a question, or when she listened to me. It made me feel interesting. Important. Loved.

"Earth to Otis?" Kiera widened her already-big brown eyes and jingled her car keys.

"That'd be great. Thanks."

Kiera's car was new – a far cry from Dara's. It had that glorious new-car smell. Dara's had that chlorine-and-old-french-fries smell.

"So you're practicing a lot out of season," I said as Kiera drove to my house. She knew where I lived without asking for directions, which I decided not to overanalyze. "Don't you usually just do mornings?"

She shrugged, squinting against the late-morning sun. "I don't mind swimming doubles in club season, if I have time. I don't know how you keep up with homework, the way you train. And don't you have, like, a four-point-oh GPA?"

"No," I said, waving her off – though it actually was pretty close to a 4.0.

We talked about our honors English class. Kiera thought Chapman was kind of a dud, but I didn't think he was so bad. "Well, sure, *you'd* think that," she teased. "You're his favorite, obviously."

I blushed and, unable to locate actual words, made a few random noises.

When she pulled into my driveway, she turned to me with that provocative smile of hers. "Hey, are you hungry? 'Cause I'm starving."

Under other circumstances, I might have said yes, but all I wanted to do was sit and watch for a message from Meg. "I'll probably just raid the fridge for leftovers," I told Kiera, picking my bag up. "I have a ton of homework." I rolled my eyes for effect.

She nodded, but I felt her disappointment.

"Thanks for the ride," I said as I got out of the car. I started up the walkway, habitually averting my eyes from the front bay window. It's where Mason used to sit, in the window seat, watching for me to get home from school. The perpetual emptiness of that window was a chronic stab of pain. It never got easier.

Kiera beeped as she pulled away, and I turned to wave. As she drove off, my eyes were drawn to the magnolia, now in obscene full bloom. On impulse, I pulled out my phone and took a picture of it.

Upstairs, I posted the photo without comment on Facebook, where I never posted anything, and made it public. If Meg ever stalked me the way I stalked her, she might see it.

I ate lunch, and then worked on my last English homework assignment for the year – a sonnet, courtesy of Chapman and our unit on Shakespeare.

Fucking sonnets. They're only ever about one thing: love.

I was screwed.

I got up and looked at the window that once was Meg's.

A ten- or eleven-year-old boy lived in that room now, but I could still envision it as it used to be: the violets-and-ivy wallpaper border, the antique quilt that covered her bed, the corner of her room dedicated to her ten thousand stuffed animals, each of whom had a name, a distinct personality, and a complicated backstory that she'd made up – or made me make up. She liked it best when I did it.

I gazed at the magnolia tree, remembering the view of it from Meg's window – framed by white lace curtains and her collection of snow globes on the sill.

Beneath your window our magnolia stands.

There it was – line one of my sonnet, iambic pentameter and all.

Froofy. I could hear Dara's voice in my head. Ignoring it, I stretched my arms, rolled my head around, cracked my knuckles, and continued.

By evening it was finished. It wasn't Shakespeare, but I thought it wasn't bad.

Magnolia

Beneath your window our magnolia stands,
Its blushing petals seem to wave and sigh,
Its branches like so many outstretched hands,
In benediction, reaching toward the sky.

Though winters stilled the beauty springs bestowed,
And shadows fell where footprints once were new,
Within my heart the heady mem'ries glowed,
As fresh and precious as dawn's sparkling dew.

This spot where souls and secrets mingled bold,
Where tender lips surrendered to the night,
Is now awash in sun's unearthly gold,
Thus rendering the scene a holy site.

New hope illuminates days dimmed by grief;
You are and e'er shall be my heart's relief.

Meg was not a terrible muse.

Waiting to see if she'd comment about the magnolia photo was killing me. She was probably out for the evening – it was Saturday night, sacred date night for couples. For losers like me, options were kind of pathetic. The guys were getting together at D'Amico's house for pizza and a slasher movie. They kept texting, cajoling me into coming over, but I wasn't in the mood. Dara texted, too, saying, *Wanna go eat?*

I was about to decline, but then Meg posted a new picture of herself with Football Guy. Apparently he also plays guitar. Fuck me. They had their mouths open in the same position, so I guessed they were singing together. Suddenly I felt like I could use a change of scenery.

Sure, I texted Dara.

I waited for her downstairs, watching the NBA playoffs with my dad, while my mom, whose sports interests centered on football, paged through some work papers. My dad and I didn't know all that much about basketball, but even we knew to root for the Bulls and to hate the Cavaliers. If Meg's dad had been watching with us, he would've yelled for Derrick Rose and complained about bad calls and commented endlessly about pick-and-rolls and triple-doubles and flagrants and other things my dad and I had little comprehension of. I wondered if he was watching the game in California, and if Meg was watching with him. Meg could holler at basketball with the best of them.

My dad and I cheered as we watched, and soon I heard the screech of Dara's brakes in the driveway.

My mom sighed loudly, then looked at me over her reading glasses. "Can't you get that girl to stop tearing into the driveway like a maniac? You tell her if she can't drive safely, she won't be driving you at all!"

Sure. I'll do that. Right after I kiss my balls goodbye.

"If you'd let me get my license," I said, pulling my jacket on, "I could drive myself."

She went back to her papers. "When you get your fifty hours behind the wheel, you can get your license."

"Nobody cares about that stupid log!" I'd turned sixteen in October – more than six months ago – but the combination of my training schedule and my mom's reluctance to let me drive in winter conditions meant I still had no license.

"*I* care." She gave me a pointed look. I met my dad's eyes; we both knew it was futile to argue with my mom over anything related to child safety. "Keep me posted on where you are," she said, glancing around for her phone.

The smell of the lilacs hit me as soon as I stepped out into the warm evening. It wasn't even dark yet; a last remnant of orange glowed at the horizon. Some kids down the street were shooting hoops and trash-talking in the waning light of dusk. It was almost summer.

Lou Reed's distinctive voice emanated from Dara's car – one of those poetic, stoned-sounding Velvet Underground songs. We were in the 1960s or 1970s tonight.

Dara sat in the passenger seat, her head tipped back, eyes closed. I peered in at her through the open window. "So what's going on here?"

"You're driving," she said without opening her eyes.

"How come?"

"Guys should know how to drive a stick."

There was probably a metaphor in there somewhere.

"The manual transmission is practically obsolete," I informed her.

"*You're* obsolete," she mumbled.

I rolled my eyes and walked around and opened the

driver's-side door. I fastened my seat belt and looked over at Dara. Her head lolled against the window, her eyes still closed.

"Are you drunk?"

She lifted a shoulder.

I gaped at her. "And you *drove* here?"

"God, would you relax? I didn't drive *you*, did I?"

"So? You could've hurt someone!"

I'd seen her drink a beer on countless occasions, but usually just one. I hadn't considered that maybe it was just the only one I *saw*.

"Where are we going?" I asked.

"I don't know. Just drive."

I eased out the clutch as I backed up. I didn't have a lot of experience driving a stick shift, but Dara had given me a few lessons after I'd gotten my permit. One night last summer, she drove us to the Ascension Cemetery and Mausoleum – thankfully, not the cemetery where Mason was buried. "Cemeteries are perfect for learning to drive," she had explained. "No one'll ride your ass for going slow, and you don't have to worry about hurting anyone – everyone's already dead." I struggled with that damn clutch for what seemed like hours, jerking us backward and forward and killing the engine more times than I could count as we both alternated between hollering and laughing hysterically. I wish all of my memories of Dara were as good as that one.

I drove down the street and came to a complete stop

at Willow, looking both ways before proceeding. Dara mumbled, "You drive like an old lady."

"Why'd you leave practice this morning?"

"Oh God. I was freaking out."

"Why?"

"I think Abby asked me on a date."

"What?" I tried to keep my eyes on the road. "Why do you think it was a date?"

"Well, duh! Because it's Abby." She put her bare feet up on the dashboard. "She asked me to go to a movie, and we're not even that good of friends. And sometimes she ... *looks* at me in the locker room. And she always wants to help me with my goggles. And my cap, at meets – she's always the one to put it on for me."

"But that's how she is." Abby was sort of the mom of the team. I'd always figured she was just being nice to Dara, not that she actually liked her. Liking Dara could be a tall order.

"Also, she touched my left arm."

I raised my eyebrows. "She touched your stump?"

"Not on the stump, but here," she said, touching her upper arm. "But nobody's ever touched that arm except you. And the doctors."

"What about your dad?"

"Please. He doesn't touch me, *period*."

I hated that man. Russian-speaking, mustached, and barrel-chested, he seemed to go through life managing to

51

avoid eye contact almost completely. I mean, I felt sorry for him, losing his wife and all. But, Jesus, Dara lost her *mother*. Man up! He was all Dara had. Except for me, I guessed, but I was hardly a fit parental substitute. Half of the time I couldn't even figure out how to be her friend.

"Well," I said, remembering to clutch as I braked for a red light, "maybe she's just hoping. Or maybe she just wants to be better friends." I was being circumspect. Of course what I really wanted to know was could Dara be interested in Abby? But I couldn't ask her outright. At best she'd ignore me, and at worst I'd be holding an ice pack to my nuts all night. "Anyway, you're graduating in a week," I pointed out. "Who cares anymore?"

"I don't want everyone remembering me that way when I'm gone! 'Dara the dyke' – I can hear it now."

"It would take the focus off your stump!"

She took a foot off the dashboard and kicked me hard in the arm. "You're a real asshole, Mueller, you know that?"

"Jeez," I said, rubbing my arm. "Sorry. I just know you hate being defined by your – by being an amputee."

I wanted to glance at her to see if I was in for another physical assault, but I had to concentrate; the light was about to turn green, and we were on a slight incline. But she laid her hand on my arm where she'd kicked me and said, "You're not an asshole. You just know me so well. Sometimes I forget."

I was so surprised I couldn't think of anything to say.

The light changed, and as I struggled to find the balance of clutch and accelerator, the car rolled backward. I cursed and sent the car shooting forward by letting up on the clutch too fast. Dara laughed.

"Where am I even going?" I asked.

She shrugged.

So I just kept driving aimlessly, past the library and the fire station, down the stretch of McCormick with all the fast-food offerings, and then up Forestway, which ran along the nature preserve. "What did you say when Abby asked you?"

"I said I was busy." She shifted in her seat to face me. "Hey. Let's just go to my house."

She reached out and laid a hand on my thigh, sliding it upward.

"What are you doing?" I took my hand off the wheel long enough to remove her hand from my leg. Driving a stick was hard enough without having to fend off groping.

"Let's just do it. We're both virgins. We could turn that around tonight."

I looked over at her, baffled. "Are you for real?"

"I just want to know what it's like! Come on – it won't take long."

"Hey," I said, mildly insulted. "What makes you think—?"

"Once when we were playing the question game, you told me how long it takes you to—"

"Okay, never mind!" *Ugh.* Now that Meg was in the picture, the wickedly private things Dara knew about me made me feel sort of sick. During that same round of our game, Dara had asked what I did with my other hand when I jerked off – sort of a cheap question, since it couldn't be reciprocated. But I'd answered it. I wished I hadn't. I wished I could turn back time and take all that private information back.

"Look, even if I wanted to, I wouldn't do it when you're drunk."

"I'm not that drunk. Come on, we should just do this. Not to point out the obvious, but this" – she waved her stump at me – "is not exactly a dude magnet."

"Oh, please. It's not your stump that keeps people away, Dara. It's you. I mean, you're cute and pretty and your ass is legendary, but, to be honest, you're kind of a bitch!"

"Yeah, but that's not the reason. Do you really think anyone would go out with me with this?" She gestured toward the stump. "People can't handle it."

"How would you know? You've never given anyone a chance."

"Well, here's your chance."

"I don't want a chance!"

A small voice in my brain knocked, asking if I was out of my fucking mind, turning down sex. Wouldn't it be good to have some clue what I was doing, for possible future situations? For an instant I imagined a skilled, confident version of myself bringing Meg to quaking heights of ecstasy with my staggering arsenal of lovemaking skills. But nothing – not my hormones, insecurities, or general cloudy judgment – could talk me into thinking sex with Dara was a good idea.

"Anyway," I said, glancing over at her, "if you're going to do it, you should do it with someone who knows what he's doing. I don't exactly see a lot of action."

"Other than with yourself." She had a way of teasing – part cute, part loaded gun – and I never knew where the balance was going to tip.

"Other than with myself," I conceded, "and even I don't think I'm that great."

That wasn't true. When I had the privacy, time, and ambition, I actually found myself to be quite excellent. But I didn't want to talk to her about that stuff anymore. Suddenly it felt … inappropriate.

I pulled over onto a side street, parking in front of a string of cookie-cutter McMansions with ridiculously manicured and lit-up lawns. I flicked the gear into neutral, then pulled up the parking brake. "What's this all about, Dara? Really?"

Instead of answering, she leaned over and grabbed me, pulling my face to hers in a hard kiss.

"Stop it," I said softly, pulling back.

"Who's gay now?" she said, enveloping me in a plume of alcohol fumes.

"Right. I'm gay. You found me out."

She moved back to her side, staring out the window. Her face was ungodly pale in the light of a streetlamp. She closed her eyes. Holy shit, was she about to cry?

I had never – not once – seen Dara shed tears. Not even in the throes of phantom limb pain so bad that I could hardly stand it.

I hesitated, then decided to take a chance. I reached out to her across the gearshift, half expecting her to punch me. But she leaned over and collapsed into me, pressing her face into my chest.

We sat like that till Dara suddenly hiccupped violently, which got us both laughing.

We went to El Grande Taco – a cheap, dimly lit, hole-in-the-wall of a Mexican restaurant, and I took advantage of Dara's preoccupied and semi-drunk condition by ordering a giant chile relleno burrito that oozed with so much cheese it made me giddy. Dara ordered a Dr Pepper and nachos and proceeded to eat salsa verde straight, dispensing it from a squeeze bottle onto a spoon.

This was yet another in a series of simple motions requiring colossal effort for a one-armed person. She propped the spoon on a few carefully arranged tortilla chips, then squeezed the salsa onto it. She then set the bottle down, lifted the spoon to her mouth, and repeated. Because she still had the hiccups, occasionally the whole spoonful sloshed onto the sticky vinyl tablecloth before it could make it into her mouth.

Watching was painful. I'd tried being one-armed a few times in the privacy of my home, just to see what it was like – doubling my arm up in my sleeve so I couldn't use it – and it was just a matter of minutes before I felt like shooting myself.

Our waitress reappeared as we were finishing up. "Can I get you anything else?" She wore a snug, low-cut T-shirt that framed her magnificent cleavage. They were a sight to behold, those breasts – jostling and beguiling whenever she poured water or set something down.

"Uh, no, just the check," I said, staring hard into her eyes to prevent my gaze drifting south and scorching my retinas. Dara's eyes, however, were glued to the splendor, at which point I found watching Dara more interesting than watching the breasts.

When the bill came, Dara pushed her purse at me. I opened it, and as usual it was a mess of crumpled bills – even some hundreds. She had no shortage of cash, that was for sure – something you'd never guess by the car she drove.

On the way home, she fell asleep in the car, despite my jerky driving. I walked her up the front steps and let her lean on me as she punched in the security code and opened the door. I handed her the car keys and gently pushed her inside. I'd have to walk home, but it was nice enough out that

I didn't mind. And I could probably use the help digesting the metric ton of cheese I'd just consumed.

"Mueller?" she said suddenly, swiveling back around and leaning out the crack of the door.

I waited, but she didn't say anything. "You want me to come in?" I asked.

She glanced down and lifted a shoulder. Her version of *yes, thank you.*

"Okay," I said, stepping inside. "But behave yourself," I added, in case she had sex on her mind.

She rolled her eyes, closing the door behind us. She dropped her keys next to a marble sculpture of some dude's head on a polished mahogany table in the foyer.

Dara's house reeked of wealth. It was modern – lots of shiny surfaces and abstract art – and sometimes there were cleaning ladies working. My modest split-level house was small by comparison – cozy, my mom called it. And it was kind of outdated – midcentury modern, my dad called it. And my mom did the cleaning (except for the laundry and ironing, which was my dad's inexplicably happy domain), although about once a month Mom went ballistic and made us all do "deep cleaning," which meant organizing closets or shampooing carpets and stuff like that. When she got this way, my dad would say to me quietly, "The smart money's on shut up and do it." He didn't have to tell me twice – not when Mom was stomping around talking about not being our goddamned personal servant and reminding us what century this was.

I followed Dara into the kitchen, which was lit only by the light of the hood range over a granite island the approximate size of Manhattan. Empty beer bottles littered the counter, and next to the sink sat a half-eaten frozen dinner, which made me feel awful. My mom was a great cook, and her part-time work-from-home job writing a medical newsletter gave her plenty of time to pursue her culinary interests. And here my motherless friend was home alone eating TV dinners.

Dara took a can of soda out of the fridge and opened a bottle of pills.

"What's that?" I asked.

"For pain."

"You sure it's safe to mix with alcohol?"

She waved me off with her stump, swallowing the pills.

I shook my head. "You really worry me."

"Don't worry about me. I hate that." She took her soda and headed up the wide, curving staircase. I followed. She went into her bedroom and then into the attached bathroom. I sat on the bed. On her dresser sat the mirror box, the magic bullet for phantom limb pain. I'd come here with her several times, when the pain was bad enough that the hand-rubbing trick wasn't cutting it. I'd seen how quickly the pain dissipated when she put her right arm in the mirror box and watched what appeared to be two symmetrical arms moving in concert before her. It was astonishing.

On the floor next to her dresser, a beat-up Stoli vodka box was filled with her swim trophies, medals, and ribbons, most collected from the years before the accident when she was virtually unbeatable. Not one of them was displayed on a shelf or hung on the wall, as mine were at home. The day I got my first ribbon at a meet, my parents put up a shelf and hooks in my room so every stupid ribbon I ever got could proudly be displayed. But Dara's were heaped in an old box on the floor like so much trash.

I heard the toilet flush, then the water running and the scrubby sounds of toothbrushing. She emerged a minute later in sky-blue panties and a paper-thin white tank top. I started to worry that she was going to try something, but she just pushed past me.

I got up as she slid between the covers. "Tuck me in?" she asked, then turned onto her side, facing away from me.

I wasn't entirely sure what she meant; she was already under the covers. I remembered the times I put Mason to bed. Usually I'd read him a story and then tickle him. I was pretty sure that wasn't going to work here. Awkwardly, I patted at the covers around her.

Dara reached out and grasped my wrist, and then guided my hand to her head. *Ah, okay.* She let go and I stroked her hair.

My eyes drifted to a framed photograph on her bedside table that I'd never really looked closely at before. A string of beads with a boxy sort of cross was draped over it, which seemed odd because Dara was about the least godly person I knew. I reached out and quietly slid the beads to the side to see the picture.

A spotlight illuminated a ballerina, onstage in full regalia, in a pose that radiated grace and discipline and beauty. My insides turned to jelly at the resemblance – that lean, muscular frame. That dark hair. That doll-like face with the small mouth.

"Who's this in the picture?" I murmured.

"Mama," she said softly.

Mama. I felt like bawling. I mean, I knew she'd had a mother, obviously. But seeing her, seeing the resemblance… The idea that Dara had once called someone *Mama*…

"She's beautiful," I whispered. "You look like her."

A slight nod.

"What are the beads?" I asked. "A rosary?"

"Her chotki," she murmured. "Same idea."

I touched the black tassels that hung from the cross. "Was she religious?"

She nodded. "We used to go to the Russian Orthodox Church."

"Do you believe in God?" I asked.

"I don't believe in anything."

I felt so empty, thinking about everything that had been taken away from Dara. As you scratched at her surface, the enormity of the hole underneath exposed itself.

"But my mom believed. I feel like if I keep the chotki with her picture, it sort of, like … blesses her."

I couldn't take much more. It was too fucking sad. I got up from the bed.

"Can you wait until I fall asleep?"

"Okay." I sat back down next to her.

"Don't turn off the light in the bathroom when you go."

"I won't."

I waited until her breathing became even. Then I crept out and hoofed it the two miles home.

4

IN ENGLISH ON MONDAY, MR. CHAPMAN
asked if anyone would be willing to share their sonnet with
the class. When no one volunteered, he glanced around the
room. "No one? Otis?"

I shook my head, my face heating up. *No fucking way.*

He shrugged and asked us to turn them in. I spotted
some Post-its on Kiera's desk in front of me.

"Hey, can I borrow a Post-it?" I whispered to her.

She tossed her shampoo-commercial hair, sending a
pleasant current of fragrance in my direction, and pulled off
a Post-it. "You can even keep it," she whispered.

I took it and wrote NOT FOR LIT MAG! on it. I stuck it
on my sonnet and passed it forward.

Kiera looked down at it and then peeked at me from
under a fringe of lashes so heavy that her lids must be

chronically fatigued from holding them up. With a coy smile, she started reading quietly, "Beneath your window our magnolia stands—"

"Hey," I whispered, lightly jabbing her shoulder. "Quit it."

She turned to me. "I love your poetry," she whispered, lingering on the word "love."

My face went from hot to hotter.

Fortunately, the guy in front of her turned around and grabbed the papers from her hands before she could read further.

She turned back to me. "I liked the picture of that tree you posted. Is that the magnolia?"

This girl was connecting the dots way too well.

"So whose window is it under?" she asked.

I fumbled incoherently for a reply, but fortunately Chapman started class.

By that night Meg's silence was really getting to me. So I sent her a riveting and provocative message:

How's it going?

I stared at the words on my screen, suddenly unable to account for my high GPA.

To kill time as I waited for a reply, I snacked, flipped through my poetry journal, and read one of Shafer's stupid links: 100 EUPHEMISMS FOR MASTURBATION! Somewhere between "mangling the midget" and "punching the clown," a response came from Meg on instant message.

> HER: *Otis? What do you remember?*
>
> ME: *About what?*
>
> HER: *Me. Us. Anything. Everything.*
>
> ME: *Everything? That's a lot of things.*
>
> HER: *Tell me.*

Good God, how was I supposed to know how much or how little to say? I wished I could see her face, have some idea what she was after – not just at the moment, but with the whole visit this summer. Why was she coming back? Was it just to help her dad settle in? And what did she want from me? Was I one of the reasons for her visit? Or just a side note, a minor attraction on her tour of memory lane?

But I couldn't ask any of those questions, not without sounding accusatory or egotistical – or pathetic. So I opted for "random" instead:

> ME: *I remember when you lost your grandmother's amethyst ring and you were terrified of your mom finding out. But she never did. (Has she?)*

I wondered if I was getting too close to the subject of her parents, of their separation. I didn't know whether to ask or pretend I didn't know about it or what.

> HER: *No, thank God. But that's probably the last thing on her mind these days. Okay, what else?*

> ME: *I remember ... that your favorite flavors of ice cream were dulce de leche and salted caramel. Really, anything with caramel in it.*

> HER: *Oh my God. Yes. Still true.*

She didn't have to prompt me to keep going; it was like I'd opened the Meg floodgates, and I couldn't stop even if I'd wanted to.

> ME: *I remember when you told me the code to your diary lock to prove to me that you trusted me. I also remember the code: 5-1-4*

> HER: *I can't believe you still remember that!*

> ME: *How could I forget? It was the day we first kissed. May 14.*

> HER: *You knew that's what it was?? I didn't even know you knew the date!*

> ME: *Some things a man doesn't forget.*

> HER: *You never told me you knew what the code meant!*

> ME: *Ha, no, because what if you'd chosen the number randomly?*

> HER: *But you knew.*

ME: *Suspected. Hoped.*

HER: *What else do you remember?*

I hesitated, suddenly feeling exposed. I could go on for days about all the things I remembered about Meg. But what about her? What did she remember about me – about us? And what was she really after, anyway? Confirmation that I hadn't forgotten her, that I would be excited to see her? Or something else?

ME: *I think I've covered enough for one day.*

HER: *Please, Otis?*

Oh God. Why did she have to do that?

ME: *Meg. Please don't say please.*

HER: *Please.*

Somebody stop me...

ME: *I remember that first kiss.*

It was like missing your exit on the highway. It's done. There's no turning back. You're on a new route now.

HER: *Oh, Otis ... I saw the picture. Did you mean for me to see it?*

I was pretty sure my heart actually stopped. I ran my hands through my hair, then pulled off my T-shirt.

I was starting to sweat. What was the right answer to that question?

She started typing before I could come up with anything.

HER: *I probably shouldn't say this. Argh, never mind.*

ME: *Please?*

HER: *Otis. Please don't say please.*

ME: *Please.*

HER: *Oh God. Okay.*

A pause – three or four seconds, maybe, that felt like an eternity. Then:

HER: *I've missed you.*

I stared at those words on the screen, feeling like my chest might explode. I was thrilled, ecstatic, and so very, very confused.

And then – fuck! – her green dot disappeared. Before she could tell me why, if she missed me so much, she hadn't been in touch for three fucking years. Before she could tell me what was up with her parents and why she was coming back to town next month. Before she could tell me that the magnolia picture did its job, which was to make her think about our first kiss.

It was a warm night in May, when the magnolia was in full bloom. A light breeze stirred the scented air, sending petals cascading down around us like mammoth snow-flakes. "Crazy Love" – from her dad's playlist – floated out from the open windows of her house. Her hair trailed loose from its ponytail, strands framing her face and grazing her neck – a look so fucking sexy that to this day it can make my eyes cross. Also contributing to my disequilibrium were her new-to-the-scene breasts, which swelled stunningly and stupefyingly against her tank top. Her legs were brown and long – at that time, she actually had a couple inches on me. The moon illuminated her blue-green eyes.

In that moment, I suddenly lost all threads of whatever we were talking about. All I was aware of was the way she was looking at me.

I reached a hand out slowly, my eyes never leaving hers. Her breath caught in a small inhale of surprise as my finger-tips skimmed her bare shoulder. I stood like that for what seemed like twenty lifetimes, in my mind begging her to kiss me, make a move, give me a sign, help me, *help me,* for Christ's sake. And I swear I do not know which of us initi-ated it or how it happened, but it just did, like the pull of the moon. I didn't understand how a kiss, how lips, could bring such staggering pleasure.

When it ended – was it seconds? minutes? – the words rose from my heart to my throat to my lips. Possibly she would not have heard them over the stereo blaring from her living room, the din of crickets, the thundering of my heart.

But her whispered reply was unmistakable.

"I love you, too."

That was the apex of my happiness, that summer. It was also the end of it.

In August, we buried Mason.

And then Meg was gone.

Each day of that week seemed to stretch longer than the last. By this point, the sun was already up when I went to morning practice and still up when I went to evening practice, which disrupted and confused my general adaptive pessimism. On the other hand, summer solstice was only a month away. It never seemed right to me that, just as the summer began, the days were already getting shorter. This was my favorite time, right now – when the days were still getting longer and all the good stuff still lay ahead.

Willow Grove High's graduation ceremony was Saturday morning, held outdoors at the downtown music pavilion. I went by myself with one of Dara's extra tickets, and if I'd known how sad it was going to make me, I might have skipped it. Not so much because Dara was graduating, since frankly I sometimes felt like I'd never be rid of her, but because it meant the fracture of the closest thing I had to a brotherhood since Mason died. It hit me hard, watching some of my teammates march across that stage and out of my life. I'd never swum in high school without those guys;

thanks to Dara, I made varsity my freshman year. They'd helped me improve, had supported me when I'd done badly and cheered for me when I'd done well. D'Amico especially. My freshman year, he was like a god to me, and when Coach put me on the "A" relay team with him this past season, I was giddy. I should have been happy for him to be graduating and moving on to the next big thing, but, honestly, I just felt sorry for myself that he was leaving.

And then there was Dara, the most talented one of us all, swimming on the "B" relay team, in early heats, battling it out with – and often losing to – girls who may have had two arms but didn't have one-tenth her strength and skill. If I'd been her, I would've wanted to get as far away from swimming as possible. But she clung to it as if it were all there was in the world. And maybe for her, it was.

And the thing was, she was still good – not the best, but better than many, even if she was technically handicapped. She had adapted and compensated. Her dolphin kick in particular was unrivaled. Whereas most high school swimmers broke out of their underwaters long before the regulation limit, Dara powered through hers until the last possible second, using her advantage for all it was worth, cutting it so close to the fifteen-meter mark that I always feared she'd be DQ'd. But she never was. She was flawless. In most races she led the pack in those first fifteen meters, only to be overtaken when she came up and started her one-armed stroking. And even though I knew it was coming, it made my throat ache, every single time. After she finished her race, she'd stand on deck, watching the final heats intently, and I knew what she must be thinking: With two arms, she would own all those girls.

I looked for her to congratulate her afterward, but I couldn't find her. A quick check of my phone showed a text from her ten minutes before: *I'm out of here. See you later.*

I figured I'd at least congratulate D'Amico, who stood outside the pavilion surrounded by family, judging by the pack of similarly tall, towheaded, blue-eyed people with him. He spotted me and stepped away, holding up a *be right back* finger to them.

"Hey," he said, coming over and giving me a hug.

"Hey, congratulations," I started to say, but to my horror, my voice broke. Still hugging him, trying to steady my voice, I said, "Good luck at Kenyon, man. You'll be great." Jesus. *Pull it together, Mueller.* If I had realized I was going to bawl, I would have texted him my good wishes instead.

"You better come see me," he said, stepping back and smiling at me. He pretended not to notice my emotional state. "You can stay in my dorm."

I nodded, not trusting my voice.

"Anyway, we've still got the summer," he said, punching me lightly in the arm. "And hey, they need guards at the pool," he added, stepping back to his family. "You should apply. We'd have fun."

"Yeah, maybe," I managed to get out.

I turned and pushed my way through the crowd, texting my dad that I was ready for a ride.

With the graduates gone, the school year tapered down for the rest of us. Summer swim club was in full swing by late May. Dara worked me like a mule, and if I complained, I got the lecture: "Three years I've devoted to you, Mueller. You're not going to crap out on me now."

"But you're not even going to be here to train me in two months," I argued. "What happens then?"

"I told you not to worry about that."

But I did worry about it. I was looking for any assurances I could find that my Dara days were numbered.

We were swimming outdoors for the summer while the high school pool underwent repairs. Summer had barely started and already I was tan. Hours upon hours I swam, thousands of yards a day. Plus Dara had me weight training at the gym until I was so sore I could barely lift my arms. I ate like a pig and slept like the dead – I had energy for nothing else. I fantasized daily about how I was going to break it to Dara that I was cutting back on training. But I could never bring myself to actually do it. For one thing, I was getting visibly stronger, which I liked. I also liked the idea of my name going up on the record board at the school pool one of these days – maybe even next season, with my medley relay team, if D'Amico's replacement was strong enough. And maybe even in that hundred breast slot before I graduated. Some fucker had gone a 59-low back in 2005, so I had my work cut out for me.

Mostly, though, when it came down to it, I could stand being achy and exhausted more than I could stand fighting with Dara. Besides, it helped me pass the days until Meg's return. And since learning that my mom had invited them for dinner their first night in, anything that distracted from my obsessing was a good thing.

The night before she came back, she sent me the following message:

> Tomorrow's the big day ... I guess we're coming for dinner?
> It was really nice of your mom to invite us.
> My dad is pretty psyched to see your dad.

My dad was excited, too, but I could tell he was trying to keep a low profile about it. My mom was tense, but it seemed like she was trying to be positive. She and I were baking a rhubarb pie for the dinner. I hoped Meg still loved rhubarb pie. How many times had we sat drumming our fingers at my kitchen table, waiting for my mom to say the pie had cooled enough to cut into, which took eons? Mason had called it "boo-bar" pie. He always insisted he wanted a piece and then never ate it. He didn't really like it – or any dessert that wasn't made of chocolate – he just wanted to do whatever Meg and I were doing. Sometimes Meg would bail on our plans to go to the pool when Mason cried because he couldn't come, too. Man, that used to piss me off. I loved spending time with her away from our parents' watchful eyes – especially when it involved a bikini. At times like that, I thought Mason was a royal pain in the ass, and to this day I hate myself for that.

I stared at the screen and cracked my knuckles, wondering how to respond. Finally, I typed:

I'm glad our dads will get to hang out again. It's been too long.

I paused, my fingers hovering over the keyboard. Then I added:

I'm glad we get to hang out, too.

I hit Send before I could change my mind. My palms started sweating as I waited for her response.

Finally, it came:

Oh, Otis. That's so good to hear. I'm nervous. About so many things. And I know it's time to face them. But it is very hard, not knowing how you feel. I'm afraid you hate me. I wish I knew what was going through your mind.

Okay, not hearing from her for three years had been heartbreaking, but I could never *hate* her. She should know that. *She* wished she knew what was going through *my* mind?

She was the enigma, and she had been since she moved away.

I was tempted to put her fears at ease once and for all: *Not only could I never hate you,* I might say, *I could never even not love you.* But she had a boyfriend. And I still didn't know what she wanted from me. I was afraid of sending her running again, before we even laid eyes on each other.

I had to err on the safe side.

> *A lot of things have gone through my mind, but hate isn't one of them.*

> *Anyway, so much has changed since we last saw each other ... You'll probably see me tomorrow and wonder why you ever cared what I think.* ☺

She immediately wrote back:

> *I will NEVER think that.*

Which was exactly what I wanted her to say, what I was baiting her to say.

And then she wrote:

> *Remember "dumb fuck"? Is that okay to bring up? :-/*
> *I don't know how to talk to you anymore.*

I pushed away from the desk. Why did she have to go there when I was starting to feel good?

Yeah. I remembered "dumb fuck."

One Christmas Meg gave Mason a dump truck, and

Mason, who mispronounced everything, hollered, "Dumb fuck! Dumb fuck!" I about peed myself laughing. I think we were both a little sad when his speech improved to the point where "dumb fucks" became "dumb twucks." He had dozens of them – they were his favorite thing.

Later, after Mason died, Meg and I would craft bald-faced lies for our parents to account for our absence when what we were really doing was riding our bikes miles down a busy highway to go to the cemetery. I just kept needing to go there, kept needing to be close to him. We'd sit at his grave, her arm around me – sometimes both arms – and we'd talk about him, about things like "dumb fucks," about things that he said or did, sometimes laughing, but most often crying. She pulled me through days that were literally unbearable.

I glanced over at the screen. What was I supposed to say to her? I didn't want to talk about dumb fucks and Mason – not now. She was asking too much – she was ruining something that was supposed to be good. I reached over and shut my computer. Not my best moment. Not by a long shot.

I picked up the photo of Mason I kept on my bedside table. It was one I had taken myself, the October he was almost two. He was sitting in a giant pile of leaves that my dad and I had raked, tossing them up around him. The sun hit his face and he was grinning, eyes closed. It was a gorgeous picture, with all the different colors and the play of the light. But the reason I loved it was because he was so damn happy.

I went to my closet and pulled a box out from under a stack of games and puzzles. Mason's stuff. Things I took from his room when he was gone – things my parents didn't even know I had. A pair of his pajamas. A pacifier. A small stuffed chipmunk named Chester. A yellow blanket that some great aunt or cousin made. The copy of *Goodnight Moon* that I bought him.

I paged through the book, remembering the parts he would recite along with me. I stared at the last page: *Goodnight noises everywhere.* We'd whisper that last line – I suppose because that's the way my mom used to read it to me, back a million years ago before Mason was even born. When my world was perfect and safe and I was blissfully oblivious of the immense suffering that lay in store for me.

I took Mason's pajamas out and held them to my face. A trace of his warm, sweet smell lingered, or maybe it was just my imagination. I closed my eyes and let the memories wash over me: His huge, dark eyes… The way his smile curved up around the pacifier he seemed to be surgically attached to… His gray Mickey Mouse sweatshirt and his puffy little elastic-waisted jeans… His little hands reaching around and hugging my legs when I walked in the door from school… His warmth as I picked him up… The smell of toast and jelly and baby wipes… The *thwuck* of his pacifier as I'd pull it out of his mouth so I could hear him talk… And that joyful little voice exclaiming, "O-mit! You home!"

Here's the truth about healing. It's a fucking myth – an idea they try to sell you on to keep you from killing yourself. You love someone and they leave, but they never entirely go away. You feel them there, acutely, like an amputated limb.

5

A BEAM OF LIGHT SHOT THROUGH THE narrow space between the blinds and the window frame, waking me from a dream about Mason. It was fading fast, but I could still hear his voice, still see his face, and I clung to the filaments of the other world until there were no strands left to cling to. It was the best thing and the worst thing, when he appeared in dreams: Being with him again was such an astonishing joy. But then, waking and remembering. No matter how much time passed, it blindsided me. Waking up from a dream and realizing he was dead never failed to feel new and terrible.

The coffee grinder whirred from the kitchen. I rolled over and looked at the clock – 7:40. As the fog lifted, I realized what day it was: June 11. The day Meg and her dad flew back to town. I was going to see Meg today – in less than twelve hours.

When I went downstairs, I found my mom pulling out her marble pastry board and wooden rolling pin. She liked the marble for pastry, but she never strayed from the ancient red-handled rolling pin that had belonged to her grandmother. *Someday this will be yours,* she would say to me, *and it will be up to you to carry on the Stratton pie-making tradition. Unless Mason turns out to be a baker!* I remembered how Mason used to throw his head back and grin, eyes closed.

"Morning," she said, turning to me, holding the rolling pin in both hands. She lifted her eyebrows, which I knew meant, *Today's the big day, eh?* "Want some eggs? Or French toast?"

"Nah." I poured a little orange juice and sat at the table.

"You get any sleep?" Her voice was gentle.

I hated it that she could see inside my head. She knew me so well that I wasn't even entitled to my own private thoughts. I nodded and sipped my juice.

She opened the pantry and pulled out flour and sugar. "You're going to help me, right?"

"Sure."

Dressed in sweats and T-shirts, both of us, we went barefoot into the backyard. The grass was lit with dewdrops, warming under the sun, and the damp-earth smell of spring gave rise to a surge of anything-is-possible feelings.

The rhubarb's heart-shaped leaves fanned out over the edge of the garden bed, big as welcome mats. My mom cut several fat stalks, removed the leaves, and handed the stems off to me. Their color was like an inverted watermelon – deep pink on the outside, pale green on the inside.

"That should be enough," she said, handing me the last stem and wiping her hands on her sweatpants. She wandered over to the lilac trees between our house and Meg's former house and trimmed a few clusters of blooms to bring inside. "I don't know why I bother," she called to me, pulling off the leaves. "They don't last."

Back in the kitchen, we made the pie, not talking much. I got the easy jobs, like measuring sugar and spices. My mom rolled out pastry dough and cut up the rhubarb. When we got the pie assembled and into the oven, my mom turned to me. "You swimming today?"

I offered my ubiquitous shrug. "I'm supposed to." I wasn't actually feeling so good. Every time I thought of seeing Meg, my stomach seized up.

"Skip it," she suggested, turning and wiping flour off the counter with a sponge.

Right. It's that easy. Practice wasn't optional, and even if Coach would forgive my missing one, Dara would castrate me. Between worries about her and worries about Meg, I felt queasy. I sat down and lowered my head onto my arms.

My mom sat down across from me. "This is a big day for both of us."

"I guess," I said into the table.

"I'm probably more nervous than you are."

"I highly doubt that."

"Otis." She paused, so I lifted my head. "You're not the only one who lost a friend, you know." She reached for the little jam jar of lilacs that she had put on the table. They were drooping already. She tried to arrange them so they stood up better. "There's a lot we haven't talked about. You and me, I mean. About what happened. But the bottom line is sometimes relationships don't weather the storms."

"Is that what happened with Meg's parents? Did they break up because of what happened?"

She shook her head. "I don't know anything about that."

"You and Karen really haven't talked?" I still couldn't get my head around that. "You guys were so close."

She kept playing with the lilacs, not meeting my eyes. A breeze floated through the kitchen window, ruffling the leaves of the basil plant on the sill.

"I mean, wouldn't you reach out to her? After you heard?" I asked.

Anger flashed across my mom's face. "Don't judge me, Otis."

Was I judging her? Maybe I was.

She shoved the lilacs back to the center of the table. "I've worked very hard with Dr. Banks to unravel my feelings about the Brandts. But suddenly Jay and Meg are coming back, and…" She turned her head away from me. "I'm doing my best, Otis."

I never entirely understood my mom's anger at the Brandts. What happened to Mason was an accident. And my mom was there when it happened, too – it's not as if they were supposed to be in charge of him. Was it just easier to blame the Brandts? It seemed impossible that she'd hold it against them this much, for this long. It didn't seem reasonable.

"Why'd you invite them over for dinner, then?" I asked. "If you don't really even want to see them?"

She didn't answer me. She stood up and got herself a glass of water at the sink, downing the whole thing in one long gulp.

And then it dawned on me. "It wasn't you," I said slowly. "It was Dad."

She set her glass in the sink and turned to me. "It's not that simple. We talked about it. I know your father wants to be friends with Jay – I know he's eager to see him. We can't just hide from this forever. Dr. Banks thought this might be good for everyone. He made me realize that Jay might be as nervous about seeing us as we are about seeing him." She leaned back against the counter and blew out a long breath. "And frankly I can't imagine what this must be like for Meg, coming back here." She crossed her arms. She had some crusted flour on one of her wrists. "I'm not sure you realize how hard this must be for her."

I knew my mom thought I was socially awkward and emotionally fragile, but I didn't know she thought I was a complete idiot. I stared at her. "Really, Mom? It'll be hard for Meg? You think?" I got up and went over to the oven, where I clicked on the oven light and stared into the window at the pie, which was still raw. The crust looked white and waxy under the oven bulb.

I heard the slap of her bare feet on the tile floor as she moved toward me. "It wasn't just ... that it happened," she said softly, avoiding saying the actual words *that Mason died*.

But I knew what she meant. It was that he died in Meg's house.

I turned to face her. "Yeah, I get it. I understand why they would have wanted to move. To another house. I get that. But why did they have to move back to California? Didn't anyone get that we—" I broke off, torn between wanting to be understood and wanting to spare myself this awkward intimacy with my mother. "That we needed each other?"

My mom turned her gaze to the floor, chewing on her lower lip. "Otis..."

"Don't you think they could have found a way to stay?" I prodded. "I mean, God! It was a terrible time for them to leave. And in the middle of the school year? Didn't her dad have any say in a job transfer – did he even try to get out of it? Maybe if he had told them he wanted to stay at the Chicago office—"

"Otis." She closed her eyes and pressed a hand to her forehead. "It's time to move on."

That was rich, coming from her. "Oh, like you're such a role model for accepting things and moving on?"

Instantly, I wished I could take it back. She looked like she'd been slapped.

I lowered my eyes. "Sorry," I mumbled to the floor.

I didn't dare look up. After a moment, she spoke. "No, you're right. I haven't moved on. And I'm not talking about Mason, because that's not something I'm going to get over." Her voice wavered, and suddenly my own eyes stung, too. I might have told her I didn't think I was ever going to get over it, either, if I could have gotten the words out without my voice breaking. "But everything else... There has never been any closure with any of us. You think I don't feel bad about Karen? You think I'm not stressed about seeing Jay tonight? You think I don't have feelings about Meg coming back? I don't even know why she's coming! Do you?"

I didn't know which point to focus on first. "What feelings? About Meg."

She gestured with her hands like it should be self-evident, whatever her feelings were. "For over three years, I have been trying to forgive her." She turned away and put her hand to her mouth.

"What do you mean?" I took a step closer when she didn't answer. "Forgive her for what?"

She just shook her head.

"You mean forgive her for leaving me like that?" I asked.

She hesitated, her eyes shifting toward me. "That was terrible for you. Not hearing from her."

It was hard not to see her point, but at the same time, I didn't want my mom mad at Meg. All I wanted was for things to be like they used to be. Except for all the parts that couldn't be. Which, I guessed, was almost all of them.

She sighed, then pressed her lips together for a moment. "Do you remember ... a few months after they left, you were so upset about not hearing from her that you wanted me to call Karen and tell her to make Meg write to you."

I closed my eyes. *Shut up shut up shut up.* I didn't want to think about that. It was bad enough as a sort of background ache, the memory of all that desperation and agony. I didn't want it sharp and in the fore. I gave my mom a level look. "You can't be mad at her for that. She was thirteen, and you yourself were just saying how hard it was for her. If you want to be mad at someone, be mad at Karen and Jay for moving away."

"Otis."

I looked at her, and her eyes were so sad. I could barely remember a time when they weren't. A mottled gray-green, her eyes were an anomaly in an otherwise brown-eyed house. It hurt her to see me suffering, I knew. That must be why she struggled with Meg: she could never forgive her for breaking my heart.

"You've been through so much, honey," she said. "We all have. I just don't want you to get hurt again." A little eleven furrowed into the space between her eyebrows, which was approximately how much she worried about me on a one-to-ten scale.

"I won't."

She watched me for a moment, then nodded. But the doubt in her face was plain.

I texted Dara that I wasn't going to swim today. She phoned me back. "That bitch is fucking up your career, and she hasn't even gotten here yet."

She called me a few choice names and then hung up on me.

I spent a ridiculous afternoon: I cleaned my room. I reorganized my bookshelves, trying to see them through fresh eyes. I tried on different clothes. I shaved. I did push-ups and pull-ups, trying to pump up a little. I took an extra shower, washing myself so many times I think I reduced my epidermis from five layers to three. All the while I mentally rehearsed what I'd say when Meg and I first saw each other. I wanted it to be smart and funny, confident and intriguing. As it turned out, the quest for perfection burned through a lot of soap.

Afterward, I went into my parents' bathroom and compared the smell of my dad's deodorant to mine. Mine was better. I put some on – and then I put some more on, because

I was sweating bullets just *thinking* about Meg, so who knew what kind of puddle I'd be sloshing around in when we actually came face-to-face.

I followed my nose downstairs to look at the pie on the windowsill. I dragged a finger through the glistening pink juices that had bubbled up on top of the golden crust. It tasted delicious, but I was still a little nauseated. I stood around nervously while my mom made potato salad and grouched at her when she talked to me. I had an odd rush of emotion when she put crumbled blue cheese and an entire jar of capers in the potato salad, because Meg loved blue cheese and capers and my mom knew it.

Back upstairs I got paranoid and decided to hide my magnolia sonnet, which Chapman had returned to me with an A in red at the top. Not that Meg would ever look through my desk drawers, but still – better safe than sorry. I glanced around my room for a hiding place and finally tucked it into an inner pocket of my swim bag.

And then it occurred to me that maybe I should give her something – some kind of welcome-back present or friendly gesture. Shouldn't I? I had always given her stuffed animals for Christmas and birthdays, usually making up complicated histories and personalities for each one. Had she outgrown stuffed animals? Probably, but I couldn't think of anything else that wasn't too expensive, too personal, or too inappropriate.

I jumped on my bike and zipped down to Willow Grove's small downtown strip. After hemming and hawing in the toy store for a good twenty minutes, I finally settled on a stuffed skunk that looked shy and mischievous and kind of sweet.

When I got home, I jotted down a story for him.

<u>Name</u>: *Herbert McGillicutty*

<u>History</u>: *unknown – claims he escaped a hostage situation overseas and arrived in a Polish ambassador's carry-on bag, but is believed to lie. Arrived at wildlife orphanage one week ago*

<u>Favorite foods</u>: *cupcakes with sprinkles, Limburger cheese, and sardine-and-peanut-butter sandwiches on raisin bread*

<u>Physical/medical/emotional problems</u>: *flat feet, prone to ear infections, exhibits irrational fear of farm machinery*

<u>Placement recommendations</u>: *would do well with a doting female caretaker and a home with nocturnal sorts. Keep separated from amphibians and exotic types. Has been known to become unruly and use foul language when provoked*

I attached his fact sheet around his neck and then got back in the shower, because bike riding is sweaty business. While in the shower, I had a sudden panic about my toenails, so I trimmed them when I got out, and then I trimmed my fingernails, too. I checked my nose and ears to make sure there were no unwanted loiterers. Then I peered farther up my nose, fretting over my nose hair. How do you know if you have too much of it? Meg was shorter than me now – she'd be able to see up my nose!

I checked the toilet to make sure I didn't leave any pee drops or pubic hairs on the bowl, in case Meg used this bathroom. Thinking about Meg using the bathroom prompted me to go through the medicine cabinet and the closet to make sure there was nothing embarrassing in there, like the acne treatment samples I'd gotten from the pediatrician at my last visit, or the lotion Meg might think I used for masturbating, which in fact I sometimes did. I hid them in the back of my underwear drawer – clichéd, maybe, but I was pretty sure Meg wasn't about to go poking around in there.

By 4:00, I was getting nervous that I hadn't heard from her yet. According to my dad, Meg and Jay should have gotten in just after one. Why hadn't she called or texted to let me know they'd landed? Had their flight been delayed, or had it just not occurred to her to text me? Or had I ruined everything by disappearing from chat last night? Fuck, what if she was mad at me?

My stomach cramped up and then, next thing I knew, I had diarrhea. After a few bouts of that fun, I decided I'd better shower again. So I took yet another shower and then examined the toilet again to make sure there was nothing gross anywhere on or in it.

Three additional costume changes later, I was dressed and ready. And shaking. I had the paranoid thought that maybe the bathroom still smelled from when I had the diarrhea, so I ran in and sprayed some air freshener. While I was there I brushed my teeth again, because you never know. And then I noticed there were splashes of water on the mirror, so I took some toilet paper and tried to wipe it off. And that's when the doorbell rang.

A gasp rattled down my throat, making me cough, and I turned left and right, not knowing where to go or what to do. Let my parents answer it? Wait for them to call me and then saunter down, all casual-like? Go down there on my own? What the hell was I going to say? Would it look weird if I hugged her in front of everyone? Would it look weird if I didn't? Holy Christ, I had toilet paper in my hand! What if I'd gone downstairs like that, clutching a fistful of crumpled toilet paper?

I flushed it and washed my hands, just in case Meg had heard the toilet flush from outside our house – the windows were open, after all – and would think it was gross that I hadn't washed my hands after. I tried to move toward the stairs, but my body didn't want to move. My breathing was labored. My lips were numb. My pits pumped out sweat like fire hydrants. This was *not* how I envisioned greeting Meg.

I took a last look at my face, my hair, my nostrils, my clothes, and I moved toward the stairs like a man sent to walk the plank.

My mom met me halfway up. She pulled me back up the stairs and into the hall.

"What?" I asked.

"She didn't come."

I stood there for long moments, trying to process. If my mom's agonized expression was any indication, I must have looked pathetic.

"What do you mean? Why?" I finally managed.

"She – I guess she doesn't want to leave the cat."

"The *cat*?"

My mom winced. "Apparently she feels the trip was traumatic for him, and she feels bad leaving him alone."

Meg cared more about a cat than about me. Things were worse than I thought.

"Otis, you have to come down."

I felt like punching the wall. "I'll be down in a minute," I told her, heading for my room.

"Make it a fast minute, Otis," she called, but I was already closing the door.

Was Meg just avoiding me? Why didn't she tell me herself? I pulled my phone out of my pocket to check for messages.

One from Dara: *You suck.*

And one from Shafer: THE MASSIVE PENIS YOU'VE ALWAYS
WANTED – IN JUST TWO WEEKS!! CHECK OUT THIS LINK!!!

Typical Shafer, with another PSA to the team. Personally,
if I had reason to be interested in penis enlargers, I wouldn't
be sending out announcements.

But nothing from Meg.

I worked on a text to send her.

> *I can't believe you're not coming. What the fuck?*

Delete.

> *How's your stupid cat?*

Delete.

> *My mom made potato salad with blue cheese and capers
> and a fucking rhubarb pie just for you!*

Delete.

Finally I settled on, *Hope your cat is doing better. See you
soon, I guess.*

I wasn't halfway down the stairs when my phone buzzed
in my pocket. She wrote:

> *I'm sorry. I should have come.*

Followed by:

Jasper won't come out from under the bed. He doesn't even care if I'm here or not.

I paused on the stairs, wondering whether I should text and tell her to get her dad to go back and get her. Damn license! Damn Dara, damn swimming for taking up all the time I could have spent getting in the damn fifty hours behind the wheel. Damn my parents for being such fascists about the stupid fifty hours. If not for all of that, I'd have my license and I'd be able to drive over.

Another text came through:

Plus I'm starving. ☹

I smiled. Of course she was. I texted, *Want me to bring food to you?* I'd have to do it on my fucking bike, but let's face it, I'd crawl naked through rusty razor blades to get to Meg, so I certainly wasn't going to let a bicycle stand between us.

She sent a smiley back.

6

I RAN THROUGH THE HOUSE AND TOWARD the deck, where Meg's dad and my parents sat with several bottles of wine for their nerd tastings and a bunch of moldy, stinking cheeses that Meg probably would've devoured with glee.

"So we thought, fine, we'll try the oh-six, and we actually liked it *better* than the oh-seven," my dad was saying as he poured wine. "It still has that eucalyptus thing on the nose. Oh, hey, Otis," he said as I stepped outside. My mom, who was slicing one of the cheeses, glanced up at me and gestured at Meg's dad, as if I wouldn't figure out to greet him on my own.

Jay jumped up and reached out a hand. "Hey, Otis. Great to see you. Jesus, have you grown!" He'd put on weight, and his hair, which was mostly brown the last time I saw him, was now thick with gray. He gave me something like a smile, but it was forced.

"Good to see you, too," I echoed, shaking his hand and trying to smile back. It struck me how strange it was without Meg's mom there, without her chatter and loud laugh. I wondered how hard the split was for Meg.

"So sorry about Meg." He turned his hands up apologetically. "That damn cat… I had to take him, though, because—" He hesitated, glancing down. "Uh, Karen's place doesn't allow pets."

"Get yourself a plate, Otis," my mom said. She gestured toward the cheese with both arms, then clasped her hands together. She seemed nervous. They all did.

"Actually," I hazarded, "I just heard from Meg and she's hungry. I thought I could bring food over there."

They all blinked at me like I was speaking in tongues.

"I could take my bike," I added.

"That's far to go on a bike," my mom said, glancing at my dad.

"It is not!" I exclaimed, exasperated. "Meg and I—"

I stopped. They didn't know we used to ride our bikes to the cemetery. My mom would stroke out on the spot. I finished with, "Meg and I would like to see each other."

"I could go back and get her," Jay said, glancing at my parents. "Would only take ten or fifteen minutes."

"Well, I think she wants to stay with the cat," I said.

Okay, that wasn't exactly true. But what had me so excited now wasn't just the idea of seeing Meg, but the possibility of being alone with her.

"Well," Jay said, "at least let me drive you over."

"It's fine," I said. "I kind of feel like a bike ride anyway."

That was a fantastic stretch, since I only grudgingly rode a bike, and only when there were no other choices – and I rarely failed to complain about it.

"But then you'll be coming home in the dark," my mom protested. "On the highway!" She shook her head. "I don't like it."

"Laura, he's not a five-year-old," my dad said mildly. He put a hand on her back. "He knows what he's doing, and his bike has reflectors."

There was an awkward moment of silence while my mom processed the idea, her forehead doing its trademark origami. "I haven't even cooked the burgers yet," she finally said. "We just sat down for drinks!"

My dad got up and turned the grill on. "I'll cook off two burgers now, and we'll do the rest later. No problem. Easy peasy."

It took everything I had not to tackle-hug him.

After a half an hour, which felt more like nine days, I had a picnic of oozy foil-wrapped cheeseburgers, Meg's potato salad, and pie. I packed it all in my backpack, where Herbert the skunk was already tucked away. I bid a cheerful farewell, managing not to roll my eyes as my mother fired off her laundry list of reminders and safety warnings. "Text me as soon as you get there," she finished, hugging me as if I were going off to war. My dad appeared and put a glass of wine in her hand, raising his eyebrows at me to acknowledge that she was kind of a case.

And then I was on my way.

It actually was a perfect evening for a bike ride. A warm breeze carried the smell of spring blossoms, and puffy white clouds scattered all over the bright blue sky.

But by the time I'd pedaled through the neighborhood and reached the highway for the longer stretch of the journey, fears began to nudge out my optimism. I thought about Football Guy, and how he probably had a nice car and loads of confidence, and suddenly I felt like a stupid little kid, pedaling along on my bike. On top of that, I was starting to sweat; after spending half the day in the shower, it seemed a gross injustice that I should end up biking to see Meg.

Cars zoomed by my left shoulder as I pedaled the last mile or so to the hotel. Of course the final leg of the ride had to be uphill, just in case I wasn't sweating enough already. When I pulled into the parking lot, I realized I didn't know where her room was. I stopped my bike by the main entrance, texted my mom as instructed to let her know I'd arrived alive and intact, and then texted Meg to figure out where she was. But of course, Meg being Meg, she wasn't sure where she was, either, and it took a few minutes of virtual Marco Polo to get me to her door.

When I found it, I leaned my bike against the wall and ran a hand through my hair. I wanted to sniff my pits, just to check, but what if she was watching me from a window? So I rapped on the door, my heart in my throat.

The door opened a tiny crack. I heard her take a breath and blow it out. And then she swung the door open.

Neurons ping-ponged in my brain, trying to piece together the visual puzzle of all the ways the girl standing in the doorway was and wasn't familiar. She was Meg but not Meg. Other than the obvious metamorphosis of her figure, I couldn't quite put my finger on how she was different. But I had the sense of her having changed more than I'd imagined, and suddenly I felt like I didn't know anything anymore.

I was conscious of the fullness of her breasts in her sort-of-clingy pink T-shirt, of the smallness of her waist, of how much shorter than me she was, but that was all in the periphery. I couldn't let go of her eyes, that fantastic aqua-sea color, the familiarity and strangeness and all the shared and unshared secrets contained in them.

"Otis." It was a whisper, an exhale, barely there.

I stared at her, not knowing whether or not to hug her. Was she the same, or was she new? Did we know each other, or not? Was a hug the right thing? The only thing more bizarre in my mind than not hugging her was the thought of how she'd feel in my arms in the bodies we were in now.

"Come on in," she said, stepping back.

I stepped inside and set my backpack on a table by the door. The smell of the room conjured an era when cigarette smoke was as popular as air and dark green stripes were the decorating rage. The TV – a modern touch, flat-screened and on a swivel base – was muted on a cooking show.

"My God," Meg said slowly as her eyes swept over me. "Is that really you?"

I couldn't think of anything to say. All I could think was how beautiful she was, and I certainly wasn't going to say that.

"You're so tall! I've never looked up at you before!" She had a look of wide-eyed wonder on her face that was giving my imagination all sorts of probably erroneous ideas. "God, you must be so strong! Sorry," she added hastily, flapping her hands. "I'm just – taking you in."

There was a lot of in-taking going on. Her fragrance had infiltrated my senses, a welcome interruption from the seeped-in secondhand smoke. Like everything else, it was familiar but different. Her damp hair hung in long waves. Had she just showered? A thought not to linger on…

"Jasper's hiding in the bedroom," she said, and there was that shy smile – the one that rendered me hopelessly and irrevocably hers the day she first showed up in my life. *That* was the same.

"Who's Jasper?" I asked a moment before I remembered it was the cat.

"He speaks!" Meg exclaimed, making me realize those were the first words I'd uttered. "It's like the first time we met," she said with a teasing smile. "I remember I was starting to think you were mute."

I blushed. "Mute" was a fairly apt descriptor for me the day she moved in. It was May, of course – the magnolia was so dramatic it managed to lure Meg over. I had never seen anything like the girl who stepped out of that green Volvo that morning. She was sunshine and sweetness, but also mystery and magnetism. My mom and Mason and I had been sitting on the front porch watching the movers, and next thing I knew, my mom was making introductions. Looking at Meg was like staring into the sun, so I averted my eyes and tried not to die. My mother's exasperation with my state of incapacity was palpable. Mason, who was one and a half, talked to her more than I did.

As luck would have it, I couldn't think of a reply now, either, so I just smiled. The moment stretched out awkwardly, and then Meg held out her arms a little, palms upturned, a question: *Hug?*

Relief flooded through me, but as she reached out to hug me, I froze. I didn't mean to, but I was suddenly wary about how badly I'd wanted to hold her, and for so long, and I didn't want to overdo it. Instead, I underdid it, and it ended up being a stiff, back-patty hug. The last thing I wanted.

She stepped back and swept her hair over her shoulders. "I can't get over how big you are!"

"I guess I was pretty scrawny the last time you saw me," I said, crossing my arms nervously and hoping my biceps looked good. I could still smell her from the brief contact. God, I wished I could have a do-over on the hug.

"Well." She smiled as if to soften the truth of it. "Comparatively. I mean, I saw a picture, so I shouldn't be surprised, but—"

"What picture?"

"It was you with your girlfriend at a swim meet."

I shook my head, confused.

She looked around, spotting her phone on the coffee table. She went over and picked it up. "Here," she said, after scrolling around a little. She handed the phone to me.

It was a picture from the local paper of Dara and me after I'd won the hundred breast at conference in February. Dara and I are standing by the blocks in our fast suits, arm in arm. Interestingly, she was on my right side, so her stump was behind my back. It was an arresting photo because I could visualize her with two arms. And because she looked so happy. We both did.

"How did you find this?" I asked.

She gestured with her hand, looking a little embarrassed. "Just basic stalking one-oh-one. Nothing creepy."

The idea of her looking for stuff about me online kind of thrilled me. "Well," I said, shoving my hands in my pockets, "she's not my girlfriend."

She raised her eyebrows.

"It's a swim thing. Dara coaches me. Sort of."

"She's a coach?" She tilted her head at me. "She looks really young."

"No. She's on the team – she's a senior. She just coaches *me*." I sighed, knowing Dara made no sense. "It's a long story."

"She's pretty."

I shrugged.

It was quiet for a moment, and I hastened to fill the awkward gap. "So, you still hungry? The burgers are probably getting cold."

"Actually, would you mind if we just sat awhile?" She fingered a rubber band around her left wrist. "I don't think I can eat right now."

"I'm pretty sure I've never heard *those* words from you before," I said, following her to the couch. She laughed, and her laugh was the same, exactly the same, which was both warming and nerve-racking. I joined her on the sofa, leaving about three feet between us. She took a breath and blew it out, eyes cast down.

"You okay?" I asked.

She gave me a tentative smile. "Not really."

"I'm sorry," I said softly, wishing I could put my arms

around her or touch her somehow, but there I sat, like a god-damned stranger.

She lifted her shoulders a little, watching me. "I can't believe I'm looking through those eyes again."

"Through?"

She nodded. "Yeah, because they're clear. Most brown eyes aren't clear. Yours are light, like honey. Your dad's are dark brown and…" She trailed off.

Mason's eyes were also dark brown. I wondered if that's what she was thinking.

"Are you thirsty?" She jumped up. "You want a Coke or something?"

She moved toward the kitchen area, barefoot. She still had that impossibly light way of walking, like she had her own field of gravity and it was less than everybody else's. She pulled open the refrigerator. "Oh! Empty. Perfect." She turned around, frowning. "There's probably a vending machine somewhere."

"Water's fine."

She filled a couple of glasses with ice and water and came back over, the ice cubes clinking like little bells. Were her hands shaking? She handed me a glass, then sat on the sofa, one leg folded beneath her, just the way she used to sit. Her ice continued to rattle in the glass.

"God," she said, glancing at me, "I'm shaking like beef."

I squinted at her. "Like beef?"

She widened her eyes at me. "Don't you remember shaking beef? From that Vietnamese restaurant in the city? We loved it!"

I smiled as I remembered. "Right. The shaking beef. God, that was good."

"We used to say that! 'Shaking like beef.' Remember?"

Before I could respond, her cell phone rang.

Meg jumped and grabbed her phone from the coffee table. "Oh!" She glanced at me apologetically. "I have to take this – I'm sorry! I'll just be a few minutes."

I threw my hands up in the air. I shouldn't have expressed my frustration, but I had a feeling I knew who was calling, and I wasn't thrilled with my place in the pecking order.

"Be right back," she said, disappearing into the bedroom and closing the door behind her.

I stared at the TV and tried to be distracted by the epic cleavage on the TV chef. She tucked a massive forkful of pasta into her mouth and rolled her eyes back in her head as she chewed. I thought about having sex with that chef right on her kitchen counter. But it was an empty thought, free of desire and barely amusing – not enough to stop me from obsessing about the conversation Meg was having with Football Guy while I sat there with my stupid cold cheeseburgers in my backpack and my stupid bike outside the door.

I wished I hadn't come. Some idiot part of me had managed to create a fantasy that the moment our eyes connected, it would all come rushing back, we'd still be *us*, and everything that had happened in the intervening years would just evaporate as we fell into each other's arms. Instead, we were strange and awkward, and I was sitting there alone in front of the TV while she talked in the other room to the guy she loved. I wanted to get up and go home, to never have come at all. To go to bed and wake up in a world where I'd let her go the day she left, where I wasn't caught in this mind-numbingly stupid pain loop.

Dara was right. Love was for chumps.

Something furry appeared in my lap. "Hello," I said. "You must be Jasper." He was long-haired, with patches of gray and white and black. He rubbed his head against my chest. I gave his back a stroke, which started him purring.

Cats are okay, but dogs. *Dogs.* I had never had one because of my dad's allergies, but I sure had loved Meg's dog.

When Cassie got hit by a car, I had picked her up and carried her – all forty pounds of her, which was nearly half my weight when I was eleven – to the animal hospital on Maple Avenue, nearly five blocks away. It was a fall day, after school, and none of our parents were home. I shook and sweated under the weight of the dog and the fear that she might be dying in my arms. Her warm blood soaked into my shirt, and her little whimpers had faded to silence. When we got there, they rushed Cassie to the back. Meg and I sat in the waiting room, holding hands and shaking. When the vet came out, he told us, "Ten more minutes and she wouldn't have made it."

But she did make it. She needed surgery and she had a bad limp for the rest of her days, but she didn't seem to mind. She was such a good girl. When my dad told me he'd seen on Facebook that she'd died, I went to my room and bawled like a baby. Not being able to connect with Meg just about killed me. I knew well enough by then that if I emailed her, she wouldn't respond. So I mailed her a sympathy card. She didn't respond to that, either.

When Meg walked back into the living room, she stopped short. "That little traitor! That stupid fleabag has refused to come out for me since we got here." She sat down close to me and petted him.

"Maybe he prefers men," I suggested.

"He *hates* Jeff. My boyfriend," she added, somewhat awkwardly.

"Oh!" I said, more cheerfully than I meant to. "Well, so much for that theory!" I scratched my new buddy under the chin, and he practically swooned.

Meg tipped her head, watching me pet Jasper. "God, your hands are huge."

I looked at them. They weren't *huge*, but they were big enough. "Good for swimming," I said. I chanced a look at her and noticed that her lashes were damp. "Hey. Are you okay?"

She nodded but didn't look up. She just continued to pet

her two-timing cat. "I just need to sleep, I think. I haven't slept well in days."

"You want to go to bed?" I asked, confused.

She looked at me, eyes widening.

"No!" I cried, startling Jasper, who leaped off my lap. "I didn't mean—"

A slow smile – understanding, sort of teasing. She knew what I meant. She knew me.

I let my breath out. "Anyway. How 'bout those burgers? You have a microwave?"

She watched me for a moment, biting her lip, thinking God knows what. Then she stood up.

We heated the burgers and dished up the potato salad. "What's this?" she asked, gesturing at the foil packet of pie I'd set on the counter.

"Guess."

"Oh God." She touched her fingertips to her collarbone. "Is it rhubarb pie?"

"Bingo."

She reached for it, smiling.

"Hey, that's dessert," I objected as she started unwrapping the packet.

"Let's have dessert first," she said, putting a plate under the foil and heading back to the living area.

"But we just warmed up the..." I sighed.

Meg.

I followed her back to the sofa and sat down next to her.

"You're lucky I ever even tried rhubarb pie," she told me.

"Why?"

"When we first moved in and you and your mom brought one over, I asked you what rhubarb was. You said it was a plant in your yard that was, and I'm quoting here, 'really sour, with poisonous leaves.'"

I laughed. That did sound like me. What a dork. "Well, obviously I talked you into trying it," I said, taking the fork she handed me.

"I don't know how." She smiled. "'Welcome to the neighborhood! Here's a sour, poisonous pie!'"

It felt so good to laugh with her. When she took a bite of pie, she moaned and her eyes rolled back, just like the TV chef with the cleavage. Why were women so sexy with eating? Jesus! What if I never developed bedroom skills that could compete with food? What if I actually got to have sex with Meg one day and she just lay back, bored, daydreaming about pulled pork sandwiches and chocolate éclairs?

"Would you believe I haven't had rhubarb pie since I lived here?" She licked the back of her fork.

"Doesn't California have rhubarb?"

"I don't know. I've never seen it. It doesn't matter, anyway. Has to be your mom's."

As I braced the plate to take a forkful, my fingers brushed

against hers. "I always think of you when we have rhubarb pie," I said.

Her eyes searched my face, like she couldn't tell if I was serious. "Really?" Her voice was soft, tentative.

"Yeah. Really."

She smiled, but she looked kind of sad. "There are things that always make me think of you, too."

"Like what?" I asked.

"Like, um … I always think of you when I get lost at my high school."

"Aw." I put my hand to my heart. "So every day?"

She elbowed me, and a sharp jab in the ribs had never felt so wonderful.

I thought maybe she'd keep talking, but instead she unmuted the TV, and we watched a cooking competition while we ate the rest of the food.

"Oh my gosh," Meg said, her fork poised over the potato salad. "Is it…"

"Yeah, blue cheese and capers. My mom made it for you."

At first I thought she was smiling, but I sat up and leaned forward when I realized she was actually crying. "Meg?"

She pushed her plate at me so she could cover her face with both hands. I set both our plates on the coffee table. "Hey!" I reached out but stopped short of touching her, not sure if it was okay. And I hated that I didn't know. "What's going on?"

She shook her head. "Sorry." She wiped her tears away with her fingertips. "I just can't believe your mom did that. For me!"

I could think of nothing to say. After a minute, she picked up her plate and started eating again while I shoveled food into my mouth in a state of complete clueless wonder.

When we finished, she stood up and brought our plates to the kitchen. My eyes followed her – I couldn't help it. She had the perfect heart-shaped butt. Not athletic and muscular like Dara's, but soft and womanly. To me, the ultimate ass aesthetic.

When she came back, she sat and turned to me. She glanced down and bit back a smile. "Your legs got hairy."

I looked at my legs, a blush creeping up from my neck. "Well, yes. That's, uh … a thing that happened."

"I mean, duh. Stuff happens. Obviously." She gestured at her chest, then rolled her eyes at herself and buried her face in her hands, which amused me. When she raised her head, her cheeks were as red as mine felt. "God. I'm sorry I'm such a train wreck."

"That's okay," I said, then realized that I seemed to be confirming that she was, indeed, a train wreck. "I mean, you're not…"

She gave me a smile that could have melted a glacier. She was close enough that I was getting a little agitated about the onions my mom had put on the burgers.

My phone dinged – my mom. I opened the text. "She says not to ride my bike home," I explained to Meg, rolling my eyes. "They're going to come get me."

"They're … coming here?" Meg fingered the rubber band on her wrist.

"Apparently."

"Oh." Our attention turned to the TV, where a judge was ripping a chef contestant a new asshole because she'd overcooked the fish.

"He's so mean," Meg exclaimed, shaking her head at the television. "I would never subject myself to one of these shows."

"Can you cook?"

"I can cook some things. I make a mean pasta carbonara."

"What's that?" I asked, relaxing back into the couch and stretching my legs out.

She ticked off ingredients on her fingers. "Spaghetti, bacon, eggs, and cheese."

My eyes widened. "Bacon, eggs, and cheese? With pasta? Oh my God, that's a swimmer's wet dream!"

I did not just say that. Did I? Meg's expression confirmed that, yes, I had actually just said *wet dream*. What was going through her head right now? Images of me, grunting and bucking in the dark and waking up with a mess in my shorts? Oh God, why do I speak?

I sought a rapid change in subject. "Hey, I have something

for you." I jumped up, ran over by the door, and dug through my backpack.

"Here," I said, thrusting the skunk out to her and sitting back down. Immediately my confidence wavered. A stuffed skunk? It was a stupid, childish gift. I wished I could rip off the idiot story from around its neck. We weren't twelve anymore.

But one look at her told me I needn't have worried. "Ohh," she whispered. "I love him."

"You still have stuffed animals?" I asked hopefully.

"Are you kidding? Every one of them. What's this?" She tapped the paper.

"See for yourself."

She muted the TV, then opened the paper. When she realized what it was, she lifted a hand to her mouth. I tipped my head to watch her face as she read.

"Oh, Otis," she said through her hand, looking up at me. "I can't believe you did this." Then she reached out her arm, hesitated, and then ruffled my hair.

Great – now I was a puppy.

I discreetly tried to fix my hair; it was bad enough from the bike ride and the perpetual chlorine abuse without supplementary agitation.

"I didn't bring any stuffed animals with me," she said, petting Herbert. "Now I have one to keep me company until I go back home."

"Right. In three weeks, you said?" And then we were in

the awkward place, where we could no longer avoid talking about what was going on.

She set Herbert on her lap and stared down at him. "I guess you know about my parents."

"I only know, like, the bare minimum. Like, your dad is transferring back? And that you're here for a visit. That's really all I know. I don't even know why…" I trailed off, not sure I wanted to say it right out: *Why after three years you suddenly wanted to come back.*

My stomach knotted up. In the silence, the sounds of the room magnified. The air conditioner hummed, and the ice maker cranked out a few cubes in the freezer. Meg's stomach made noises, which I pretended not to notice.

"Well," she said, running her hand along the underside of Herbert's giant fluffy tail, "we lived in corporate housing. And then my parents split, and my mom has this little apartment."

God. That sounded awful. "Do you live with her?"

"I live with my dad. I see her on weekends, usually. I have to be back in three weeks because she gets a week with me in July."

I must have looked confused, because she explained, "Custody agreement."

Why? I wanted to ask but couldn't. Why was she with her dad? Why had her parents split up? Why was she here? "That must be rough."

She raised her eyebrows, staring into her lap. "There isn't a single thing that hasn't been rough. Not since I was thirteen."

My stomach dropped. "I can imagine. I mean. Same for me. Obviously."

She kind of looked me up and down. "You seem like you're doing okay."

I thought about it. "What's 'okay'?"

She smiled a little. "Right. That is a good question." She fingered a lock of her hair. "Anyway. You're probably wondering why I came. But too polite to ask."

I blushed as though I'd been caught out. God, she knew me.

"I just … I really needed to see you," she began.

My heart jackhammered while my mind spun out fantasies. She hadn't stopped loving me all these years. She wanted to get back together. She—

"We need to talk, Otis."

And just like that, my wild hopes were dashed. Nothing good ever follows "we need to talk." It means you fucked up, or you're fired, or you're dumped. It means something you are not going to want to hear.

"I know I have some explaining to do," she said into her lap, her hands still clutching the skunk. "And some apologizing – to put it mildly."

"I guess there's lots that we could talk about," I said. *Like why you disappeared on me right when I needed you most.*

My stomach started to churn. "We don't have to get into that stuff tonight," I said. "You're tired. There's always tomorrow. Or some other day." Or never.

I was such a wimp. For three years I had longed to talk to Meg, and now that she was here I was too chickenshit to face what she might want to say.

She opened her mouth to respond.

I braced myself.

And then voices. The sounds of a key card swiping the lock and the door creaking open. And there were our parents.

I can't say I was sorry to see them.

Meg stood, but then seemed rooted to the spot. My mother was also frozen. My dad pushed through and greeted Meg, giving her an awkward hug. He looked back at my mom, who finally inched forward.

"Meg," she said, trying to smile. She moved toward her in hesitant steps. And then they were hugging, and my mom was crying – and not subtly. My mom doesn't do "subtle" where emotions are concerned.

When my mom finally let go of Meg, she said, "It's good to see you. You're just beautiful."

Meg wiped her eyes, and I realized she was crying, too. She looked at my mom like she wanted to say something, but she couldn't get words out.

Suddenly it overwhelmed me, the weight of the past, all

the Mason in the room. In some ways, the last three years had been an infinity. But in other ways, the passage of time seemed to count for nothing.

I scrambled to my feet. I didn't want to leave Meg, but I wanted this scene to end – and end fast. I grabbed my backpack, and my mom moved toward me, wiping away tears.

"Everything okay?" She spoke softly, doing a rapid analysis of my face and posture to calculate my psychological status.

"Yup," I said, shouldering my backpack. "Your teeth are black."

She made a face. "Petite Sirah. Like ink."

"Well, we'll get out of your way," my dad told Meg's dad. "You must be tired. Give me a shout tomorrow."

"I will," Jay said, clapping my dad on the shoulder. "Thanks for tonight. It was great to see you."

My mom, still sniffling, went over and gave him a hug.

I froze. To hug Meg goodbye, or not?

But Meg made the decision for me by coming over, arms extended, and giving me a very sweet hug. This time I didn't stiffen up. Figures – we finally got it right, and it was while our parents were watching.

My mom moved toward the door and said to Meg's dad, "Let me know if you want the name of that Realtor."

He glanced at Meg. "As soon as Meg decides if she's moving back. Otherwise, I'll probably get an apartment in the city."

I stood there like a dolt, blinking at Meg. "You... You might move back?"

She stood with her mouth open for a moment, blinking. "Maybe. That's what I was going to tell you," she said weakly, crossing her arms. "I have to figure that out."

The room was way too quiet. Finally, my mom broke the silence by saying how late it was. "Come on, Otis. You drive home."

I followed my parents out into the cool night, all of my mental whirring adding up to zero comprehension. We loaded my bike into the trunk and my dad handed me the car keys.

I drove home on autopilot. Nobody spoke.

7

I DREAMED I WAS AT A SWIM MEET BUT MY arms didn't work – I just kicked in the water, panicking, and straining to catch someone's eye so they'd help me before I drowned. Finally, I noticed Dara, sitting in one of the chairs on the deck. She just smirked at me as I went down, down, down.

I awoke gasping for air, soaked in sweat. I kicked off the covers and waited for my heart rate to come down.

What I had wanted was to dream of Meg. Of us kissing, of the desperate tangle of mouths and arms and legs.

My subconscious was unsatisfactory.

I picked up my phone. Time: 7:51. I reread the messages Meg had sent while I drove home from the hotel.

I'm sorry you found out that way. I was just about to tell

you myself, but then our parents ... Anyway, I probably
should've brought it up earlier. I meant to. But seeing you
again – it was kind of overwhelming. Great, but over-
whelming. You know?

But yes, I have to decide whether to stay in CA with my
mom or come back to Chicago. And to do that, I need to
figure some things out. To see if I can be okay here. And
okay with you.

Well, I guess you're busy – or maybe too mad to write back.
I'm exhausted, so I'm gonna go to bed. I'm sorry, Otis.

When I'd gotten home, I had reached out with a quick
Sorry, I was driving – I'm home now message, but apparently
she had gone to sleep already.

I didn't know what things she needed to figure out, but
I was determined either to convince her to come back or to
die trying.

I went downstairs, cell phone in my sweatpants pocket,
following the sound of my dad's cheerful whistling. I found
him in the kitchen, messing with the espresso machine he'd
recently bought so he could stop contributing to Starbucks'
unholy wealth. Decked out in a faded Grateful Dead T-shirt,
a Cubs hat, and his Budweiser pajama bottoms, the man was
a mess. I had to smile.

"Hey, Ot, want a latte?" he asked. They must love him

at the office. He was so damn likable.

"Sure." I stood over his shoulder and watched him assembling parts, wondering if he had a clue what he was doing. "Where's Mom?"

He affixed a little plastic tube to a nozzle. "Grief support group." He poured milk into a small metal pitcher.

"I didn't know she was still doing that." Almost four years later? Mom kept talking about moving forward, but in some ways it looked more like she was going backward.

He glanced up at me briefly. "Yeah. She still does."

He turned on the machine and lifted the pitcher of milk to the wand, which made the milk bubble and sputter. I crossed the kitchen and looked out the window. Two squirrels played chase in the backyard, twirling up and down the old birch tree. The thermometer outside the window read sixty-six already. I lifted the window open and was rewarded with a breeze that smelled of fresh-cut grass.

"You going to see Meg today?" my dad said loudly over the noise of the machine. "You guys seemed like you were hitting it off okay last night, huh?"

Was my dad playing matchmaker? This was quite a contrast to my mom, who I sometimes thought might have been happy if I never saw Meg again. Okay, maybe not *happy*, but less stressed, anyway. My dad wasn't such a worrier. They balanced each other out like that.

Maybe that's what marriage was, in essence – an unspoken

agreement regarding division of neuroses and quirks so that the bases were covered and neither partner stepped on the other's toes. *You be the worrier and control freak; I'll stay cool and be flexible. You tolerate my love of everything retro and my tendency toward slovenliness, and I'll try to be cheerful when you're down and stay out of your way when you're moody. I'll deal with moldy food in the containers in the back of the fridge, but you will not ask me to deal with bugs or spiders. You'll cook awesome meals, and I'll do the dishes. I'll let you weigh in on what wine to open, and you'll never open anything without checking with me first so God forbid you don't accidentally open something epic that should be cellared for another five or ten years.* Those seemed to be aspects of my parents' unwritten agreement. Somehow it worked.

"I'll drive you if you want to go to a movie or wherever," he said. "I know Jay is meeting with work people today."

"I don't know." I sank into a chair at the table. "I have to swim."

"Oh, come on." He poured the milk over the espresso. "On a Sunday?"

Dara calls it seventh-day swimming. She says when I'm God, I can rest on Sunday. Besides, I blew off the day before, so skipping again wasn't an option.

My dad continued. "I'll bet even Michael Phelps took days off when he was training."

I scowled and accepted the mug he handed me. "Not even Christmas Day."

My dad whistled. "I guess you have to be that devoted to make it to the Olympics."

He wasn't helping.

He gestured toward my mug. "Not too shabby, huh?"

The foam at the top of my mug was creamy and billowy. "It is a thing of beauty," I told him.

"Starbucks ain't got nothing on your old man." He kissed his bicep – a gesture my mother couldn't stand, but it must have been part of their unwritten agreement, because he still did it.

He was showing me how he could grate whole nutmeg onto our lattes with the wood rasp from his tool box when my cell phone rang. I glanced at it with dread, expecting Dara.

It was Meg. I lunged for my latte, almost knocking it over, and headed toward my room, answering the phone as I went.

"Hey," Meg said. "Am I calling too early?" The familiar, sweet sound of her voice made me desperate to be close to her again. She had a way of pronouncing her consonants, light on the tongue, that always made me want to get my ear right near her lips.

"Ha, I'm a swimmer, remember? There's no such thing as 'too early.' How'd you sleep?"

"I was sleeping fine, until Jasper peed on my bed! I don't know if he couldn't find the litter box or if he's just pissed at me, no pun intended."

I groaned. "Ugh, that sucks."

"Seriously, *nothing* gets that out. You know how they say nothing lasts forever? It should be amended to 'nothing lasts forever, except cat pee.'"

I laughed.

"I have a feeling that the Extended Stay will be revising its pet policy soon." She heaved a sigh.

I set my coffee down on my desk and pulled opened the blinds, squinting against the sun. "Have you seen how bright it is outside?"

A door creaked open on the other end of the phone. "Oh, wow. We have this little patio thingie off the back door." She yawned. "I could use a latte."

"Ha! Guess what I'm drinking right now?"

"You so are not drinking a latte."

"I so am! My dad made me one. He has a new machine." I took a noisy slurp.

She made a disgusted noise. "Lucky."

"You're welcome to come and put my dad to work. Nothing makes him happier than being productive."

"That is a true thing. Remember how he was always getting my dad to do house projects?"

I smiled. Meg's dad would rather watch TV and hire a handyman, but my dad always wanted Jay to be his project pal. "Well, your dad got my dad to sit and watch sports sometimes, so maybe it was good for both of them."

"Yeah, it was. I think they've missed each other. I hope they'll, you know, hang out again and stuff."

Unanswered questions hung heavily in the air. The question of our mothers' friendship. The question of mine and Meg's. The question of whether Meg would also move back and what, exactly, she needed to figure out before she made that decision.

"Anyway," she said after a moment. A chair scraped and cars whizzed by in the background. "What are you doing today?"

"Swimming," I said. "For a while, anyway."

"I'm dying to see you swim," she said, which made my stomach leap. "Could I watch? Is that allowed?"

"Well, I should warn you that, as much fun as training with Dara is, I think watching would be even less fun."

"I don't think so. I'd love to see how you train, meet Dara … all that stuff."

My stomach twisted thinking about "all that stuff." It could be amazing to have Meg there – or it could be the worst day ever, depending on how Dara behaved.

"And then maybe after … we could talk?"

"Sure," I said, as if I didn't fill with dread at the very thought. "Let me find out when Dara wants to practice." She'd probably yell at me for not referring to her carefully constructed schedule, which I had long since misplaced or possibly tossed.

I hung up with Meg and texted Dara, letting her know that Meg wanted to watch me practice. I phrased it as a statement so that it was clear I wasn't asking for permission. But I figured I'd better give her a heads-up.

She called me right away. "Training is not a spectator sport," she said by way of a greeting.

"Jesus, Dara. What's the big deal if she comes? The pool is open to the public, you know."

"Fine, whatever. But you're putting in your yards. Don't expect me to go easy on you just because she's there. I'll pick you up in ten minutes."

"No! I'm not ready. Anyway, I'm going to have my dad drive me so we can pick up Meg."

"I'll pick her up after I come get you."

I hesitated, dreading the intersection of Dara and Meg. But it was probably inevitable.

I turned to the mirror. My hair looked like roadkill in a windstorm, and my mouth tasted like coffee mixed with garbage. "I need to shower."

"Don't be ridiculous. You're going straight into the pool. You'll shower later."

"Just give me a half an hour, okay? And could you not drive like such a maniac?"

She snorted and hung up.

When she picked me up, I was freshly scrubbed and combed and minty. She was in a bitchy mood, but I did my best to get a friendly vibe going in the car. "What did you do yesterday?" I asked.

"I knitted a scarf."

One of her favorite rejoinders: naming things that can only be done with two hands. *I practiced guitar. I shucked oysters. I gave myself a manicure.* "Ha-ha. Seriously."

"I slept."

"All day? Go to Sanders." I pointed at the upcoming intersection.

"I know where it is," she grouched.

But when she pulled up at the hotel and saw Meg waiting out front, Dara's expression changed. I don't know what she expected, but she looked surprised.

I jumped out of the car, wishing I could throw my arms around Meg and take a big whiff of her, but instead I just stood in front of her, grinning like a dummy. "Hey."

She was wearing a summery dress, black with a flower design. It tied behind her neck and clung to her waist. I tried not to stare.

She reached out and poked me lightly, just once, right below my shoulder. "Hey, yourself." Her bright eyes sparkled, and she had shiny stuff on her lips that caught the sun. She gestured with her head toward Dara's car. "Should we go?"

"Right!" I turned and hesitated for a split second about whether to put Meg in the front seat, which under normal circumstances was the polite thing to do, or spare her Dara's proximity and put her in back. I went with manners and opened the passenger door for Meg.

Had I told Meg about Dara's stump? It stuck straight out toward Meg as Dara leaned into the backseat to move her stuff so someone could sit back there. Meg did a double take, then glanced at me, still standing by the door.

"Hey, Dara," she said as she climbed in. "Nice to meet you."

Dara sat back and glanced at Meg, looking flustered. "Hey."

"Thanks for picking me up."

"No problem."

I buckled in behind Meg and prompted her to fasten her seat belt.

"Mueller thinks I'm a hazard behind the wheel," Dara explained, pulling out of the lot with less hazard than usual. "I am actually a very skilled driver."

"Well, that makes one of us," Meg quipped. "Though I'm guessing you're a great driver, Otis," she added, turning to glance back at me.

"I'm not bad," I said, hating that I couldn't show her myself.

"Well, you've got me beat in driving and swimming, that's for sure," she said.

"You could improve at swimming if you wanted to," Dara said.

"I don't know," Meg said. "If after three years in California all I can do is doggie paddle, I think it's safe to say I'm hopeless."

"Well, you come by it honestly," I said.

Meg laughed. "True." She explained to Dara, "My dad can't swim. He's petrified of the water."

"You should have seen Mueller three years ago," Dara said, pulling up to a red light. "He couldn't do any of the strokes – and he belly flopped when he tried to dive. Believe me, if he can learn, anyone can."

Thanks, Dara. Heat bloomed in my cheeks and ears.

But Meg craned around and smiled at me. "The dark horse. I'm not surprised."

"What's that?" Dara said.

"You know … the unlikely one who turns out to be amazing. That's so Otis."

My face warmed. *Yes, okay!*

"Well, he didn't do it on his own, you know," Dara grumbled.

"Oh, I didn't mean to imply that he did," Meg said quickly. "My dad was telling me this morning about all the medals and ribbons Otis has won; you must be an amazing coach."

Dara grunted, and that was the end of the car conversation. On balance, I considered it a win – but only because Meg was so awesome.

At the pool we found a table with an umbrella. Meg pulled a chair into the sun and settled in.

"Did you stretch already?" Dara asked, pulling off her "Shut Up" T-shirt.

I hadn't. I'd been too busy grooming this morning – and examining my body from various angles in the mirror. I also tested how the Speedo/drag-suit combo handled a complete erection, in case of an emergency. Not good. Not good at all.

So Dara and I stretched while Meg dug around in her purse – trying to look busy, I suspected, because it was frankly kind of awkward, especially when Dara worked on the two-person stretches she liked to use on me. Her comfort in handling my body, our familiarity, suddenly felt way too intimate.

When we finished, Dara handed me her goggles.

"You coming in?" I asked Meg, holding the elastic on Dara's goggles as Dara adjusted them. Technically it was open swim time, but the pool often roped off a strip on the far ends of the deep end for lap swimming.

"Maybe later."

I stepped out of my shorts and peeled off my T-shirt, acutely aware of Meg's eyes on me. Drag suits cover up slightly more skin than Speedos, but they still don't leave much to the imagination. I hoped Meg was thinking, *Wow, he's hot,* but I worried she was thinking, *Wow, what a tiny package he has!* Because I didn't think girls knew about stuff like the complete insignificance of non-erect package size or unfortunate situational realities such as shrinkage. This was a grave injustice. In my opinion, these things should be covered in health class.

"There're your boys," Dara said, gesturing with her chin. Shafer, D'Amico, and Heinz strolled in, towel-snapping each other's asses.

Shit. They weren't supposed to be here. They never swam on Sundays. "Why?" I asked Dara.

Dara stretched her shoulders. "I told them I'd help you guys work on exchanges if they came today. I think you guys can take first at River Park, but, man, your exchanges suck."

"They don't suck," I argued. "Only Shafer sucks on starts."

"Plenty of room for improvement on yours," Dara said. "Come on."

I waved at Meg and headed to the pool. I dived in and had barely started warming up when Shafer jumped in and grabbed my ankle after my turn.

"Who's the girl?" he demanded when I came up. "You know her?"

Heinz appeared, too. "Yeah, who is she?" he asked. "Man, she's hot as fuck."

"Shut up," I snapped. "You guys are such assholes."

They exchanged confused glances. "What the fuck?" Heinz asked.

Dara appeared. She wiped her goggles off rather than pulling them up, which would mean all the trouble of getting them back on. "Swim or get out of the pool. We're not here to fuck around."

Shafer ignored her, slapping me on the chest with the back of his hand. "Come on, Shakespeare, who is she?"

D'Amico walked over by us. "Hey, are we doing this or what? I have to start work in half an hour."

"Yes, we're coming," Dara told him. She turned to Shafer and said, "She's his childhood friend. And she has a boyfriend, so back off."

Shafer shrugged. "Hey, just because there's a goalie doesn't mean you can't try to score."

I was tempted to punch him, but Dara shoved me and it was back to swimming.

I kept one eye on Meg as we practiced starts, and then after, even as I swam, turning in her direction when I breathed, trying to see whether she was watching me. Shafer and Heinz swarmed her, not about to waste their time swimming or deferring to Dara when there was a beautiful mystery girl in the vicinity.

"Quit grabbing the gutter!" Dara yelled. She stood by the wall, checking my turns.

"I didn't!"

"Yes, you did," she said, gesturing wildly with her one and a half arms. "If you can't break that habit, you're going to be fucked at trials. And how many times have I told you to tuck tighter on your turns? I swear you've got two seconds tied up in these fucking turns."

I glared at her, worried Meg could hear Dara handing me my ass, but I doubted she could make us out over Shafer's mating calls and the piped music and the yelling and splashing of the kids who'd gradually filled up the pool.

After a while, when I couldn't take Dara's shit anymore, I faked a leg cramp. Pathetic, I know. But it was the only excuse I could think of that stood a chance of getting Dara to give me a break.

Dara gave me a look that could have bent metal, but I climbed out and walked – limped – over to Meg. I pulled up a chair right next to her, crashing into Shafer to move him the hell away from her.

"What happened?" Meg asked me. She looked so concerned that it made me feel bad. And good.

"Just a leg cramp," I said, toweling off. I grabbed my swim bag and took out my water bottle.

Meg opened her mouth to say something to me, but Shafer interrupted.

"You totally have to come back and go to Willow Grove in the fall." He was practically drooling all over her. "It'll be so awesome. I'll show you around."

Meg smiled. "Thanks, but if I come back, I've already got a tour guide lined up."

"Who, Shakespeare?" Heinz said.

Meg looked at him quizzically.

"Mueller," Heinz said, nodding his head toward me. "He writes poetry."

I rolled my eyes. "It's a stupid nickname."

"Anyway," Shafer continued, trying to get Meg's attention back, "I'd be a much better tour guide. Shakespeare barely talks – he's more the brooding type. I, on the other hand, am engaging, entertaining... Some even say irresistible."

"*Nobody* says that," I countered.

"Will you forget it, Shafer?" Dara exclaimed, appearing out of nowhere. "She has a boyfriend! Get a life!" She grabbed my water bottle out of my hands and took a long drink.

I watched Meg watching Dara and wished I knew what she was thinking. She leaned toward me and whispered, "Are you going to go back to swimming laps, or can you play now?" Her breath tickled my ear, and I checked to make sure my towel was in reach. *No poolside boners.*

I glanced at Dara, who was screwing the cap back on my nearly empty water bottle. Before I could say anything, Meg rolled her eyes and asked Dara, "Can Otis play now?"

Dara looked at Meg, and time held still for a second. "Well. I guess we're not going to accomplish much today, anyway. Not with Mueller's *cramp*." She tossed my water bottle to me.

Meg stood up and reached an arm back to untie her dress, but stopped when she realized all eyes were on her. "I'll just go change in the locker room," she said.

"I'll show you where it is," Shafer said, scrambling to get up.

"That's okay," Meg said. "I used to swim here! But thanks."

We all watched her walk away. Past the kiddie fountain and wading pool, past the locker rooms, toward the concession stands.

"Uh, where's she going?" Heinz asked.

I smiled. "She'll get there eventually."

Meg.

The guys started in on me, asking how well I knew Meg, how long she was in town, if she really had a boyfriend – an endless barrage of questions.

"What're you guys up to today?" Shafer asked. "Wanna hang out?"

"Sorry, we have plans," I told them.

"You do?" Heinz asked. "What are you doing?"

I shrugged. "You know, just—" I started to say, but Dara interrupted.

"I'm having people over tonight. I forgot to tell you guys."

Since when? "But it's a Sunday," I said, which apparently

was a dumb thing to say, judging by the guys' snorts.

"Anyway," she continued. "You guys should come." She glanced at me. "You can bring her," she grumbled.

Heinz and Shafer loved that idea, but I wasn't so sure. "Maybe," I said. Desperate to escape the hot seat, I walked over to the pool and jumped in.

It was a good thing I was in the water when Meg returned – boner bets were off. Her purple bikini clung to her kind-of-staggering curves. I was blinded by legs and stomach and chest and arms and shoulders. I cringed to think how many times Football Guy had seen this much of her, let alone what he had *touched*.

D'Amico was working now, up in the guard chair. I thought about what he said about applying for a job. It looked like a pretty good gig, as jobs went, and maybe I'd see him more, too. Heinz and Shafer were kind of asshats, but D'Amico was a genuinely good guy.

Meg came over to the edge of the pool, Heinz and Shafer flanking her like bodyguards. "Is it cold?"

"It's not so bad," I said. "You'll get used to it fast."

She lowered herself into the water, inch by inch, holding on to the side. "It's freezing!" she exclaimed, her lips holding the shape of a small "o."

It was killing me not to reach out for her.

"Hey, Shafer," I said, "why don't you show Meg some of your famous dives? Meg goes wild for diving."

Meg held back a smile as Shafer and Heinz scampered out of the pool and wasted no time making fools of themselves on the diving board.

Dara said to Meg, "So what are we doing after this?"

Meg glanced at me, confused.

I was furious at Dara's tactics, but I was stuck. Meg and I didn't have actual plans – there was nothing I could say.

"I had hoped to spend some time with Otis today, actually," Meg said. "We have a lot of catching up to do."

Dara stared Meg down. "I can imagine," she said. "You haven't talked to him in over three years, right?"

Meg blinked, presumably processing that Dara was being a total bitch to her.

There was a mighty splash and loud laughter. A moment later, Heinz popped from the water like a jack-in-the-box, said, "Hi, Meg!" and promptly disappeared underwater again. The three of us hovered at the edge of the pool, watching the guys and their idiot dives. Shafer had one where he charged full speed off the board and thrust himself into a sideways roll, splatting randomly in the water. From there, they just got stupider. At one point D'Amico blew his whistle at him for jumping too high on the board. Repeatedly. Shafer blew D'Amico a kiss and bowed, which even I had to laugh at.

"Am I the only one who's starving?" Meg asked.

"You're always starving," I teased.

Dara poked me in the chest. "Don't even think of pigging out on crap."

And before I could even think of a reply that would suggest I ever make my own choices in life, Dara added, "Be there around nine tonight." She turned and swam away from us with a splash.

Meg turned to me.

"Why do you let her treat you that way?" She seemed genuinely puzzled. She let go of the gutter with one hand so she could turn and face me better. Her hair floated in the water in amber strands.

"It's complicated," I said lamely. "She's pretty serious about my swimming."

She bit her lip. "Hey, not to be rude or anything, but ... what happened to her arm?"

I hesitated, afraid to say anything about Dara. Especially about her arm. It was no secret a little Internet search wouldn't turn up, but I didn't feel at liberty to talk about it.

Before I could answer, Shafer swam toward us. "Hey, Meg," he said. "Party at Dara's tonight. You have to come. I'll give you a ride. Shakespeare can't drive yet."

I couldn't believe how inconvenient not having my license was proving to be. I didn't even want to go to Dara's. I wanted to do something else with Meg. Something private. This day was turning into a fucking train wreck.

"I might not actually be invited," Meg said matter-of-factly.

"Oh, you're invited," Shafer said. "For sure. Pick you up around nine?"

To my surprise, she turned to me and gave me a *why not* shrug.

"I don't know, Meg," I said softly, moving closer to her. "This might not be your scene. There'll probably be drinking and … who knows what."

She raised an eyebrow. "Well, yeah."

Apparently this was not her first rodeo.

"Pick you guys up around nine," Shafer said, swimming off.

Meg and I were left hanging there on the side, in awkward silence.

"Do you go to parties much?" she finally asked, her legs pedaling slowly in the water.

"Not that much." More like not ever. "You?"

"I used to," she said. "And then I stopped. But Jeff's, like, super social. So I sometimes get dragged along." She gazed into the water.

"Aren't you getting tired of hanging on?" I asked.

"Huh?"

I gestured with my head to where she held the gutter. "To the side."

She laughed. "I thought you meant Jeff."

Yeah. That, too.

Meg made her way to the ladder while I climbed out the side and went to our chairs, moving them close to each other and turning them toward the sun. The day was bright, but cool enough that the hot sun felt like heaven. Meg scurried over, shivering. I felt bad that she was so cold, not that I could do anything about it. She pulled a huge towel out of her bag and wrapped it around herself. After she had dried off a little, she laid the towel down on the lounge chair and settled in next to me.

It was surreal: Meg actually there, with me, at the pool we spent so much time at when we were kids – sometimes with our moms and Mason, sometimes just us. We had possibly sat in these very lounge chairs at some point, on the same patch of concrete, near the same tables. And now, here we were, together again.

Meg turned to me. "Weird, huh?"

It was as if she read my thoughts. I nodded. "But, you know … good weird."

She reached out and briefly put her hand on my arm, then pulled her sunglasses down and lay back. I leaned back, too, tingling with warmth from the sun, and from Meg's touch.

"You need a ride home or what?"

I opened my eyes to find Dara standing in front of me, toweling off her hair so hard you'd think it would leave a bald spot. I had just been starting to feel a little woozy and dreamy. She was like a bucket of ice water over my head.

I glanced at Meg.

"I feel like staying awhile," she said.

I shrugged at Dara. "Thanks, though."

Dara leaned over me and gave my stomach a couple of loud smacks. "Don't eat junk. See you tonight." She swished off.

And then the guys left, too, but not before confirming that Meg was coming to the party. Twice.

It wasn't long before Meg got up and returned with loaded hot dogs and strawberry éclair ice-cream bars – a lunch that was high in fat and even higher in subtext. We ate it all, soaking up the new summer sun and talking about anything except Dara. Or us. Or Mason. Or her parents. There were a lot of elephants in the room. And we were doing an admirable job of avoiding all of them.

And then it all went south. Above the boisterous din came a piercing scream from the kiddie pool. And then another.

Meg clapped her hands to her ears, her face going chalk-white.

"What's wrong?" I asked, shifting to face her. Another series of screams sliced the air.

Two lifeguards jogged past, one saying to the other, "It's that autistic kid. He screams when he gets overstimulated."

I turned back to Meg, who was still clutching her ears.

Beads of sweat bloomed on her forehead. As the screaming continued, she started snapping a rubber band on her wrist and mumbling to herself.

I leaned in toward her. "Meg?"

She jumped up, so I stood up too, but she took off for the bathroom.

The minutes ticked by as I waited for her, wondering what the hell had just happened. The screaming eventually stopped, but there was still no sign of Meg. At one point I walked over by the bathrooms, but, with no recourse, I just went back to our chairs and sat down. I was considering asking a girl to go check on her for me when she appeared.

"Meg? What happened?"

She shook her head, shoving her things into her bag. Her eyes were pink and swollen. She took a deep breath and held it before letting it out. Finally she said, "Could we just go to your house, maybe? We really need to talk."

"Sure. I'll call my dad for a ride."

I was bombarded with warring emotions: Concern for Meg, who seemed like kind of a wreck. Joy at the prospect of spending the afternoon together. And terror at the threat that seemed to cling to the words "We really need to talk."

8

MY DAD DROPPED US OFF AT HOME AND
headed straight to Starbucks, of all places. He claimed he
planned to work there on his laptop for a bit, but I was pretty
sure he was either doing recon to figure out how they make
fancy espresso drinks or just giving Meg and me some space.
My mom apparently was doing lunch and a movie with
someone from her support group.

As my dad pulled away, Meg paused in the driveway. Her
eyes went to the magnolia, then to the blossoms in the grass,
shriveled and browning, and then, finally, to her old house.
Her lips moved as she plucked at that rubber band around
her wrist.

I stepped closer. "You okay?" My hand hovered near her
back, not yet able to make the leap to touching her.

"I don't know yet." She took a slow breath, exhaling

through pursed lips, then followed me up to the front door. I pulled the house key out from under the doormat.

"You still keep that there?" Meg exclaimed. "That's the first place a burglar would look!"

"Look at you, thinking like a criminal."

"But I'm right!"

"I didn't say you weren't."

Meg followed me inside, pausing to look around. I set my bag down quietly, watching her.

"Everything's the same," she said, her eyes scanning the living room to our right. She bit her thumbnail. "Except this." She stepped into the living room and pointed to my most recent school photo, framed on the wall with the others. "And this." The year before. "You always did photograph well."

I gave her a *say cheese* smile, and she smiled back.

"And you never even wore braces," she said.

"Nope. Want some iced tea?" I asked, going into the kitchen and opening the fridge.

"Sure." She went to the cabinet and took down two glasses.

I smiled as I took out the tea. Meg may not have known north from south, but she knew exactly where the glasses were in our kitchen.

"What?" She tilted her head at me, noticing my expression.

I shrugged, then stared into the pitcher of tea. "It's just …

you remember where things are."

"I know. It's weird. It doesn't feel like time has passed here. Popcorn." She walked over to the cabinet over the stove and opened it. "Check. Cereal." She opened the pantry door and pointed left. "Check."

She closed the pantry door and turned back to me. "Otis."

"Check," I said softly.

Our eyes locked for a moment. She looked away first. I went to the counter and filled the glasses with ice from the dispenser in the freezer door. I was pouring the tea when Meg said, "Oh, shoot!"

When I turned to look, she had her dress strap pulled to the side, where a strip of pale skin revealed the crimson surrounding. She shook her head. "I thought I'd be fine since I already have a base tan, but I guess that was a lot of time in the midday sun."

I winced and set down the pitcher. "Should you put something on it?"

She pressed her finger into her shoulder and let go. An oval glowed white, then flashed back to red. She frowned. "A cold compress might be good."

I ran a kitchen towel under cold water and squeezed it out.

"Thanks," she said, reaching for it. She dabbed it on her shoulders, drawing in air through her teeth.

"Your back is burned, too," I told her. "Here." I took the towel and hesitated. Her hair was in the way, but moving it seemed maybe like taking too many liberties. But she did it herself, sweeping it over her left shoulder. I gently laid the towel on her back. "Is that okay?" Touching her, even through a towel, made me a little shaky. The smell of her hair wafted up to me, fruity and flowery.

"I'm such an idiot," she said, glancing back at me. "How come you didn't burn?"

"I don't really burn. I just tan."

She made a face and mocked the words back at me, making me laugh.

"Hey," she said, turning back around. "I'm sorry. About earlier. I ... I didn't mean to freak out like that."

"It's okay." But I wished she'd explain. Why had that kid's shrieking bothered her so much? Just when it felt like she was the exact same Meg, something like this came along to remind me that in some ways she was a stranger to me.

I handed her the towel back, and we took our iced tea downstairs to the family room and turned on a station that ran old TV shows. I excused myself to change into shorts and a fresh T-shirt, wishing I could shower but not wanting to leave her alone for that long. Instead I just slathered a thick layer of deodorant on and hoped for the best.

When I rejoined her, her phone rang, a meditative spa-like ring tone. She grabbed it and said apologetically,

"I was waiting for this. Sorry. I'll be right back." She stood and ran up the stairs, waiting till she got there before she answered. It didn't take a genius to figure out who it was.

I sat and sulked. After a few minutes, I decided to head up to the kitchen for some more iced tea – and maybe for some masochistic eavesdropping while I was at it.

"I'm at his house now," she was saying, so quietly I could barely hear her. "I'm gonna talk to him soon... I know, I know." A deep, shuddering breath. "And he's being so *nice* about everything."

She said it like it was weird that I was being nice. Why wouldn't I be nice? Was I not always nice? And I hated that Football Guy was in on whatever this talk was she wanted to have with me. Was she going to tell me that she'd never really liked me *that way* and that she could only move back if I promised to keep my distance?

Just then the central air clicked on, and I couldn't hear her over the blowing. I closed the fridge and headed back down the stairs.

She came down a few minutes later and sat next to me, pulling the flower-patterned quilt off the arm of the couch. "I always loved this quilt," she said, laying it over herself. "The crotch-et quilt."

I laughed. "Shut up." In fifth grade, reading aloud in class, I had the misfortune of coming across the word "cro-cheted" for the first time, which I pronounced *crotch-et-ed*.

How was I supposed to know? Meg used to die laughing every time she remembered it.

She leaned back and closed her eyes. "Maybe we should take a nap."

I blinked in confusion, unsure if she was serious. The words "we" and "nap" in the same sentence led to some hopeful and unlikely interpretations in my head.

She opened her eyes and gave me a tiny smile. "On separate sofas, I mean." She yawned.

"Obviously," I said, trying to get my heart rate back under control. "I'm sure Jeff wouldn't appreciate even an innocent, platonic nap between friends."

"Ha. Probably not."

I couldn't help myself. "Doesn't he trust you?"

Her eyes flicked briefly to mine. Just when I thought she wasn't going to respond, she said, "Why is she so stuck on you?"

"Huh?" Man, she could switch gears.

"I mean, don't take that the wrong way; I totally get how a girl could get stuck on you. But Dara – it's different. Obviously."

I was still processing the line she'd tucked in the middle, about how she totally got how a girl could get stuck on me. I would have liked to plumb that compliment deeply.

"The Olympics." I traced lines down the condensation on my glass of tea. "She's trying to get me to the Olympics.

That's why she spends all her time training me. It's her obsession."

"The Olympics?" Meg said, eyes widening. She shifted to face me, leaning her back against the arm of the sofa. "Are you that good?"

I snorted. "No. But try telling her that."

"Why does it matter so much to her?" She leaned toward the table to pick up her glass of tea.

So I told Meg the story of Dara.

When I got to the part about the shark attack, a look of recognition crossed her face. "Oh my God... I remember seeing stories about her on the Internet. That was when we were, what, like eleven?"

I nodded, setting my glass down on the table.

"She's not from here, though, is she?" Meg asked.

"No, she lived in New York. She moved here after the accident."

Meg raised her eyebrows. "Wow. I mean, I feel bad for her. But still ... the way she treats you..."

Dara would find Meg's disapproval deeply ironic, given her opinion of how Meg had treated me.

I picked up the remote from the sofa next to me and examined it. "Maybe I wouldn't like the way Jeff treats you, either," I said, as if it were an apples-to-apples comparison.

"He makes me laugh," she said quietly. "I need that."

Great. He was good-looking *and* funny. I hated him.

"Anyway, he's my boyfriend. Dara's not your girlfriend. Right? Just your, what, boss?"

I glanced up at the loaded remark. "Friend," I said carefully, still fingering the remote. "Friend-slash-coach. I don't know – it's complicated."

"So you keep saying."

I shrugged.

"There must have been someone," she said, watching me. "If not her."

"What do you mean?"

She gave me a *come on* look. "You're sixteen and a half. And look at you!" She looked pointedly at my body. "There must have been someone. All this time?" Her sunburned nose glowed red in the warm light of the lamp on the end table. She tipped her head to the side, waiting.

Was this the talk? Was she about to pull the rug out from under me? "So what if there was? What would it matter?"

"I don't know," she said quietly, picking fuzz off the quilt. After a moment, she scooted down and laid her head against the arm of the sofa, curling up on her side. Apparently she was actually going to nap?

I slid to the end of the sofa to give her more room, plucking a Hershey's Kiss from the green glass candy dish my mom liked to keep on the end table – her grandmother's. "For what it's worth, no. There hasn't been anybody."

She turned her head to look at me. "How can that be?"

"Impossible standards, I guess." I held the chocolate out to her. She lifted her head to see what it was, then backed away. "No. No, thank you."

"What?" I unwrapped it and popped it in my mouth. "Since when do you turn down chocolate?"

"I don't like it anymore."

I stared at her as if she'd said she no longer breathed air. "Since when?"

She didn't answer.

"That doesn't even make sense, Meg," I said, unwrapping another Kiss. When we were kids, chocolate was one of the four major food groups. "Who *are* you?"

I was sort of joking, but she apparently wasn't in a humorous mood.

"I think I'm going to sleep now." She laid her head back down.

"Seriously?"

Crickets.

I sat there for a few minutes, rolling the foil wrapper in my fingers and watching her. She radiated exhaustion. I got up and arranged the quilt over her. At the very least, I could continue to be "nice."

I went upstairs and rummaged through the linen closet until I found the caddy of stuff we brought on vacations – mini shampoos, sunscreen, that kind of stuff. I found a travel-size bottle of aloe vera.

I went into my room, tidied up a little, and then messed around on the computer. My mom texted me: *What are you two up to?*

Transparent enough? I thought about texting back, *We are having sexual intercourse, try back later,* but I knew how well that would go over. I told her the truth: Meg was downstairs resting, and I was on the computer. She said she was on her way to meet my dad at the nursery to buy some flowering plants for the deck, and then they were going to bring home Thai food for dinner in an hour or two.

Dara had sent me three emails with links to pages about improving breaststroke, subject lines: STUDY THIS!! She said nothing else, other than *See you tonight. Don't forget.*

I lay down on my bed, wondering about the changes in Meg. Screaming freaked her out. She didn't like chocolate anymore. Chocolate! I thought about how many jillions of s'mores we had eaten together over the years, all those summer barbecues…

I turned to my side and looked at the picture of Mason. My chest ached. That smile of his – it broke me wide open. Sometimes it could still surprise me, the fact of his being gone. I probably was in no position to judge my mom for how stuck in her grief she seemed to be. Maybe hers was just more visible. I generally made a point to show as little as possible. Of everything.

I must have fallen asleep, because I woke up, aware of a presence. I got up and found Meg hovering in the hallway outside Mason's room.

"Hey," I said, running my hands through my hair. When I came closer, I saw her eyes were wet. I marveled at how fragile she seemed to be now; when we were kids, she almost never cried. I was the big baby.

She gestured toward the room. "When...?"

"Recently," I said, stepping past her through the doorway and picking up a geode paperweight from the desk. I ran my finger along its sparkling, jagged interior. "We actually kept it exactly the same until a few weeks ago."

"Oh my God. Really?"

I glanced up sharply at the alarm in her voice. I shouldn't have told her that.

She put a hand to her chest. "This whole time?"

I shrugged. What could I say?

From the hallway she pointed to the picture of Mason and me, the one where I was reading him *Goodnight Moon*. She smiled, but her face was filled with pain.

I set the geode down and went over to her. I hesitated for a second, then put my arms around her, reminding myself that we were not strangers, we *knew* each other, dammit. She shook a little, her arms folded against herself, but after a moment she slid her arms around me and rested her head on my chest. Despite the fact that it was kind of an excruciating moment, it felt so good to hold her.

And it gave me an idea. I had no clue how it might work logistically, though, since I didn't have my fucking license. Maybe Meg would borrow my mom's bike…

"Hey," I said softly. "Maybe we could go to the cemetery this week."

She pulled away from me in a single move, shaking her head.

I frowned. "What? Why?"

Bafflingly, her expression became angry. She turned and walked into my room, so I followed her.

"Look," she said, spinning around to face me. "I loved Mason, you know that. But I don't know if I can go back there." She took a couple of tissues out of the box on my desk and wiped her eyes. She examined the tissues, probably checking to see if her makeup was coming off. It was.

"Okay," I said. But it wasn't okay. Nothing was okay. The more time I spent with her, the more of a puzzle she became. I wanted to stay away from things that upset her. I wished someone would give me a list of what those things were so I could avoid them. "So," I said, wanting to change the subject, "did you sleep?" I glanced in the mirror and ran my hands through my hair again, pointlessly. I wished I'd gotten a haircut before she came back.

"Slept and dreamed, too. I am so sleep deprived."

"What did you dream?" I asked, desperate to feel a

connection to her again. I felt totally cut off.

She lifted a shoulder. "Just … stressful stuff." She dropped the tissues into the wastebasket and took another one.

I went to my dresser and picked up a pack of cinnamon gum. I unwrapped two pieces and popped them into my mouth, in case the smell of chocolate on my breath might bother her.

She examined my display of swim medals and trophies.

"You won all these?" she asked. She picked up a trophy and held it sort of tenderly. "Most improved," she read.

"Freshman year."

She put it back and fingered some of the medals hanging on ribbons. "Wow. They're heavy."

I sat down in my desk chair and swiveled to follow her as she walked over to the bookshelf on the other wall.

"Hey, I remember these."

My rock collection – much of which had been procured with Meg at Lake Michigan. My mom would pack picnics and take Mason and us to the beach. Sometimes we'd bring Cassie and go to the dog beach. I thought of the time Mason pointed to Cassie's bum leg with concern, telling us, "Tassie weg hurt." The memory made my throat ache.

"I gave you this one," she said, holding up a smooth, dark red rock.

I smiled, knowing exactly what was coming.

"It's a *heart*," she said emphatically.

"Still looks like a kidney to me."

She shook her head, returning my smile for a brief, glorious second. "Haven't you changed at all?" She set down the rock and picked up another, her expression once again serious. "You seem the same in so many ways."

Well, that sucked. I had hoped she'd see me as new, exciting, older. Big and strong. Confident, sexy, and mysterious would be a bonus. Instead she saw me as the same?

"Have you changed so much?" I asked.

She looked out the window, eyes fixed on her former bedroom window. "Yeah." She rubbed at a smudge on the window with the tissue she was holding. Then she turned and put the rock back on the shelf.

I spotted the aloe on my desk. "Oh! Here." I held it out to her.

I was rewarded with another fleeting smile. "Thank you." She took it from me and squeezed some into her hands. It made a farting noise. I refrained from making a joke.

She started rubbing the aloe into her arms and shoulders. Her eyes flicked self-consciously in my direction as she rubbed some in the V-shaped area of her dress.

I cleared my throat. "I can, uh ... help with your back." Of course that had been in the back of my mind since I started looking for the aloe, but I wasn't sure I'd have the cojones to offer.

She craned around and looked at her back in the mirror over my dresser. She rolled her eyes. "Christ on a bike."

I stood. "Here," I said, reaching my hand out for the aloe. I felt shaky just thinking about touching her. But I'd rubbed sunscreen on her back a hundred times. It was no big deal, right?

She sat on the bed.

I sat next to her and she shifted so her back was to me. "Can you untie this, do you think?" I asked, tugging on the fabric of her dress where it tied around her neck. "It's in the way."

She did, without a word. When the ties were undone, she pulled them over her shoulders and held the front of her dress to her chest. My heart hammered away. I hoped she couldn't hear it. From inside my head it was deafening.

With trembling hands, I slid some strands of her hair over her shoulder to the front, noticing that she shivered a little. "Are you cold?"

"No, I'm fine."

"Okay. I'll be gentle."

And then she said, so softly I barely heard it, "I know that, Otis."

I rubbed the aloe between my palms to warm it up a little, then hesitated, my hand hovering over her hot shoulder. I couldn't help remembering our first kiss, which started with my touching her shoulder. Did she remember that?

I laid my fingers on her shoulders and, as lightly as I could, smoothed the aloe over her hot skin. She sighed, and I couldn't tell if she was registering pleasure or pain. Just in case I was hurting her, I said, "Sorry."

"No, it feels good," she whispered.

My stomach flipped over. And my shorts seemed to be shrinking.

"Hey," I said after a minute. "I'm sorry if I upset you. About the cemetery thing."

She reached behind her and laid her fingers on top of my hand. I held still until she pulled away a moment later. I had no idea what was going on in her head, but for now, at least, it seemed that everything was okay.

I continued with the aloe, venturing over the tops of her shoulders a little bit. And then I forgot to pay attention to where the burn was and I just smoothed aloe everywhere. Her breathing was audible. I leaned around to peek at her face. Her eyes were closed, her lips parted... I remembered those lips. The shape, the softness, the taste... It made me think about kissing her, and once that thought was in my head, it was hard to vanquish. I kept slathering that damn aloe on, my fingertips skimming her skin as gently as possible, hoping it would keep absorbing until I either ran out of it or I imploded, whichever came first.

I must have sat there reapplying the aloe half a dozen times while I went through these mental gymnastics. A field of electricity buzzed around me, and my breath kept catching in my throat.

Outside, a car hauled by with the music cranked up so loud I felt the bass thumping through the bed. And that broke the spell. Meg opened her eyes and turned her head. "I guess that'll do it!" She laughed. "Thank you." She stood up.

"No problem," I croaked. My face felt hot, and I was starting to sweat. I licked my lips and hoped I didn't look as wrecked and crazed as I felt. I was in a ridiculous state of full-body excitement.

She tied her dress back up behind her neck. I could see her nipples straining through the fabric, and it made the last few drops of blood in my head drain out and go to the one place I would have sworn couldn't accommodate any more.

I shifted, trying to hide the Loch Ness monster in my pants. "Hey, my parents are bringing Thai food," I said, by way of distraction. "I forgot to tell you."

She gasped. "I love Thai food." Her face glowed – she was fucking beautiful. Then her eyes widened as if she'd thought of something dire. "Do you have sriracha sauce?"

I couldn't not smile. "I think so."

"Let's check." She slipped out of the room ahead of me, giving me a merciful moment to adjust myself before following her to the kitchen.

* * *

During dinner, which was almost unbearably spicy because Meg insisted on squeezing sriracha sauce all over everything I ate, I told my parents that the team was going to hang out at Dara's later. My mom had barely stopped chattering the whole time, to the point of being kind of annoying, so it was hard to get a word in edgewise.

When I excused myself to grab a quick shower while they were all still picking at the food, Meg glanced at me with what looked like alarm. I hesitated. Maybe she didn't want to be left alone with my parents? There was a time when our parents were practically interchangeable. I was shocked again by how different things were.

But my dad gave me a wave and asked Meg if she'd like a demonstration of his new espresso machine, so I made my escape.

I showered as fast as humanly possible, still trying to think of ways to get out of going to Dara's, but it seemed like Meg wanted to go, for reasons I could not fathom. She tapped on my door before I was finished getting dressed. I opened the door in nothing but shorts.

"Taste," she said, stepping in and holding out a mug.

I peered in at the foamy top, covered in spices, and sipped. "Oh my God," I said, making a face. "How can you stand it so sweet?"

"That's how you make it taste good," she said, taking it

back. She sipped it and made *mmmmm* sounds. "Anyway, it's my dessert."

She sat on my bed, watching as I pulled on a T-shirt. She complained about not being able to change her clothes.

"I never meant to wear this all day," she grumbled. "I wish I could drive already. I'd go to the hotel and change."

"As if you could find the way to your hotel," I teased, pulling on a lightweight hoodie over my T-shirt.

"I could!" she objected. "I have the navigation lady." She spoke in a voice that was at once elegant and robotic: *"In one-quarter mile, merge onto Highway Forty-Three."*

She sounded exactly like the Google navigation voice. "That lady's gonna save your life," I predicted.

"Yeah, no kidding." She caught my eye in the mirror. "Hey, do you have an extra toothbrush, by any chance?"

"No, sorry." I leaned against the dresser. "You could – well, that's gross."

"What? Borrow yours? Would that gross you out?"

"No, I thought it would gross *you* out."

"It wouldn't gross me out." Her lips curved into a small smile. "It's not like I haven't used your toothbrush before."

"True," I said with a laugh. She once drank some chocolate milk that my mom had left in the fridge way too long. I still could see her flapping her hands, her tongue hanging out of her mouth, making noises like a cat hacking up a hairball.

"So you don't mind?"

"Nope."

She followed me into the bathroom, and I rinsed my toothbrush under hot water for her, glad I'd just gotten a new one. My last one had been pretty mangled, due to my exemplary habit of chewing on it while I walked around during brushing.

In my room, I listened to the sounds of her brushing across the hall, which was weirdly thrilling. Someday we could be married and this would just be a normal, comforting, daily sound, Meg brushing her teeth in the bathroom. Also, I liked her teeth. They were pretty. I liked her lips. I liked her whole mouth. I liked that my toothbrush was in it.

A mean voice in my head pointed out that this was probably the closest I'd ever get to swapping spit with Meg again.

9

SHAFER WAS LATE, AS USUAL, WHICH GAVE me the opportunity to give him shit about his late starts in our relays.

There were more cars at Dara's place than I'd anticipated. I wondered if her parties were always this packed. It was hard to imagine her actually inviting so many people into her home.

We parked on the street and found the front door open.

"Wow." Meg glanced around the foyer and into the enormous living room, taking in all the art and shiny surfaces.

Shafer felt up the breast of an African sculpture in a lit-up nook by the door. "Yeah, Dara's richer than God."

We headed downstairs to the finished basement, following the music – The Clash, I was pretty sure, so maybe we were in the eighties. Half the team sat in a circle on the floor with a mess of beers and a couple of vodka bottles. The room was lit in strings of Christmas lights, and there was a mini fridge along the wall near a leather sofa. Dara, who was seated in the circle and wearing a "Simon Says Go Fuck Yourself" T-shirt with the sleeves cut off, raised a shot glass at me, her expression flat, and tossed back the contents like water. Some party: she looked about as festive as a funeral.

Kiera spotted me and waved me over. "Come on. We're playing Kiss or Shoot. Martin's invention, naturally."

Kiera was one of the few people who called Shafer by his first name. It was the only thing that made me remember he had one.

She saw Meg and her face fell.

"Uh, this is Meg," I said, keeping it simple. I hung back, but Meg nudged me to go sit down and followed along with me. The circle expanded to accommodate us.

"Meg! Meg!" Heinz and Shafer chanted.

"Are you Otis's girlfriend?" Kiera asked Meg, looking so stricken it was almost comical.

"No, no," Meg said, waving her off as if it were a ridiculous question. "We're friends from years ago. We used to be neighbors."

"Meg Brandt?" Marla Rubinoff said from across the circle. "Oh my God!" She crawled over and hugged Meg.

As the junior high reunion continued, I asked Kiera, "Um, what's Kiss or Shoot?"

Kiera smiled mischievously. She clearly was somewhere north of .00 on the blood alcohol scale. "It's Spin the Bottle, but if you don't want to kiss the person, you have to do a shot."

"And it's gender-blind," Heinz said, making a face. "Glad I'm not driving…"

Gender-blind? I couldn't imagine Dara, the most homophobic possibly-gay chick in town, would have given the nod to that. I scanned the room for Abby and spotted her across the circle, blowing lightly into a beer bottle.

Marla returned to her spot, and Meg settled in next to me. I didn't want to kiss anyone but her, and not in front of these idiots, but I certainly wasn't going to do shots of vodka. Would Meg? Or would she kiss these guys? And what if she landed on me but opted for the vodka? Possibilities bombarded me, each worse than the one before.

It was decreed that Meg should go first. She crawled forward and spun an empty vodka bottle. Time slowed as it circled for what seemed like a hundred times. I leaned toward her. "What are you doing?" I whispered. "What about Jeff?"

Meg ignored me, watching the bottle intently. Someone set a couple of beers in front of us. The vodka bottle slowed. Shafer and Heinz got up and ran around the circle, strategizing to plop themselves down where the nose landed.

"No cheating," Dara barked. "Sit your asses down."

After several eternities, the bottle stopped, pointing

right between Marla and Nate Russell. Nate was probably the shyest guy on the team, so he didn't fight when Dara called it Marla.

"Wait, what kind of kiss?" Meg twisted her thumb. "Is there like a minimum time or something?"

"Not really," Marla told her, "but if it's too short, you get booed."

Meg shrugged. "I'm game. You?"

"Sure," Marla said. "It'll be my welcome-back kiss."

They crawled toward each other and gave each other a kiss that lasted about a nanosecond. They laughed when they got booed.

How did I get myself into this? And why the hell did Meg want to play such a stupid game? The idea of her kissing Shafer or Heinz was just plain sick. But would I rather watch her do shots? I guessed I would.

"Let Otis go next, since he just got here," Kiera said. Her diction was not exactly crisp.

"No fair rigging the bottle, Kiera," Marla called out. Kiera flipped her the bird without even looking her way.

"Uh, I'm not playing." I held my hands up in a *not me, no thanks* gesture.

There was a general uproar in response to that, most vociferously by Kiera, but they all shut up when Dara shouted.

"Hey! Mueller doesn't have to play if he doesn't want to."

Kiera turned her big, pleading brown eyes to me. "Why don't you want to play?"

I glanced at Meg, who was regarding Kiera with a look that smacked of disdain, unless it was my imagination.

"I'm just not feeling it."

More booing. Wow, what fun parties were! Tragic that I'd been missing out on this. I stood up and went and sat on the couch. A strand of lights was draped across it, and I fingered the bulbs, which were warm. On the other side of the basement was a bunch of exercise equipment. Maybe I could go over and get in a workout and everyone would forget I was even there.

"Come *on!*" Kiera said. "That's not even fair. Everyone has to play."

"Just kiss Kiera, Otis, and get her to shut up," Heinz called out.

She turned toward me hopefully. I waved them off, shaking my head. I felt terrible. She was a nice person. Honestly, at that moment I had no clue what she even saw in me.

The game was actually pretty amusing as a spectator sport – and it reflected some weird politics: no girl would kiss Abby, which made me feel bad for her. Kiera chose a shot over kissing Shafer (points for taste). A fairly involved kiss occurred between Heinz and a tall freestyler named Melanie – it got applause and shouts of "Get a room!" Other than that, I worried about the bottle landing on Meg. It never did, despite some of the guys' best efforts to cheat. On her next turn, she landed on Dara.

Dara poured two shots before Meg had a chance to even speak and passed one down to her. Meg stared at it for a moment, then gave me a little *what can you do* shrug and tossed it back. She made a face and clutched her chest. I took some comfort in the fact that she didn't seem accustomed to hard liquor. Unlike Dara, who could probably drink an army of Cossacks under the table.

After a while, Dara took her bottle of vodka and sat away from the group. She leaned against the wall next to a bookcase and took a slug from the bottle. How the hell much was she drinking?

She and I each sat alone, together in our separateness. I let the music from the speakers fill my head as the game devolved into pairs sneaking off, new drinking games emerging, and rumors of someone throwing up in the bathroom.

Meg came my way and sank into the sofa next to me, holding a beer. "Hey, Otie."

"Mary Margaret, are you drunk?" I was trying to be funny; "Mary Margaret" was actually her full name, and it's what her mother always called her when she was in trouble. Once Meg got *Mary Margaret*-ed for dropping an f-bomb while yelling at basketball on TV. Her dad rushed to Meg's defense. *Oh, come on, Karen – you didn't see the call! His foot was on the line! It was total bullshit!*

"Ugh, my mom." Meg stared into her bottle, then took a sip.

Ugh? I couldn't tell if that meant her mom was off-limits, or if she was bringing her up because she was finally ready to talk about her. "How's your mom doing, anyway?" I asked gently. "I'm sorry about ... that situation."

She picked at the label on her bottle. "She's not doing so great. She's still kind of messed up. From ... you know."

Oh God. Because of what happened with Mason?

"She has depression and ... kind of a drinking problem." She glanced at me and I felt kind of sick. Jesus. That's not how Meg's mom was at all, apart from all the wine geekery among our parents. She was a full-time social worker and did volunteer work, and she was always busy, always moving quickly, always had a loud and ready laugh.

"So why would you want to...?" I trailed off, realizing how callous my question was.

She sighed. "Live with her, you mean? I don't want to, not really. My dad is the stable parent, as my therapist would say. He thinks it would be better if I were with my dad, despite..." She gestured with her beer bottle, and I knew she was encompassing all of Willow Grove. "And he's right. I know he's right. But..." She bit her lip. "I don't know if I could really live back here. Sometimes I feel like I'm just fucked either way. And like I'll always be fucked, you know?"

As I searched for a reply, the music changed and I became

aware of all the voices around us. I was so absorbed in Meg that I'd almost forgotten where I was for a minute. I wished I could find my way to just hugging her, but I was too aware of all the people milling around.

And then people were tugging on her and trying to get her to go play some stupid game.

She leaned toward me so I could hear her. "Come with."

I looked away, irritated. "Yeah, no, thanks."

She rolled her eyes. "Why did you even come, if you don't want to be with people?"

"I didn't want to come! *You* wanted to come." I shifted away from her. I felt defensive, like an outcast in a roomful of the socially adept, of whom Meg was a member and I wasn't.

"Well, excuse me," she sort of yelled over the music. "You know, it's not easy, thinking about starting over at a new school. I thought I should take advantage of the chance to get to know some people. Is that so terrible?"

I actually had not considered that. "No! It's just … not my idea of a good time."

"Well, what *is* your idea of a good time?"

I shrugged. "What's Jeff's idea of a good time?" Why? Why do I allow myself to speak? "Is he allowed to play kissing games, too? You modern couples…" *Ugh. Nice job, Mueller.* Not only was I an epic drag, but now I was sort of an asshole, too.

"I'm sure he's having a good time. He's a lot of fun."

What did he do that made him so fucking fun? Tap-dance and tell jokes? Pass out Hula-Hoops and bubble gum? If there was one thing I hadn't been since Meg arrived, it was fun. "Well, no offense to him, but I think parties are pretty stupid."

Her eyes flashed. "Well, why don't you go home if you're having such a terrible time? Don't let me stop you."

This was so unexpected, and stung so sharply, that a familiar burn bloomed behind my eyes and all I could do was stare at my legs and try to recover.

"Oh God, I'm sorry." I could barely hear her over the music, but I was pretty sure that was what she said. She laid her hand on my shoulder and leaned closer. "Otis. I didn't mean it. I just – I feel like I'm disappointing you."

I couldn't even meet her eyes; the last thing I wanted was for her to see mine threatening to spill over.

"I'm not the same girl you used to know, Otis. Okay? She doesn't exist anymore."

She stood up and headed for the stairs. I don't think five seconds passed before I got up and went after her. Dara sat in the corner, rotating a cap between her fingers, her pale blue eyes following me.

Meg, of course, had no luck finding her way out of the house. I found her circling through the dining room into the kitchen. "Where's the stupid door?" she wailed.

"Come on," I said. I held out a hand for her to take,

wanting desperately to make things right with her. She only hesitated a second before she reached out. I took her hand and led her through the living room and the foyer and out the front door.

It was like stepping into paradise. The cool night smelled of earth and tree blossoms and smoke. A pearl sliver of moon flashed in and out of the branches of the trees as they rustled in the breeze.

"There's a gazebo in the backyard," I said.

She headed that way, pulling away from me. I followed her, wishing she hadn't let go of my hand. When we reached the gazebo, we sat on the wooden bench inside, the strains of music from the house faint against the drone of the crickets or cicadas or whatever the hell bugs were doing their mating calls.

Meg took out her phone. "I'm going to ask Shafer for a ride home."

"Meg, come on. Wait," I said, moving closer. She was leaning forward over her phone, opening a gap in the top of her dress. The round of her breast glowed in the moonlight, making my heart speed up. "Can we talk?"

She let out a breath, an almost-laugh. "That's sort of the problem, Otis."

What the hell did that mean? "I thought you wanted to talk," I said. "To figure some things out. There's stuff I'd like to figure out, too, you know." I didn't want her to leave, so I pressed where I might not normally have gone. I leaned my head in front of her, forcing her to meet my eyes. "You were everything to me, and then you left and I never heard from you again." I made a *what the fuck* gesture with my hands.

"I know." She said it softly and turned her eyes downward. "I don't blame you for hating me."

I sighed in exasperation. "I don't hate you, Meg. I just want to understand."

She kept her eyes on her lap. "There are things you don't know, Otis. And if I tell you, it will change how you feel about me."

"It will not. That's ridiculous."

"Don't be so sure. Your mom hates me."

I stared at her. "Are you for real? My mom doesn't hate you! How can you say that?"

She looked at me. "What do you know about how Mason died?"

I blinked. "What?"

"What did your parents tell you? Do you know how he died?"

"He – he choked." I stood up and started to pace. "Why are you doing this?" What the hell was she after? When Meg said she wanted to talk through some stuff, I guess I was thinking she meant about our past and our complicated feelings for each other. Not this. Why was this necessary? Was I not sad enough for her? Had I not suffered enough? I was supposed to be trying to move on, not dredging up the past.

"This isn't going to work, is it?" She said it quietly, as if she were talking more to herself than to me.

"What isn't?"

She shook her head slowly. "This was a bad idea. All of it."

"What was?" Panic crept into my voice. Did she mean coming back at all?

She stood up. "I'm going."

"With Shafer?"

"I don't know. I'll figure it out."

"Shafer's been drinking, in case you didn't notice." I stepped closer to her. "Let me call my dad."

She bristled. "God, Otis, I'm not going home with your dad! *You* go with your dad. I'll see you later."

And she turned and headed across the grass to the house, the white flowers on her dress bright with moonlight.

I watched her go, my head spinning.

Why did she bring up those things about Mason? Why did she want to relive all of that? What the hell did it matter anyway?

I wanted to go home. But I wanted her to come with me – I wanted her to *want* to come with me. What did it say that she'd rather hang out with a bunch of drunk strangers than be with me?

Someone turned up the music – any louder and the

neighbors would probably call the cops. I texted Dara to let her know I was leaving, but didn't hear anything back. I thought about going inside to check on her, but I couldn't bring myself to do it. I was an outsider, an interloper, a joke.

So I stood up and walked home. It took approximately forever, which gave me a lot of time to obsess about what Meg might be doing.

When I got home, I raided the kitchen, as usual. If I were a drinker, I'd have poured myself a stiff one to drown my sorrows, especially after seeing the bottle of sriracha left sitting on the table. Instead, I ate peanut butter out of the jar, then a hunk of cheddar, and finally some mint chip ice cream. I kept my phone at hand, but no messages came.

I wished I could talk to Meg, wished I could fix everything that had happened that night. I thought about her question – what was my idea of fun? – and it bothered me that I didn't have an answer. Maybe I just didn't think in terms of fun. Honestly, apart from a few rogue moments, the last time I really had fun was probably before Mason died. When Meg was still here, living next door. Looking back, it was almost surreal, how good we had it.

She moved to town the spring I was ten. Our parents hit it off from day one, so we were together all the time while they barbecued, played their music, drank their wine. You know what was fun? Pushing each other on the tire swing in her backyard. Building forts in my basement with sheets and blankets and flashlights. Making snacks and watching TV on rainy days. Catching fireflies. Toasting marshmallows. Stargazing.

Kid stuff, I guess. But the truth was that most of those things still sounded fun to me. More fun than parties with obnoxious people and endless vodka and stressful games. Maybe it was true I hadn't changed. Maybe I had a case of arrested development. Maybe I was still just a kid.

When I went upstairs to bed, I overheard arguing from behind my parents' closed bedroom door. I hesitated in the hallway, then crept closer. My parents didn't really fight. Usually their version of fighting was my mom yelling about something and my dad trying to placate her. But this time he sounded a little worked up, too.

"I'm sorry!" he said. "It seemed like a good thing, a nice gesture."

I heard a drawer slam, then my mom's voice: "How could you do that, Scott? Without even asking me first? You think that's my idea of a vacation? Being stuck in a crucible with the people who stress me out the most?"

Whoa, whoa, whoa. Vacation, as in Michigan? Had my dad invited Meg and her dad to Michigan? I could barely begin to process what that would mean.

"You're right, I should have asked first. But I'd had a couple of beers and Jay and I were having a really good time and Michigan came up and it just happened."

"Just when it was starting to get easier, being there again. This would have been our best year there since…"

She still couldn't say it. *Since Mason died.*

My dad said, "I'm sorry, okay? What do you want me to do, un-invite them?"

Mom made an exasperated sound. "Don't be ridiculous. There's nothing you can do. I'll just have to deal with it."

And then there was silence.

I tiptoed into my room, deciding not to bother letting them know I was home. My mom would check for me soon enough anyway. I collapsed onto my bed and thought about Meg and me, together in Michigan again. It seemed too good to be true. Maybe this would give us the chance to work things out, to recapture the way we used to be. Maybe it would convince her to come back to stay. I closed my eyes, thinking of all the things we loved about Silver Lake, all the things we did together when we were there: The fireworks on the Fourth of July… Kissing behind the raft where our parents couldn't see… Walking over to the swampy area at the end of the road, looking for frogs and turtles… Going to the Sugar Bear for ice cream… Taking the rowboat out to the water lilies so Meg could lean over the side and pick them…

That was my idea of fun.

And dammit, it used to be hers, too.

10

IN THE MORNING I TEXTED DARA TO LET HER know I was ready to swim whenever she was. Coach Brian was out of town, so there was no club practice that day. It would just be Dara and me – oh, the joy. I waited to hear back, wondering if she was hungover or maybe even still partying. Maybe I'd be able to go back to sleep for once. But no, she texted back within a couple of minutes and said she'd pick me up in ten.

I waited for her under the magnolia. A thick mass of pale gray clouds obscured the sun; if they didn't clear, it was going to be a chilly practice.

She pulled into the driveway without the usual drama. She wasn't in a chatty mood, which wouldn't make it easy for me to get information about the remainder of Meg's evening. I tore the wrapper off what I assumed was meant to be my breakfast, since I'd found it on my seat – an all-raw spirulina and chia seed bar.

"So what time did the party wrap up?" I asked her, biting into the bar. It tasted like seaweed blended with crunchy dirt.

"I went to bed a couple hours ago," Dara said. "They were still going. Some of them are still there now."

I wanted desperately to know if Meg was still there when Dara went to bed, or if she'd left with someone, or what she'd been doing... But Dara didn't say and I didn't ask.

The pool was practically deserted – it was just Dara and me and a few others who hadn't been at the party. Dara cut me a lot of slack. She gave me an easy set, swam a few laps herself, then got out and lay on a lounge chair with a towel for a blanket.

When I finished my set, Dara was asleep. I thought about sneaking over to the office to apply for a lifeguarding job. I liked the idea of making some money, but I liked even better the idea of having an obligation that would force me to spend some time away from Dara.

I took one more look at her, and, maybe because her sleeping appearance was deceptively serene, I decided to go for it.

In the office the director of the swim program – a frizzy-haired, middle-aged woman – told me she needed swim teachers more than she needed guards, and since I was a swimmer, was I interested? I had already envisioned an easy summer of sitting up on the guard chair, wearing the whistle of authority and getting tan, but then she mentioned that teaching paid better and I came around. As long as my references were good, I'd have a five-hour training session on Wednesday and then I could start.

Dara was awake when I came back. "Wanna get some breakfast?"

I rapidly calculated that not only was I very hungry, but that maybe if I told her about the job in a public place, she wouldn't yell or kick the shit out of me.

At the pancake house, I tried again to get Dara to tell me about the goings-on after I left the party. I waited as she squeezed lemon into a glass of tomato juice, then dropped the lemon in. She picked up the Tabasco sauce and shook some into the drink. When she reached for the pepper, my patience ran out.

"So what happened?" I asked. The waitress set a tall glass of chocolate milk in front of me – one of my few Dara-sanctioned pleasures owing to its magical formula of carbs, protein, and electrolytes. "Did Meg stay long?"

She shook her head. "The guys crawled all over her like maggots on trash. At some point she scraped them off, and next thing I know, she's fucking crying on Abby's shoulder."

Crying? On Abby's shoulder? "Do you know why she was crying?"

Dara sprinkled salt into her tomato juice and stirred it.

"Girls like that are always crying for no reason. Makes me sick."

I leaned across the booth. "What do you mean, 'girls like that'?" I was still bristling about the "maggots on trash" comparison.

"Drama queens," Dara said, sipping her juice and meeting my eyes. "Girls who feel sorry for themselves even though they have everything."

She was baiting me and I was taking the bait, even though I knew that in Dara's mind, if you had two arms, you pretty much had everything.

"And of course Abby totally fell for it and was all, like, hugging her." Dara banged the spoon on the side of her drink so hard I couldn't believe she didn't crack the glass.

Our food came. I was pissed off at Dara but starving. I drowned the waffle in syrup and slid my over-easy eggs on top, stabbing the yolks to mix with the syrup and sprinkling the whole thing with salt and pepper. "You don't even know Meg," I said, not looking up.

"You don't know her, either," Dara said pointedly, pulling the top off a whipped butter packet with her teeth.

I wanted to argue, but I didn't have much supporting evidence. "Who'd she go home with?" I asked.

"Abby."

I glanced up at the irritation in her voice. "Abby was drinking," I said, torn between feeling guilty that Meg got a ride with someone who'd been drinking and feeling mad at Meg for doing it.

"Oh, please. She walked around with the same beer all night. Abby's not a drinker."

We ate without talking for a few minutes while I tried to figure out how to tell her about the job. Finally I just said it. "So I'm going to be teaching swim lessons."

Dara looked up, a single blueberry speared on her fork. "What?"

"I was just gonna see about a part-time job guarding, because I could use the money. D'Amico said I should apply. But teaching lessons is what I was offered. Just very part-time," I added, finishing more with a whimper than a bang.

She set down her fork. "When did this happen?"

"At the pool. While you were sleeping." I took a bite of bacon and wiped my fingers on my napkin.

She sat back and stared me down. "What hours?"

"I don't know yet. Whatever they give me. Don't worry, I'll train around it." Dara's unblinking gaze was starting to unman me.

She tilted her head at me, which in no way resembled Meg's head tilt. Meg's always seemed to say, *Tell me, Otis, I'm listening, I can't wait to hear what you think.* Dara's version was more like, *Jesus, Mueller, how can you be such a bonehead?* "Do you realize how annoying that's going to be? Trying to teach unfocused little brats how to swim?"

I shrugged. "It'll be okay."

She didn't say anything more. I examined my paper place mat, a study in consumer-targeted advertising. It was covered in ads for a cremation service, a power scooter, an assisted living facility, and a hearing aid. When I looked up, a little bird of an old lady with a metal walker was standing at our table, hunching over toward Dara.

"Dear. I hope you don't mind my asking—"

"Lawn mower," Dara said loudly, not looking up from her pancakes. "Terrible accident." She turned to the woman, waved her stump at her, and said, "Have a nice day."

The woman patted Dara on the shoulder and said something about what a brave girl she was. Someone of sounder body might have gotten an ass-kicking, but even Dara wasn't going to attack a lady so old she was practically dead.

"Let's get out of here," Dara grumbled, pulling some bills out of her purse.

I started shoveling down the rest of my breakfast as fast as I could because Dara was already getting up. I grabbed the last few slices of bacon as Dara threw a few crumpled twenties down.

"I'll get your check," the waitress called, hurrying toward us.

"It's all set," Dara said without turning around.

She pushed the revolving door with her foot and exited. I followed behind, emerging into a light rain.

"You okay?" I asked through my packed mouth as she yanked open the car door.

"Peachy." She slammed the door and started the car, jamming the gearshift into reverse. She was backing out before I'd even gotten the damn door closed.

We rode in silence, apart from the squeak of the wiper blades. When she dropped me off at my house, she said, "Don't bother me, okay? I'm going to bed."

My mom was in the kitchen when I came in, taking muffins out of the oven. The house smelled like bananas and spices. "Hey," she said, glancing up. "How was last night?"

"Fine." I paused, realizing I was weirdly empty-handed. I had left my swim bag in Dara's car. Crap.

"Are you and Meg … doing okay?" She set the pan of muffins on a cooling rack and pushed her hair out of her eyes.

"I dunno." I reached for a muffin.

She held out a hand to stop me. "Too hot."

I turned to go.

"Wait."

I gave her an annoyed look and hovered in the doorway.

She leaned against the counter, oven mitt still on. "Well, tell me about last night. What was the party like?"

"I told you it was fine."

"I see," she said in a clipped voice. She hated it when I did that – gave answers containing no information. "What time did you get home?"

"Not that late. Why?"

She raised her eyebrows. "Apparently Meg ignored her curfew – along with the texts Jay kept sending her." She paused, apparently waiting for me to say something, but I'm good at not saying something, so I just waited her out. "Do you really think you should have left her there?" she asked.

Oh, that was rich. "It wasn't my idea that she should stay." I glanced down and scraped some egg yolk off my shirt. "I'm not the boss of her."

"Listen." She sat at the table and nodded to the chair across from her.

I sighed and sat down, knowing I was about to hear about the Brandts coming to Michigan. I'm a terrible liar; I couldn't fake ignorance even if I wanted to. "I already know about Michigan," I said.

"You do? You know that Meg and her dad are coming?"

"Yup."

"Meg told you?"

I shook my head. "I heard you and Dad arguing when I got home last night."

I watched her process that.

"Oh," she finally said. "Well, I was upset. Your father didn't even ask me first."

"I know. I heard." I stood to go.

"Well, wait." She leaned toward me, and I noticed the dark smudges under her eyes. "How do you feel about that?"

"Fine." She flinched, and then I felt like a dick for being so short with her. "Oh," I said. "I applied for a job today. At the pool."

Her face brightened. "A job? For the summer?"

I told her about it, which seemed to ease some of the tension between us, and then escaped to my room. I tried to read, but I couldn't concentrate. I kept thinking about Michigan, and how Meg might feel about it, if she even knew yet. I thought about how much my mom didn't want Meg and her dad there with us. What would it be like, having us all back there together – minus Mason and Karen? Would the place remind Meg and me of the good times we used to have, maybe rekindle the way we felt about each other? Or would it only highlight how much had changed, how different we were now?

I never heard from Dara – and I didn't text her because she'd said not to bother her – so I went and swam by myself in the afternoon, half because I was hoping to spy on some swim lessons to get a clue. I had to wear an old jammer and crappy goggles because my stuff was in Dara's car. And there were no lessons while I was there.

I made it almost to bedtime before the temptation to text Meg started to overwhelm me. On the one hand, I was nervous that she *wasn't* excited about this Michigan news; if she was, wouldn't she have texted me about it by now? Maybe she didn't want to spend a week trapped in the middle of nowhere in a dilapidated old lake house with me. If that was the case, I could live without knowing.

But, on the other hand, she had a sunburn, she had cat problems, she was convinced my mom hated her, her parents had separated, her mom had a drinking problem, and from the sounds of it, Meg had had a shitty time at the party last night. Probably in part because she'd had a fight with *me*. If I wanted to be friends, shouldn't I be acting like I cared?

So I texted her. After about seven hundred aborted attempts, I settled on *Hey, just checking your pulse. Bad cat, sunburn, trouble with parents, possible hangover? Hope things are looking up.*

She didn't respond.

In the morning, I had six messages. One from Dara, saying she'd bring my swim bag when she picked me up for practice. And five from Meg, which she'd sent right after I went to bed, naturally.

> *I'm sorry for the way I acted. The last thing I wanted to do was fight with you. None of this is going the way I hoped it would.*

*Did you get home okay? I ended up getting a ride home
with a really nice girl named Abby. I think I might have
given her an earful at the party...*

*I know I probably seemed like a mess. I want you to know
that I'm not normally like that. I usually don't even drink.
The idea of being like my mother... Ugh. No.*

Anyway, my dad is pissed. I'll be laying low for a few days. ☹

Okay, well, I guess I'll catch you later.

No mention of Michigan. I wasn't sure what to make
of that. Maybe Jay hadn't told her yet. Maybe he was recon-
sidering going. I hoped not.

But I had no time to think about it anymore and certainly no time to write much. So I fired off: *Sorry I missed your
messages – I was asleep. Anyway, I'm around.*

Over the next few days, I didn't see or hear from her.
Was she grounded? Would her dad really ground her when
she was only here for three weeks? I didn't want to ask my
parents; after the argument I'd overheard, the last thing I was
going to bring up to them was Meg's dad. But with every
day that passed that I didn't see her, I was frustrated over
the lost opportunity to try to make things right with her. *For*
her. So she'd be okay. So she'd move back. But time was of
the essence, especially because I didn't want things to still be
weird between us when we left for Michigan. That trip was

going to be messed up enough as it was. And after Michigan, her three weeks were up.

In the meantime, I was busy with swimming and training for my new job at the pool. I would be teaching lessons three days a week. Outside of that, I wasted time on the computer and got a head start on some of the books we'd be reading in junior AP English. I started with Dante's *Inferno*, figuring hell was something I could easily identify with.

Friday afternoon I was teaching my last lesson – a three-year-old girl named Amanda who had dark blue eyes, blond ringlets, and a fear of the water that didn't exactly make my job easy. Her mother told me that she'd had lessons already, but no one could get her to put her head underwater. I was starting to feel the pressure of failure before I even started. I couldn't get Amanda to put her head underwater, either, although I did get her to blow bubbles.

"Come on," I told her, squatting down across from her in the shallow end as she hung on to the side. "How about … if you put your whole head underwater, I'll give you a pony ride!" Bribery was never discussed during my training, so I assumed that meant it was fair game.

She smiled. She liked that idea.

"Okay, I'll be waiting for you in here." I took a breath and ducked under the water. I waited so long I could hear her laughing. Finally she started poking the top of my head. I came up, tossed my hair out of my face, and said,

"Where were you? I waited and waited!"

"Nooo!" she exclaimed, reaching for me. She put her arms around my neck and said, "I want a pony ride."

"You have to put your head underwater first. Didn't you see how easy it was?"

"I can't!"

"Yes, you can. You just have to hold your breath. Can I see you hold your breath?"

Still holding on to me, she puffed her cheeks out, her blue eyes perfect circles, then blew the air out and started panting hard. I couldn't help cracking up.

I glanced up and my eyes caught a pair of tanned legs a few feet away. I knew those legs. I stood up, Amanda still wrapped around me. "Hey!" I called out. "When did you get here?"

Meg's eyes were hidden by her sunglasses, but she was smiling. "A while ago. I've been observing your teaching technique."

"Great," I mumbled, embarrassed. I hoisted Amanda up a little higher on my waist.

She waved at Amanda. "You like Otis?"

Amanda nodded. Then she buried her head in my shoulder, suddenly shy.

Meg watched us, her smile fading.

An ache bloomed in my chest. I knew what she was thinking. It was impossible for me not to think about Mason as I dealt with Amanda. Honestly, though, I kind of liked the reminder. The small voice, the giggles, the familiar weight of a kid clinging to me. In a way, it felt good.

"Amanda's gonna go underwater," I informed Meg.

Amanda lifted her head. "And then I'm going to ride Otis like a horsey."

Meg summoned a smile, for which I was grateful.

It took another ten minutes of cajoling and negotiating, but I finally got Amanda to do it. She came up after about a billionth of a second and clapped her hands to her face, rubbing her eyes. "I did it! Mama!" she yelled before she even opened her eyes. "Did you see that?"

Her mom clapped her hands and praised her from her lounge chair.

Shafer, Heinz, and D'Amico, taking a break from swimming, also clapped and cheered.

"Horsey time," Amanda informed me.

Wonderful.

I maneuvered her onto my back and started galloping through the shallow end. Words cannot describe how stupid I felt. When Amanda started telling me to make horsey noises, I felt like I had no choice but to keep her happy.

"Neigh!" I yelled, bringing loud laughter from my teammates, who had gathered around to watch. I couldn't bear to look at Meg as I pranced around. My humiliation was boundless.

"Giddyap, horsey!" Amanda yelled, smacking me on the head.

"No hitting, Amanda," her mother called. "That's enough. Leave poor Otis alone now."

I took Amanda to the edge of the pool and handed her off to her mom, hoping my tan concealed the blush I could feel burning in my face.

"I have a feeling they're not paying you nearly enough for this," her mom said apologetically. "I hope your boss knows what a great teacher you are."

I waved her off, embarrassed. "See you Monday, Amanda. Good job today."

I jumped out of the pool and was heading to grab my stuff when someone called, "Hey, horsey."

I turned. Kiera strutted toward me in a black swimsuit with a neckline that plunged to somewhere near Australia, a silver hoop holding the top together at the crucial point. "I thought you should know," she said, her eyes twinkling, "every girl here officially wants to have your baby."

Good thing my face was already red. I couldn't think of a word to say. She bit her lip, then gave me a smile so seductive it made my eyes cross, before turning and walking off.

I grabbed my towel and went over by Meg. She had her sunglasses lifted, her eyes following Kiera. "Subtle, isn't she."

I toweled off my hair, wondering if – or more like hoping – she was jealous.

"See?" she said. "I knew you were the dark horse."

"Ha-ha," I said, but I couldn't help grinning. She could make me feel so good with just a tiny remark, or even sometimes just a smile or a look. I sank into a chair next to her and tried to fix my hair with my fingers.

"You're gonna be such an amazing father someday." She said it so softly, I wasn't even sure I heard her right. I turned to look at her.

She wasn't smiling anymore. She reached up and lowered her sunglasses over her eyes.

"You'll be a great mother, too."

She shook her head. "Nope. I don't want kids."

"What?" No disguising my surprise – it was a total shock to me. "When did you decide that?" My first reaction was, indefensibly, a feeling of betrayal. As hysterically funny as it might be, the plans we made as kids for future procreation – a son first, then twin daughters two years later – were something I had not dismissed, apparently.

She shrugged. She pulled her legs up and wrapped her arms around herself, resting her chin on her knees. Two little kids ran by, shrieking with laughter, their wet feet slapping the ground. I stared at the fading footprints they left behind.

"Well, I hope you change your mind," I said, wondering if I was crossing a line. I traced a tiny moon-shaped scar on my knee – acquired one summer in Michigan from a piece of clamshell, when Meg and I were crawling around in shallow water trying to catch minnows with a kitchen strainer.

"So," I said. "Michigan."

She nodded. "I can't believe we're going."

I felt a rush of relief – Jay hadn't backed out after all! – followed by uncertainty. I wanted her to say she was excited, that she was looking forward to it. But her tone was matter-of-fact.

"Maybe it'll be good," she said, glancing over at me.

"It'll be great," I said. "I'm excited."

She tilted her head and smiled at me a little. Then she turned and lay back. She hummed along to the music piped overhead, and she sounded so good. "Hum louder," I said.

She smiled without looking at me. "Now you made me self-conscious."

"Don't give me that. You have a beautiful voice." I knew from Facebook that she was in choir at her school in California. I thought about telling her that Willow Grove had, like, five choirs she could choose from if she decided to move back, but I wasn't sure my agenda needed to be quite that transparent.

She turned to me. "Hey, our parents are going to some wine thing downtown tonight. I'm officially off probation, so we could hang out, if you want. I think…" She took a breath. "I think we should try this talking thing again." She leaned on her side to face me better. Because she was mostly reclined, her breasts scooted together, creating an unreasonable situation. It wasn't like Kiera cleavage – a dark, deep line you could tuck your whole hand into – but *almost*-cleavage, round and ripe and shadowy. Jesus. I grabbed my towel and laid it over myself.

"Unless you have plans or something."

I blinked, suddenly aware that Meg had been talking.

"Yeah, you're probably going to a party," she said, a small quirk of her mouth telling me she was teasing.

"Wait, what did you say?" I said, nervous at the prospect of getting busted for being distracted by impure thoughts.

"Weren't you listening?" She lifted her sunglasses to give me an exasperated look. "I said, I could come over and make spaghetti carbonara for you tonight. If you wanted."

How did I miss that? I imagined Meg cooking me dinner, just the two of us, alone. I imagined her falling into my arms and doing all the things we should have been doing for the last three years. I imagined convincing her to move back to Chicago.

I knew I was just setting myself up for disappointment and misery, because my mind was already going in all sorts of ridiculous directions. I'd probably end up with my heart in a sling. By the end of the night I might feel like shooting myself.

"That sounds awesome," I said.

And I meant it.

11

IT STARTED THE WAY SO MANY GOOD THINGS
do: with bacon. Our parents had left. Meg stood at the stove,
the pan in front of her sizzling and popping, and I sat at the
table with my feet up on another chair, sipping not just any
lemonade, but homemade lemonade with fresh mint and
ginger – Meg's own invention and a stroke of refreshment
genius. Meg had gone home for a few hours after the pool so
I'd had time for a shower *and* a nap. I felt pretty darn good.
Rested. And a similarly uncharacteristic sense of freedom,
since I hadn't seen or heard from Dara since she took off
after our morning practice.

"Could you crack those eggs into a bowl?" Meg asked,
turning the bacon over.

"Sure." I jumped up to help. I was a little overzealous in
my cracking; I brought an egg down so hard on the edge of

the bowl that it broke clear through and the egg splattered onto the counter.

"You Ironmen." Meg smiled, shaking her head. She was in a good mood.

I wiped up the egg with paper towels and tried again. When I had three eggs in the bowl, Meg told me to whisk in the Parmesan cheese.

I squinted at her. "Did you ever read *Tom Sawyer*?"

"No, why?" Her poor nose was peeling from her sunburn, illuminated by the lightbulb in the stove hood.

I started mixing the cheese with the eggs. "He's supposed to whitewash a fence, but he hoodwinks the other kids in the neighborhood into doing the work. You'd make him proud."

"You could grind in some pepper now."

"See?"

She laughed.

"I mean, come on," I said, picking up the pepper mill. "You're standing there in front of the stove, just looking pretty, and I'm doing all the heavy lifting."

"Oh, boo-hoo. Cue the violins."

"How much pepper?"

"Tons."

When she finally said I could stop grinding pepper, I stood behind her, watching over her shoulder as she dropped spaghetti into a boiling pot of water. She wore a red-and-white polka-dot shirt and jean shorts, and she looked unreasonably cute. Also, I could smell her hair.

"Where'd you learn how to make this?" I asked.

"Jeff's grandmother. She's from Italy."

Why'd I have to open my mouth? I just killed my own buzz.

"She's an incredible cook." Meg set the stove timer to nine minutes. "Jeff's got it made. All the women in his family are great cooks."

The idea of Meg immersed in his world gave me an ache.

But minutes later, when we stirred the creamy, cheesy egg and the crispy bacon into the steamy pasta – and threw in handfuls of extra cheese – I was distracted from my misery.

"This is unreal," I told her, twirling up a giant forkful. "This might be the best thing I've ever eaten."

"I know, right?" She kept grating more cheese into her bowl until I finally had to laugh.

"How 'bout some pasta with your cheese?" I asked.

She stuck her tongue out at me.

We ate it all – every delicious bite. Then Meg set the pot between us and we fished out the last strands of spaghetti with our fingers. When there was nothing left to pillage, we cleaned up.

"Otis? It's kind of scary," she said, running hot water into the pot, "how much you can eat."

"Ha! From the girl who eats like it's her last day on Earth."

She smiled. "Touché."

I was never so happy washing dishes in my life.

When we finished, we went downstairs to watch TV. I sat close to her on the couch, deciding to pretend Jeff didn't exist.

"Feels like old times," Meg said. "Doesn't it?"

"Well, not exactly," I hazarded, flipping channels with the remote, settling on an old black-and-white Katharine Hepburn movie. She gave me a quizzical look.

"I mean," I said, "if it were old times, there'd probably be some hanky-panky going on."

She chortled. "Oh, Otis. You're so funny!"

I wasn't really going for funny. I was trying to rekindle a fucking flame.

"Who says *hanky-panky*? You're like an old geezer trapped in the body of a Greek god."

My head spun; she had insulted me and flattered me in the same breath. "What, you don't remember all the...?" I raised my eyebrows suggestively.

The smile fell off her face in an instant. She looked away. "I remember everything," she said softly. "The magnolia. Michigan. Of course I remember."

"I don't know what you remember," I said, suddenly feeling an edge. Because after all that kissing, all that in-love-ness that we were awash in, she disappeared and never looked back. *Why?*

Some angry energy was blooming inside of me; was I

really going to ruin the best, most promising evening I'd had in years?

"So how is it with Jeff?" I heard myself ask.

Yes. Yes, I was.

"What do you mean?"

"I don't know. Is he a good kisser?"

I was such an asshole. And an idiot: Why did I ask questions that I didn't even want to hear the answers to?

"It's different, I guess." She gazed at the floor. "Jeff kisses … like a man on a mission. You…" She glanced at me for an instant before looking away. "You kissed me like you thought I might break."

My face flushed with heat. Great. So I had no clue how to kiss. So be it. Fuck it all anyway. Fuck Michigan. Fuck my hopes. Fuck me.

I picked up the remote and turned up the volume.

"Wait," she said, taking the remote and muting it. "Don't take that wrong – please."

"Don't worry about it," I said, staring at the silent screen.

"I wasn't dissing him," she said. "Really, I wasn't."

I blinked. Dissing *him*?

"I'm sure things are never, you know, like the first time."

Just as I was beginning to process this unbelievably amazing revelation, my phone dinged. I picked it up to silence it, but the displayed message stopped me short. "Oh, shit."

"What? What is it?"

"Shit." I stood up. "It's Dara."

"Of course," she mumbled.

"I have to go." I headed for the stairs. "There's been an accident."

I pedaled through the dark, ping-ponging between fear and anger. Damn Dara for pulling me away from Meg at such a crucial moment! But what if Dara was seriously hurt? What was I going to find when I got there? Her texts were hard to decipher. If she'd totaled her car and hit her head on the windshield, she could be dead by the time I got there. Or maybe she was just being dramatic and her texts were garbled because she was tipsy. God – I was finally getting somewhere with Meg. *Fuck.*

My mind twisted and leaped as I rode toward the forest preserve, cars whipping past me in the night. Stopping for red lights seemed to take an eternity. Maybe I should have called Shafer or Abby or someone else who could drive – and help me with whatever I was in for – but I didn't even know where Dara was or if I was overreacting. When I finally reached the start of the forest preserve, I called her, trying to find her. Between her confusion and her slurred speech, she wasn't much help. The only thing she was clear on was "don't call nine-one-one."

But finally, I found her car, or what remained of it, where Forestway Drive winds around the lagoons.

The front of the Corolla was crumpled into an enormous weeping willow – the hood was lifted and bent, and the driver's-side windshield had a bloated spiderweb pattern embedded in it. No seat belt, probably, the dumbass. How many times could this girl cheat death?

I found her huddled under a nearby tree, dressed in a white tank and shorts. Her face was covered in blood, her hair caked with it.

I jumped off my bike and ran over to her. "Dara!" I grasped one of her shoulders and shook her a little, my heart pounding. "We need an ambulance."

"No. No police."

"We have to. All we have is my bike. Your car is totaled. Jesus, Dara – you could have been killed!"

"You know what I never told you?" Her head listed to the side. "There were signs posted that day."

I knelt down next to her. "Where? What are you talking about?"

She touched her hand to her head and looked at the blood. "In Hawaii. They posted warnings. That sharks had been sighted."

"You knew there were sharks that day?"

She nodded.

"Why did you do it?" I asked, picking up her hand, which was wet. Now I had blood on my hands. "What are you saying?"

She waved her hand limply. "I thought it would be fine. I always did stupid shit. Climbing water towers, stealing, messing with fireworks... Nothing ever happened to me. I thought, you know, they just cover their asses and post signs and whatever." She stared at nothing. "Sometimes I still can't believe it happened. In my dreams, I still have two arms. That's mostly why I drink. The more I drink, the less I dream."

Jesus. It wasn't just the phantom limb pains. It wasn't just the loss of an arm. Waking up every day and rediscovering that your arm was gone – having to face that over and over and over again? The thought made me weak. I had my own version of that waking-up-and-remembering, and it was unspeakably terrible.

She leaned her head back against the tree. "S'another way I ruined his life. He was my swim coach, you know. Before..." She gestured with her stump.

Her dad. Yes. I did know that, although I'd forgotten.

She closed her eyes and her head lolled again. "Now I swim like a fucking freak."

There was nothing I could say to that. And I was still reeling to think she had done so many other reckless things. Climbing water towers? Fireworks? Jesus. Did she have a death wish?

"And now his freak of a daughter is a..." She hung her head.

"A what?"

"Nothing," she whispered. "Just a fuck-up." She leaned her head back, her eyes closing.

Choosing her probable wrath over her possible death, I got up and called 911. I paced while I talked, checking on Dara to make sure she was still breathing. When I hung up, I sat next to her and talked to her about anything I could think of, trying to keep her with me.

Through the tangle of trees over our heads, a jillion stars sparkled against the black sky. I had never felt more alone.

It's funny how even the most un-religious person will turn to prayer when the chips are down. As Dara bled onto my shirt, I pleaded with the Great Whomever to let her be okay. I felt guilty because I had wished her away countless times, but not like this! I never wanted anything bad to happen to her. It hit me hard, how fucked up she really was, and what a shitty friend I'd been. I mean, who did she have, except for me? And what was I doing? Ignoring her. Thinking of myself and wishing she'd leave me alone. It occurred to me that, before Dara, I'd only ever really loved two people, not counting my parents, and I'd lost both of them. Dara was the third person I'd ever loved, as complicated and messy and unpleasant as it often was. I couldn't lose her, too.

The cracked windshield of Dara's beloved Corolla gleamed in the moonlight like the facets of a diamond, a galaxy of its own. And of all things, that's what finally triggered the overflow of the well inside of me – which is pretty fucking nuts, if you think about it. My brother was dead, things with Meg were fucked, Dara was bleeding away on me. But somehow, it was looking at her crumpled-up car that broke me. She had loved that car more than just about anything. I'd been riding around in it since the summer after eighth grade. I couldn't imagine her not hauling me around in it. I couldn't imagine *her* without it. Whatever happened now, nothing would ever be the same. A chapter of my life had just ended, and I had no idea what the next one would hold.

When the twinkling of stars gave way to the flashing of lights and the panicky sound of sirens filled the still night air, I stood up, propping Dara straighter against the tree. I was scared shitless and thinking I should have called my parents.

Two cops questioned me, one about a foot taller than the other and probably twenty years younger. I answered as best I could while the EMTs moved Dara to a board and put some plastic contraption around her neck.

"Had she been drinking, do you know?" It was the younger of the two cops, Officer Garrett.

I really, really didn't want her to get busted and lose her license, but I was a terrible liar. "She's on all these medications. For phantom limb pains."

He nodded knowingly, his mouth twisting into a grimace. "Fucking prescription medications. The wife had knee surgery and the doctors doped her up so bad that she had a car accident, too."

He bought it. Maybe there was a God.

He took a good look at me and asked why she'd called me, a kid on a bike, for help.

"I'm kind of her best friend." I stuck my trembling hands in my pockets. I was shaking – shaking like beef, Meg would have said – either from being cold or scared or both.

Officer Garrett put an arm around my shoulder and said some comforting things, I don't remember what. He took information from me while Dara was loaded into the ambulance.

"Her dad's out of town," I said. "I don't know his cell phone number."

"What about the mother?"

"Dead."

"Brothers? Sisters?"

I shook my head.

He whistled through his teeth. "So you're basically the closest thing to family we have, eh?"

Just when I thought I couldn't feel any guiltier. "I guess so."

"All right. Come on – I'll take you to the hospital. You have parents to call?"

"Yes, sir."

I called my dad, knowing how my mom would freak, and then texted Meg an update from the cruiser. It was hard not to feel like a criminal in the backseat of a police car – the last place I ever thought I'd be. It felt sort of like being put in a cage.

My parents met me at the ER. Officer Garrett introduced himself and then made himself scarce, probably because my mother looked like a cannon about to blow.

"Oh my God! Is that blood?"

I looked down at my shirt. I looked like an ax murderer.

My dad gaped at me. "Why the hell didn't you call us, Otis?" He didn't exactly sound mad – more baffled and disappointed.

"I didn't know how bad it was," I said as they sat down. "I didn't want to wreck your night without even knowing what the situation was."

A fluorescent light over my head flickered. I shifted in my seat. When I'd arrived with Officer Garrett, a guy was vomiting on the floor of the waiting area, and even though it had been mopped up, I could still smell it. My stomach churned.

My dad got up and went to the water dispenser, where he drank a cup of water and then refilled it and brought it to my mom, who sat on my other side.

She held it, not drinking. And then she hissed, "You could have been *in* that car. I knew she wasn't a safe driver!"

She sounded livid, but her eyes welled with tears. I wished I could escape – fly, apparate, vaporize, anything. I'd rather be anywhere than near my mom when she was upset.

"But I wasn't," I whisper, leaning in.

She shook her head and blinked, and both eyes spilled over at the same time. "You don't understand anything."

I did understand, even if she didn't know it. I was her only remaining child. I *got* it.

She dug in her purse for tissues. "How is she?" She sat with her legs crossed, her black high heel wagging back and forth at a frenetic pace. They must have been at a nice restaurant when I interrupted, because her shoes were generally of the comfort-is-the-only-concern variety.

"I don't know," I said.

I took out my phone and texted Meg again to give her an update. She responded, *Okay, hope she's all right.* Who knows what she was really thinking.

After a while a doctor came out and told us that they'd be observing Dara throughout the night.

"Can I see her?" I asked.

"Tomorrow," he said, tapping a file folder against his hand. "She's not going to wake up tonight anyway."

"Did anyone reach her dad?" I asked. "His number must be in her cell phone."

"He's flying in."

Oh boy. I was afraid of how angry he might be at Dara. Once when I was in eighth grade, he came to a swim meet and yelled at Dara in Russian after her two hundred free relay. I don't know what he was saying, but he was *mad*.

People stared. What kind of asshole yells at an amputee for not swimming right? She didn't cry, although I almost did. That was the last time I ever saw him at a meet.

The drive home was quiet except for once or twice when my mom exploded about how I was never to get into a car with Dara again, and why couldn't I stay away from girls who were so *troubled*? Girls, plural. A statement about Meg, too? I didn't pursue it.

Later that night Mom tapped on my door, then pushed it open. She held a glass with about an inch of something amber in it. My dad had probably poured her a medicinal Scotch.

"Can we not?" I asked, anticipating another tirade about Dara. I stood up from my desk. "Can't it just wait until tomorrow?"

"It's about Michigan."

I crossed my arms. "Let me guess. Meg's not coming."

"No, she's coming."

Relief. But why did my mom's expression still telegraph doom?

She slowly walked over and sat on my bed, holding the glass in both hands. Definitely Scotch. It smelled like peat smoke and Band-Aid adhesive. "Not just Meg, though."

"Yeah, her dad – I know, you told me."

"Not just Jay."

"Karen's coming?" I could see why my mom was so upset.

But my mom shook her head.

"Well, who, then?"

She took a sip of the Scotch and grimaced, staring at the floor. "Apparently Meg's boyfriend will be joining us."

12

THE NEXT MORNING I SAT IN THE WAITING area in the hospital and played games on my phone, trying to distract myself. When I wasn't worrying about Dara, I couldn't stop fuming about Football Guy. Hadn't he ruined enough things for me? Now he was going to ruin my vacation, too – and my chance to get close to Meg again? The thought of actually having to *live* with this guy, to see them together, to be the third wheel while *they* had a romantic reunion... It made me sick just thinking about it.

Apparently it was a birthday gift from Meg's mom, sending Jeff to visit. My mom had apologized, saying she couldn't exactly tell Jay and Meg that he wasn't welcome at the Michigan house, when they knew full well that there was plenty of room.

"Why the hell not?" I had kicked my garbage can hard,

flipping it over and sending crumpled-up paper and granola bar wrappers tumbling. "It's our vacation. They have no right bringing him."

"If it's any consolation, Jay felt bad about it."

Yeah, that was a huge consolation.

I informed her in no uncertain terms that I would not be going. She informed me in no uncertain terms that I *would* be going and to suck it up, buttercup.

I lay there half the night, trying to figure out a way to get out of it. Finally, somewhere around three a.m., I had to face the reality that I was not the master of my universe, not the captain of my ship. I was going to have to go on this stupid vacation. And it was going to suck harder than a Hoover.

"So, who are you here for?"

I startled at the raspy voice. A powdery old woman with apricot-colored hair had been sitting kitty-corner from me in the waiting area all morning. She wore pink running shoes and baggy sky-blue pants, and her head wobbled just slightly.

"A friend," I mumbled. I didn't want to talk, so I didn't reciprocate the question, which I felt bad about. Maybe her husband was lying on the brink of death and she was lonely. Scared.

I sucked.

Dara's dad was in her room – I knew, because the nurse had told me Dara already had a visitor and, at one point, he came out to get some coffee. I had raised a hand to greet him, but he didn't even look my way.

My phone vibrated and I jumped about a mile, startling the woman. I smiled sheepishly at her and opened the message. I was hoping for Meg, but it was Abby.

> *Hey, any idea what's up with Dara? She stood me up last night and she hasn't answered any of my messages.*

Stood her up? As in, they had a date? Would Dara not tell me something like that?

I hesitated, thinking I should call her rather than text the news, but I was uncomfortable talking in front of the old woman, who kept smiling at me anytime my eyes caught hers, and I didn't want to leave. So I texted back and told her about the accident. After asking me a long string of alarmed questions, she said she'd been worrying that Dara was mad at her. *We had such a good time the other night,* she wrote.

The other night? Dara went out with Abby?

She continued. *I couldn't figure out what happened! What's her room number? I'll come when I get back from the city.*

I gave her the information, wanting to ask about what had happened between them, but if Dara didn't want me to know, it was probably none of my business. But my head was kind of reeling. Yet another thing Dara hadn't told me.

I shifted in the uncomfortable plastic seat. My back hurt and my stomach was starting to growl – nurses were delivering lunch on wheeled carts and it smelled good. Just as I was thinking about going to find some food, Dara's dad came out and told me in his gruff Russian accent that I could see her. I didn't even know he realized I was there. He disappeared before I could say anything, and I edged into Dara's room, nervous.

I had tried to prepare myself for what Dara might look like, but it still stopped me in my tracks. White bandages covered her head, and her eyes were purple and swollen. She watched me watching her, but otherwise didn't acknowledge my presence.

The room looked just like hospital rooms on TV – lots of white and tubes and screens that made beeping noises. It smelled like disinfectant but with something sickish underneath, all mingled with a TV-dinner smell. Dara's lunch sat on a tray, unmolested. It didn't look too bad – something in gravy with rice and a plastic cup of green Jell-O. I'd been waiting there for hours and I was starving.

"Hey," I said weakly, walking over to her bed. Apart from her bruises, she was almost the same dull white color as the hospital gown she wore. "So … what's the damage?"

"Concussion. Nine stitches. Fractured ribs. Contusions." She shrugged. "I've been worse."

I sat in the chair by her bed. "What happens next?"

"Not sure yet."

"You gonna lose your license?" I envisioned myself having

to drive her everywhere once I got my license. *Oh, please, God, don't let her lose her license.*

"I'm sure my dad'll take care of it."

"What did he say?"

"He said..." Her expression went hard and she ranted in Russian. She met my eyes and said, "Basically, I fuck up one more time, I'm dead to him."

That bastard. I wondered if being gay would count as "fucking up." The thought made my stomach hurt. I scooted my chair closer. "You just need to hang on until August. Once you get to college, you'll be okay. Your whole life will turn around."

Crickets. I mentally counted the beeps from one of the machines hooked up to her. Carts clattered by outside, and laughter emitted from the nurse's station in the hall.

"What happened last night?" I asked.

She tapped her finger on the surface of her Jell-O, leaving dull fingerprints on the shine. "It was my ampiversary."

I stared at her in confusion. "Your ... what?"

"My ampiversary," she said, still staring at the Jell-O. "The day I lost my arm. Yesterday was five years."

"Oh," I said. I tried to process what she was saying.

She looked up at me brightly. "Five years is wood. I looked it up."

"Wood?"

"You know, traditional anniversary gifts? One year is

paper; fifty years is gold... That stuff."

The possible connection between "wood" and "tree" nudged at my consciousness, but my mind was working much too slowly.

"Anyway," she said, leaning back in bed, "I have to have a psych evaluation. Bet you love that."

"Hey," I said, getting up and going to sit on the edge of her bed. "I just want you to be okay."

"Well, apparently having a bipolar mother who killed herself doesn't bode well for 'okay.'"

"Wait, what?" Her mother committed suicide?

She started tapping on the Jell-O again. "I never told you this story? It's a good one: Promising young dancer, rumored to be in the running for the rare title of *prima ballerina assoluta*, gives birth to an unwanted bundle of what turned out *not* to be joy, ending her career and ruining her life. So she hangs herself. The end."

My mind whirled. I hadn't known any of this. I mean, I knew that Dara's mom was a ballerina and died when Dara was little, but that's about it. I certainly never had any idea it was suicide. Or that Dara thought she was the reason.

She met my eyes, her expression intense. "If you really want me to be okay, then train. Train like it's a matter of life and death." She softened a little. "You really could do it – you're just too dumb to know it. You still have so much room to grow. You've only been swimming for three years!

You're tall and you're gonna get taller! You have wingspan, and big feet and hands! You're tough and you're disciplined. You could be epic if you applied yourself."

I shook my head. "I'm a good swimmer, but I'm no Dara Svetcova."

I wished I could call it back. It was such a stupid thing to say, which I realized just a moment too late.

Her eyes flashed. "So what if I used to be good? What good does that do me now?" In one motion, she picked up the Jell-O and whipped it across the room at the wall. Jewel-like green blobs fell everywhere. She lowered her head, then turned to me. "I can't compete with two-armed swimmers, and I don't want to swim with the fucking freaks and idiots." She collapsed back against the pillow and closed her eyes. "Don't you get it? You're all I have."

If that was true, then we were in trouble. Because one thing I knew for sure was that I was never going to be enough.

The following week moved by in a lonely blur of water. I trained hard, wanting to do well at next Saturday's meet for Dara's sake. When I wasn't swimming, I was teaching other people how to swim. I'd even gotten Amanda to paddle a few strokes and to float on her back. Two new kids signed up for lessons with me that my boss told me came from referrals. It was nice to not suck at something.

I didn't see Meg for a few days. She sent a brief message

saying she had things to do in town, but that was pretty much it. I didn't know if she was annoyed with me and Dara, or if she wasn't happy about having me hanging around while she and Football Guy had their romantic reunion – during *my* fucking vacation. Or maybe she just didn't want to talk to me. It was probably just as well, because I was so mad about Football Guy coming with us to Michigan, I could hardly see straight.

But then, in the midst of the silence, she started sending me pictures of places she was – weird places, like Dairy Queen or Chuck E. Cheese's – with captions like, *revisiting* or *a lot of memories here*. Mostly those places reminded me of Mason. I couldn't think of anything to say back, apart from *Why the fuck are you going to those places?* So I said nothing.

Dara was released from the hospital with stitches, bruises, painkillers, antidepressants, and a standing date with a psychiatrist twice a week. Her psych evaluation basically concluded that she had depression complicated by chronic pain and unresolved trauma. I didn't think it took a genius to diagnose that.

She seemed to have skirted any legal repercussions; maybe they didn't check her blood alcohol level. She probably had me to thank for that.

Her dad bought her a new car. One with an automatic transmission. She dubbed it the Stupidmobile. And not just because automatic transmissions were stupid, but because what could be more stupid than giving a fuck-up like her a fancy new car that could pay for some poor kid's college education? "I'm going to trade it in for something cool," she'd said. "I loved my old car. This car is embarrassing."

Only Dara would think a shiny new BMW was embarrassing.

With my dad's help, I talked my mom down from her hysteria about my driving with Dara – but only until I got my license, which was probably a couple weeks at the most.

Saturday morning Dara let me drive the Stupidmobile to the River Park meet, which was a nice long drive – close to an hour. I never knew a car could be so awesome. I was accustomed to the practical, energy-efficient, unsexy cars my parents drove – never quite new and minimally upgraded. This car had me fucking high from the smell of new leather, the comfort, the fast acceleration and tight handling.

Dara sat in the passenger seat, legs folded under her, eating Cap'n Crunch from the box. Her head was a mess of bandages and zombie-like bruises.

"Sucks I can't swim since they're doing relays today," she said through a full mouth. "I would have been in the earliest heats for once."

I kept my eyes on the road. There was nothing to say to that.

"So," she said, turning toward me. "Guess who came to visit me in the hospital?"

I played dumb. "Who?"

"Abby."

I looked over at her. "Yeah?"

"And," she said, grinning, "guess who came to see me last night?"

"Um … Abby?"

She glanced at me and nodded, then shrugged like she didn't know what to make of the whole thing. "She just started an internship at Children's Memorial, did you know that? She wants to be a doctor."

"That's great."

"Yeah, wouldn't she be a great doctor? Better than these clowns I have to deal with. She's, like, *really* nice."

I squinted at her. "She's always been nice. This isn't news."

"I know, but … this is a different kind of nice." She closed the cereal box and tossed it on the floor. "We talked for a long time in the hospital. And then last night…"

I turned my head to stare at her.

"Eyes on the road!" She gestured out the windshield, laughing. "You need to get on two-ninety-four – get in the left lane."

I signaled and changed lanes. "Okay, tell me everything."

"I don't know," she mumbled.

I glanced over at her. She wiped some crumbs off her seat.

"What?" I said. "Come on!"

"Okay, okay. We had this amazing talk. I told her stuff… Stuff I don't talk about." I looked over at her, and she met my gaze. "I told her about my mom."

"Wow." I had known Dara for years, and she'd only just told me about her mom. But she already told Abby?

"Abby almost cried."

She said it like she couldn't believe it. But I could envision that. Abby has this expression, a certain angling of her eyebrows, that makes her look sort of chronically concerned. She's the kind of person who will reach out to touch your arm when you tell her something good or you tell her something bad. I was glad that if someone besides me was going to care about Dara, it might be Abby.

"And then she took my hand."

Hand-holding? Wow. "I can't believe you didn't mind. You get so pissed off when people feel sorry for you."

"No, you don't understand. This was different. It wasn't about my arm. I felt like it really *mattered* to her, what had happened to me. Like she really cared. You know?"

"She does. You can tell."

She ducked her head.

I leaned forward a little to see her better. Her bandage obscured one of her eyes. I poked her in the shoulder and grinned. "This is awesome."

"It's not all awesome," she said, her smile fading. "I go

back and forth between being excited every time I think about her and wishing I could just be normal and like guys."

"Hey. It's okay to like Abby." I slowed to get into the 294 turn lane.

"You don't know my dad."

"Fuck your dad."

"Yeah, right."

"He's an idiot. Lesbians are, like, the greatest idea ever. Ask any guy."

"I'm not a lesbian." She sighed. "I'm not an anything."

"Okay, you're not an anything."

"Hey," she said softly, reaching over and tugging on my sleeve. "Thanks. For always being there for me."

I glanced at her bruised and bandaged head and thought, *Not always.*

"How's your stupid job?" she asked, putting her feet up on the dashboard. Her toenails were painted a teal green.

"I like it, mostly."

"Kids. Blech. That'd drive me nuts."

I rolled my eyes.

"You can't keep missing doubles, you know. If you have to work in the afternoon, then swim in the evening. Senior Champs is coming up."

I didn't respond.

We arrived at the pool and got out of the car. It was clear that a brutally hot day was in store – not a cloud in the sky, and no shade to be found other than the umbrellas already claimed by swim teams. The sun was fierce, the thermometer already soaring. I felt sorry for Dara that she couldn't swim. At least the rest of us could cool off.

When I finished warming up and got out of the pool, I spotted Abby and Dara, sitting side by side on a towel, Abby in her suit and Dara in shorts and her team T-shirt. It was clear Abby liked her – I could see it on her face, in her smile, in the way she leaned close when they spoke. *Like her back, Dara, dammit!* I wanted her to be happy, no matter how mad she sometimes made me. If she were happier, maybe she wouldn't be such a bitch. And if she and Abby were together, I would no longer be "all she had."

"So." Shafer stood next to me, eating green grapes out of a plastic container. "What's going on with Meg?"

"What? Nothing. Do my arms." I turned my back to him.

"She hasn't come around the pool this whole week," he said, putting down the grapes and stretching my arms. "And you ditched her the night of Dara's party. You fighting or something?"

I gritted my teeth. I didn't *ditch* her. It was more like she sent me home. But Shafer was the last person on Earth I'd confide in.

"You guys were childhood sweethearts, huh? That's what she said."

"Something like that," I muttered, pulling away.

He picked up his grapes and popped one in his mouth. "Well, I don't know why you're not trying to get her back. If I were you, I sure would be. I mean, yeah, she has a boyfriend. But how can you not have feelings for her?"

I did not dignify that with a response. I certainly wasn't about to discuss the breadth and depth of my feelings for Meg with Shafer.

He and I were both swimming the fifty free, although he was in the last heat and I was a few heats before him. As I went to line up at the blocks, a girl's voice yelled, "Go, Otis!" I turned. It was Kiera. She smiled and waved. It occurred to me that she was really nice. And pretty. And didn't have a boyfriend. And was unambiguously into me. She wasn't Meg, but only Meg was Meg – and Meg had a boyfriend. A boyfriend whose grandmother taught her how to cook. A boyfriend who was flying out to spend a long weekend with her, even though she was due to return home – to him, in California – the next fucking day.

When I got up on the block, I was kind of psyched. My training had taken a bit of a hit lately, but that could be good – sort of a fake taper. I wasn't as sore as usual. I meant to take full advantage of it. I swung my arms and adjusted my goggles, waiting for the start.

At the buzzer I got off a solid dive, and I swam like it was a matter of life and death, like Dara said. I kept myself to two breaths for the whole race, and I hoped Dara was watching

– I'd never done a fifty on two breaths. I always ended up taking a last breath too close to the end of the race, which made Dara nuts.

I touched in and came up, turning to look at the clock. The first thing I processed was that I'd taken first in my heat – handily, too, which was exciting because my seed time had placed me fifth of eight. I pulled my goggles off and did a double take at the clock. Personal best by two-tenths.

When I climbed out, Kiera was cheering for me from the sidelines – I recognized her "Woo-HOOOO!" Coach Brian came up to me, throwing his arms up in a *what the hell was THAT* look. Behind him, Dara was hurrying toward me. I probably had seen more smiles from her in that single morning than in the three years I'd known her combined.

She took a running leap and jumped on me, almost knocking me over. "Fuckin' A, Mueller!"

She was embarrassing me, but I couldn't help smiling.

"Ow, fuck," she said, wincing. "I think I just refractured my ribs." And then she leaned back and grinned at me. "Two breaths? You see? See what you can do?"

And that's when I spotted a familiar figure, standing apart from the crowd, watching me. I thought I was seeing things. Meg? What was she doing here? How had she even gotten here?

Dara turned to see what I was looking at. "Oh, for fuck's sake. What's she doing here?"

"I didn't know she was coming," I said, my gaze locked on Meg. She looked like she'd been smiling a moment before, but it had faded.

"I'll be back in a minute," I told Dara, already walking away.

"Don't you dare let her fuck up this meet for you."

I made my way to Meg, pulling off my cap and weaving my way through the crowd. "Hey!" I stopped in front of her, squinting. "What are you doing here?"

"You invited me – remember?"

I scratched my head. "Oh, right. That was a long time ago." My hair felt like a tangle of wet steel wool. I tried to run my fingers through it, but it was hopeless.

She looked worried. "Is it okay that I came?"

"Yeah! Of course." I guided her back a few feet from the pool – we were in the way of some girls who were cheering for a teammate at the pool's edge. "I just – I didn't expect to see you here. How did you get here?"

She smiled and tossed her hair over her shoulder. "I asked my dad to drive me to your meet without fully disclosing the location until we were in the car."

I laughed.

"I am seriously down in the polls with him. He's hoping I'll get a ride home with you."

Oh boy. Dara would not be happy with that arrangement. Unless she was so happy about the Abby thing, she maybe didn't even care. "We'll figure it out," I said.

She gazed at me, her eyes lit by the sun. "You were amazing." She shook her head. "Watching you swim just slays me."

My eyebrows shot up. "It *slays* you?"

She blushed. "You're like a different person when you swim. You look like such a man."

I grinned. I might not act like a man or kiss like a man, but apparently I looked like one.

I didn't think I was imagining the sweep of Meg's eyes over me. *All* over me. I'm pretty sure my heart actually stopped for a few seconds before it started back up in double time. After all, I was in a Speedo and that's all. This thought almost never occurred to me. Only in Meg's presence was I conscious of the fact that I was practically naked.

"I guess I'll get to see you swimming a lot in Michigan," she said.

"Right." I nodded. "And your boyfriend, too!" Obviously I just couldn't help myself.

Her eyes widened for a moment. "Right. Apparently."

"That's a nice gift. I guess."

"Ha." Her expression suggested she didn't think it was a nice gift at all, which gave me a moment's hope, but then she said, "My mom has an agenda." She ran her hand up the back of her neck and lifted her hair for a moment. The heat was brutal. "I'm sure she's just trying to remind me of what

I'd be leaving behind if I move back to Chicago."

"Oh." It was hard to imagine her mom being that manipulative. But if she had a drinking problem… I guess that changes people. "What year is he, anyway?"

"He'll be a senior."

Fuck. I'd hoped he'd just graduated. Maybe heading off to college in New England. Or actual England. Or maybe Siberia. "Well, I hope he likes Silver Lake. It'll be different having him there – not exactly like old times, huh?"

She held my gaze. "It'll never be like old times, Otis."

Fuck me. "Well, gotta go," I said loudly, taking a step backward. "I have an event coming up."

"The two hundred IM?" she asked, holding up a heat sheet. There were ink circles on it; she'd found my name and marked my events.

"Yup," I said, walking away. Not my best event, the IM, since I sucked at fly. My fly looked like a robot with epilepsy.

It wasn't a great swim, but no surprise there. I came out at about the same time as usual. My hundred breast was much better – good enough to place in the top five.

One event left: the medley relay at the end, which we stood a good chance of winning. Heinz and Shafer were pretty damn fast, and D'Amico was epic – a state-qualifying backstroker for two years.

I stood with the guys while we waited, drinking water and sucking on sliced oranges, trying to stay cool when we weren't in the water. We still had a good ten minutes before our relay, so I wandered over to Meg.

"Hey, congratulations," she called out, jumping up from her chair. She tipped her sunglasses back on her head and ran to meet me. To my surprise, she hugged me. Heat radiated from her, and she was damp with sweat. "Oh my God, your breaststroke is so fast!"

I couldn't help beaming like an idiot when she pulled away and smiled at me. She picked up the hem of her shirt and waved it a little, trying to cool herself. "It's so hot. I had forgotten how psychotic Chicago weather is."

"It's actually supposed to rain later," I said, squinting to the west. "You should go inside when you can, cool off a little. Are you drinking enough water? You have sunscreen on?"

She didn't answer, but she looked at me with an expression that resonated with something in the recesses of my memory. Finally, I placed it: it was the same expression she'd had that time she'd gotten lost in the hallways and I'd taken her to the classroom. Just like then, I wasn't sure what was behind that expression in her eyes. Also just like then, it stirred up feelings in me.

Abby appeared out of nowhere, panting. "Otis! It's Dara."

I heard her before I saw her – a high-pitched scream. I turned and scanned the place. She was curled up on the ground by the girls' team, clutching her arm.

I had never heard that kind of sound from Dara. Not ever. If Dara couldn't stop herself from screaming, from drawing attention like this in a public place ... I couldn't even imagine how bad it must be.

Meg clapped her hands over her ears, her face going white. Oh, shit – the screaming.

"Come on!" Abby pulled me by the arm.

I couldn't attend to both of them. With an apologetic glance at Meg, I took off after Abby.

When I reached Dara, a crowd was gathering – the thing she hated most. I pushed through and knelt on the concrete beside her. Between the bruises and the bandages and the agony on her face, she was a heartbreaking sight.

"Let's get you out of here." I gathered her up in my arms and stood. She jerked and twisted. "I'll take you to the parking lot. We'll do the hand thing."

"The box," she managed to get out.

The box? I hesitated. The box was at least forty-five minutes away. I still had the relay. But she knew that.

"Let's try the hand thing first," I said. "I still have the medley relay."

"Box," she repeated, louder.

If she was asking me to miss the relay, things must be dire. "Okay." But it wasn't really okay. I wished it were an individual event and not a relay, because I was costing the guys the race.

As I turned to head out, my eyes lit on a single face: Meg's. She was watching us, her lips moving. She stood plucking that hair rubber band that always seemed to be on her wrist.

Oh Jesus. I was supposed to get her home, too.

Abby appeared and stroked Dara's head. "It's okay," she murmured. "You'll be okay." She turned to me. "I have a relay! Otherwise I'd come." Then she mouthed, *You have a relay, too.*

I glanced around and caught Meg's eye. I gestured her over with my head.

Dara twisted in my arms, eyes shut tight, and let out another shrill cry. Meg approached, hands hovering by her ears.

"Can you get my stuff from Shafer and bring it to us in the parking lot?" I asked Meg. "I need to drive Dara home. I'm sorry – I think you have to find another ride."

"I can give her a ride," Abby said, nodding at Meg.

Meg looked at Dara for a moment, then shook her head. She looked at me. "I'll come with you."

"Christ," Dara said tightly, twisting her head to glare at Meg. "Seriously?"

"Yes," Meg said, looking not at all sure that was a good idea. It probably wasn't. It probably very much wasn't. "I can help," she said, nodding as if trying to convince me, or maybe herself. I certainly wasn't convinced. What if Dara screamed all the way home? What then?

"I'll get your stuff and meet you in the parking lot," Meg said, backing away and then breaking into a jog on her way to find Shafer.

Abby handed me Dara's bag. She stepped close to Dara and stroked her head one last time, saying, "I'll come see you after the meet, okay? Hang in there, sweetie."

I pushed out of there as fast as I could, the asphalt of the parking lot burning my feet. Dara was crying now, occasionally spitting the word "fuck" out. Honestly, to me, her crying was almost worse than the screaming. This was such a bullshit way to live. I couldn't believe nobody could figure out how to cure phantom limb pain.

The interior of the Stupidmobile was a sauna. I started the engine and got the AC blasting, leaving Dara sitting in the passenger seat with the door open. I walked around to her side and squatted by the open door.

She reached out a clammy arm to hold on to me, a slightly sour smell emanating from her. She buried her face in my shoulder. "This fucking sucks."

"I know. We'll get you home to the box."

I glanced up. Meg was headed our way, wilted and stressed, her arms full of things.

I whispered to Dara, "Okay, let's go." But she clung to me. "Come on," I prompted her gently, trying to extricate myself. "Here comes Meg." When Dara finally released me, I couldn't bring myself to make eye contact with Meg, who stood by the car. She held out my bag to me.

I took my clothes and flip-flops out of my bag and pulled them on, then tossed the bag into the backseat.

"I want the back," Dara said, crawling in back and moving my bag to the floor. She curled up on her side, holding her stump.

I waited for Meg to climb in the passenger seat. She bit her lip, then opened the other back door and climbed in next to Dara.

"What the fuck?" Dara said.

Ignoring her, Meg opened her bag and pulled out a towel and a bottle of water.

I still stood outside the car, staring in. Towel in hand, Meg scooted closer to Dara and dabbed her face. "Your bandage is coming loose," she said softly, leaning over and pressing the edges lightly. Dara eyed Meg suspiciously, but she didn't stop her. Meg opened the bottle of water and held it out to Dara.

Dara was lying on her arm, so she had to shift and sit up a little. She took several long swallows. "God, that's good," she muttered, wiping her mouth with her forearm. "So cold."

I sat in the front seat but turned to look at Meg. "Where'd you get cold water?" There hadn't been time for her to go inside to the vending machines.

"From a cooler."

I bit back a smile. "Whose cooler?"

"I didn't stop to get names, Otis."

"You steal the towel, too?"

"'Steal' is a harsh word. I gathered supplies."

I glanced at Dara, who I knew was impressed but trying not to show it. She handed the water bottle back to Meg and lay back down.

I set my phone to navigate home, since I wasn't sure I knew the way. Then I started the car and pulled out.

Dara was sniffling in the backseat, and I knew how much it must be killing her to cry in front of Meg. It was going to be a long ride.

"Sit up," I heard Meg say. When Dara didn't respond, Meg repeated, "Come on, sit up."

What was she doing?

There was a rustling and then a small click. I glanced back, but I was going to crash this beautiful piece of machinery and possibly kill us all if I kept staring into the backseat.

I heard Dara ask softly, "How did you know?"

Meg responded, "Otis."

I heard some more movement and murmuring, and then things grew quiet. When I came to a red light, I looked back. Meg sat close to Dara, and Dara stared at something, calming down.

Meg held a mirror steady as Dara opened and closed her hand next to it, watching.

Meg.

God, she gave me such an ache. She said I didn't know her anymore, but that was bullshit. She hadn't changed as much as she thought. This was Meg to the marrow. She had always understood what was important – had always been able to put other people before herself.

A horn startled me. The light was green.

We drove back to town in silence, save for the navigation lady who piped up with directions. Occasionally, Meg repeated after her softly, in the damnedest exact same voice. After a while Dara fell asleep.

When we got to Dara's house, Dara leaned on me as we went up the long walkway, Meg following behind.

"Four-seven-six-three," Dara mumbled, and I pressed the code onto the panel and went inside.

"Pills." Dara waved her arm toward the kitchen.

Meg and I exchanged a look, but we went into the kitchen. Dara swallowed a couple of pills from a prescription bottle with a glass of water that was already sitting on the counter.

"I'm so tired." She slumped over onto the counter, her head resting on her forearm.

"Come on," I said softly, herding her toward the stairs. Meg followed behind.

"Do you want the box?" I asked Dara.

She shook her head. "It's not so bad now. I just want to sleep."

"Want me to close the curtains?" Meg asked. When Dara nodded, Meg pulled the curtains closed, then came around the bed to stand next to me.

"The dosage was one," Meg whispered. "I looked at the bottle. One capsule."

I let out a sigh. I mean, what was I going to do about it?

Dara seemed three-quarters asleep already, but she looked up at me. "Don't turn off —"

The bathroom light. "I won't."

She closed her eyes. Her breathing slowed and became regular, and soon she was all the way asleep.

13

THE BANK OF WINDOWS IN THE LIVING room was a study in gray: the sun had vanished and the sky grew ever darker. Meg sank onto the sofa – butter-soft leather, of asymmetrical design. It probably cost more than both my parents' cars put together. I sat in a nearby chair, having no idea what range of proximity would be welcome or appropriate.

"What if she calls out or something?" Meg said. "We need a baby monitor." As soon as the words were out, her hand went to her mouth, and then she dropped her face into her hands.

No. Not this. "I'll check on her in a while," I said, craning my head to look toward the stairs. "She'll probably sleep hard." I whipped my head in the opposite direction and stared out the window at the deepening gray. Anywhere but at Meg. Anything but this. Why did it always come back to this?

The fact was, I didn't know the exact details of Mason's death. All I knew was that at 1:30 he was in Meg's room, supposedly going down for a nap, and at 2:00, as I tore through our basement looking for a video game, sirens were screaming, emergency vehicles piling up on our street. I went to the front door to see what was going on. Meg's dad stumbled over, white-faced. He intercepted me before I could go outside. I don't remember what he said. He steered me back inside and sat with me in my basement. We watched old episodes of *SpongeBob*. One of them was the one with jellyfishing. That I remember. I must have been worried. I had to have been. But I can't remember what I knew, what I was thinking or feeling. I remember getting caught up in *SpongeBob* after a while – I remember laughing at it. I laughed, and I looked at Mr. Brandt, wanting him to laugh, too. But of course he didn't. And to this day, I think, *How could I have laughed? How the fuck could I have been laughing?* Even now, I cannot bear the sight or sound of *SpongeBob*.

Unfortunately, I also can't forget the look on my mother's face when they got home. If I live to be a thousand, I hope I never see that look again. She sank to her knees in front of me, her face pressed against my legs. It was weird. Embarrassing. Terrible, barking noises came out of her; in another context, the sounds might have been comical. My dad stood limply in the middle of the room, a faraway look in his eyes. Like he wasn't really there. Just his body.

We kept a baby monitor at the Brandts' around that time, since we sometimes stayed there past Mason's bedtime and let him go to sleep in Meg's bed. Maybe, if the monitor had been on, they would have heard the signs of trouble. Maybe, if it had been on, Mason would still be alive. I could only guess that's what Meg was thinking.

There was much I was spared. I know that he choked to death. That was all I knew. I didn't ask anything. I didn't want to be left with images, questions, ammunition for assigning blame. He was gone and he was never coming back. Nothing else mattered.

But the truth would always be this: I wasn't there when Mason died. But Meg was.

I stood up and went to the window. The trees leaned hard with the wind, as if they were trying to pull free. "Did your dad really get transferred back to California?" I said.

I tracked her approach: The sticky sound of the leather releasing her legs as she stood. Her footfalls, light like always. Her hands on my shoulders, her forehead pressed against my upper back.

"I didn't know what else to do."

My mind reeled. I was losing my sense of time and place. She couldn't possibly be telling me that they left because she *wanted* to? That she lied to me when she told me it was because of her dad. Maybe they had all lied to me, including my parents.

Outside, the wind picked up, the sky a deep gray-green. The color of my mother's eyes.

I pulled away from Meg and walked out the front door. On the porch I watched the low, dark clouds rolling in. The wind smelled of rain and ozone, of summer memories from my childhood, happy times from another life.

Meg came up behind me again as the first drops plunked down. I could feel her there.

She put her hands on my arms and turned me around to face her. She took one of my hands and held it in both of hers, clutching it to her chest. Her hair whipped in the wind, strands crossing over her face. "I'm sorry." She blinked as her eyes filled. "I couldn't tell you the truth, because it would mean telling you what happened."

"I don't want to know!" I said, pulling my hand away and turning my back to her, afraid of what she might say.

"You never wanted to know!" she shouted. "But did it ever occur to you that maybe I *needed* you to know?"

The rain seemed to increase relative to Meg's emotional pitch. It flattened the little pink flowers that encircled the base of the big oak tree.

I stepped off the porch and onto the grass, letting the rain soak me. Again, Meg was right there. She moved in front of me, pulling on my shirt, pleading. "I kept *seeing* him,

Otis. I couldn't make it go away. I had nightmares. I started sleeping with my mom! I missed school all the time – do you remember? Did you notice? I lost weight. You didn't even notice!"

The rain washed the mascara off her lashes, charcoal rivulets running down her face.

I tried to remember details from those awful months – to remember *Meg* specifically – but I couldn't. I barely remembered going to school myself, apart from the agony of having to bear up to people's nervous glances – and my teachers' soft words, their offers of support and leniency. They didn't seem to understand that talking to me about it was the worst thing they could do. Their kindness was unbearable. I just wanted to be left alone. As for Meg… All I remembered was that she was there, by my side, through it all. Until she wasn't.

"Your parents stopped talking to my mom and dad." She was shivering, her teeth chattering. "Your mom…" Her face crumpled. "I *begged* my parents to move." She wiped water and tears off her cheek.

She talked about her dad's boss agreeing to a temporary transfer, but I wasn't really listening anymore. I felt strangely calm, blank. Somewhere inside, a storm was brewing. But I couldn't face it. Not now. Maybe not ever.

"I have to check on Dara," I said, backing away from her.

"I told you, Otis!" she cried, her voice breaking. "I told

you you wouldn't like me anymore! This whole thing was a terrible idea. I could never come back here."

"Come inside," I said firmly, loudly, over the rain.

She followed me, choking back sobs. We were soaking wet and the air-conditioning in Dara's house was set to "tundra." I grabbed a towel from the kitchen and handed it to Meg, then turned and went upstairs.

Dara was still asleep. She had pulled off her shirt; it lay on the floor beside the bed. Bruises covered her chest and ribs – awful, purple bruises in places, others fading to yellow and green. Her tiny bra was tugged slightly to one side, exposing one of her nipples. I pulled the sheet up to cover her. Her face was so relaxed, her expression serene. At that moment, I almost would have traded places with her.

I sat down on the floor by her bed, pushing away thoughts of the things Meg had just said. I picked up Dara's mirror box. It was heavy, a fairly crude construction of unfinished wood – pine, maybe. I put my right hand in. Two hands, ta-da. I twisted and turned my hand, watching its twin obediently copy every motion. What was the source of this magic? What mysteries of the human brain does a mirror reveal?

I set the box aside and lowered my head into my hands, unable to fight the onslaught of information, of thoughts.

Meg was right. I didn't remember her missing school. I didn't notice she lost weight. My grief was a river that drowned me, a black hole that sucked me in, a fire that devoured me. I was consumed with losing my brother; I didn't think about Meg's loss – Meg, who loved Mason with all her heart. Meg, who had to live in the place where he took his last breath. Where one of them found his body. Was it Meg? I hadn't asked, because I didn't want to know. I *still* didn't want to know.

No wonder she wanted to leave, no wonder she never talked to me again. When I went through the hardest time of my life, she was there for me, as constant and strong as she could be. But *she* was also going through the hardest time of *her* life. And I was blind.

And I finally saw the truth of it: It wasn't that Meg wasn't there when I needed her most. It was that *I* wasn't there when *she* needed me most.

"Hey."

I looked up. Dara watched me with one groggy eye.

"What's wrong?" she asked drowsily.

I shook my head.

"Don't cry, Mueller." She rolled toward me so she could reach me with her full arm. She tried to pat me but managed only to jab her thumb into my ear.

There was a rap on the door. Abby peered in, looking worried. "Can I come in?"

I quickly wiped my eyes.

Abby raised her eyebrows at me, a question. "What happened?"

"Nothing," I said. "Dara's been sleeping."

She hesitated, as if deciding whether or not to pursue a line of questioning. "Meg's downstairs." She glanced at me. "Also crying."

"Were they mad?" I asked, sitting up a little. "About the relay?"

Her eyes flicked over to Dara. "They understood."

But I could tell that she was downplaying it. For Dara's sake.

She sat next to Dara on the bed. "Your bandage is coming off." She leaned in and peeked under it. "Oh, honey," she said, wincing at the stitches. She gently replaced the bandage and sat back, taking Dara's hand.

Dara gazed up at Abby. "Thanks for being nice to me," she said softly. It was an eerie, kind of beautiful moment – Dara devoid of defenses. Just feeling. Just being.

"You don't have to thank me, silly," Abby responded. Their eye-lock made me feel like I should make my exit. I stood up quietly, but Dara turned to me.

"Hey. Thanks."

I picked up her mirror box, turning it over in my hands. "You know, we should devise a portable mirror box – something you could carry with you at college. I think I might be able to figure out how to build one."

She pulled her hand from Abby's and rolled away, pressing her face into her pillow.

"Dara?" I stepped closer, trying to see her face.

"You might as well both know," Dara said into her pillow. "I'm not going to college."

Abby and I exchanged glances.

"What do I want to go to college for?" She turned back over and faced us. "I won't have any friends, I don't want to take classes, and I'd suck at college swimming. They'd only let me on the team for the PR. Or out of pity."

"You're just nervous," Abby said, leaning in and smiling. "So am I! It's normal. Cut yourself some slack—"

"I never even applied!" Dara yelled, startling Abby.

I stared at her. "You never applied? But – what about Grinnell?"

She closed her eyes, her forehead creasing. "Everyone was always asking… It's all anyone could talk about this last year. I just … I'm sorry. I was gonna tell you…"

Abby stared uneasily at a spot on the floor. Dara turned to me nervously, waiting for a reaction.

"Well," I finally said, "what are you going to do?"

"I just want to keep training you."

No. No way. But how could I tell her now that I wanted out? I couldn't. Not in front of Abby, not after the day Dara'd had. But there was no way I was going to be her full-time job. That was fucked up.

"I guess you both hate me," Dara finally said, staring down at the sheets.

"I don't hate you," I said. "I'm just worried about you."

"Me, too," Abby said.

"Well, don't be," Dara said.

I glanced at Abby. "Could you give us a minute?"

"Sure."

"I don't want to talk about college," Dara said, after the door had closed.

"You lied to me." I shook my head at her. "Jesus, Dara."

"I didn't mean to. I just didn't know how to tell you." She looked away. "Could we just... Could we not do this right now?"

I sighed and set her mirror box down on her dresser. "We have to talk about it at some point."

"Not today."

I knew what *not today* meant. It meant that she'd avoid it forever if possible. "Fine, not today," I said. "Are you okay now? I think I'm just gonna go."

She bit her thumbnail. "I think I might ask Abby to stay."

I glanced at her with interest, a smile creeping up. "Oh?"

"Shut up," she said, cracking a smile.

"Where's your dad?"

"L.A." She made a face. "Back tomorrow night."

"He didn't waste any time, did he?" I grumbled. "Okay. Well, I'll see you later."

"Wait," she whispered. She craned her head toward the door, listening, then pulled down the sheet. "Does this look sexy?"she asked, glancing down at her bra.

I bit back a laugh. "Yes," I said, nodding. "Yes, it does."

She grinned and yanked the sheet back up.

"Are you gonna seduce her?" I couldn't resist asking.

"*Pff.*" She rolled her eyes. "I wouldn't know how to seduce a monkey into eating a banana."

Ha, that sounded about right. "I'll send her up."

She held out her fist.

I reached out a fist, shaking my head. I see her through one of the worst days she's ever had, and she gives me a fist bump.

When I went downstairs, Meg and Abby were in the living room, talking quietly on the couch.

"She's asking for you," I told Abby.

Abby gave Meg a quick hug, then ran up the stairs.

I sank down on a chair across from Meg.

"How's she doing?" It was hard to meet her eyes, knowing how much pain was behind them.

"Better," I said.

"Shafer says he'll come get me," she said softly. "He'll take me home."

"Shafer is a piranha."

"Well, he's a piranha with a car."

Couldn't argue with that.

Meg bit her lips together, making them disappear. I hoped she wasn't going to cry again. "I wish I'd never come back."

"Hey." I navigated around the coffee table, a giant round puck of what looked like hammered brass, and sank in next to her on the sofa. I touched her shoulder to get her to look at me. Her eyes were bright. "We're gonna figure this out."

"How?"

"Somehow." I sighed. "The thing is, I really don't want you to go back to California. Unless you really want to." *Please don't want to.*

"Do you really think we can be friends, after all that's happened?"

I didn't honestly know what I thought. But what I said was, "Yes."

Her phone dinged and she glanced down. "Shafer's here."

I stood. "I'll get a ride from him, too."

"What about Dara?" Meg stood and picked up her purse. She tossed her damp hair behind her shoulders.

"She wants Abby to stay."

"You know," Meg said, tilting her head, "I kind of think Dara might be gay."

"Oh yeah?" I grabbed my swim bag.

"How else could she resist you?"

I laughed. Gay or not gay, I'm pretty sure Dara would always be able to resist me. But I liked the sentiment behind Meg's theory.

We ran out to Shafer's car, the rain pouring even more

heavily now, my flip-flops splashing through puddles. I opened the passenger-side door for Meg before flinging myself into the backseat.

"Dude." Shafer leaned back in his seat, glaring at me. "What the fuck about the relay, man?"

"Did you see Dara?" I asked, buckling up.

"Yeah, but—"

"Then kindly shut the fuck up and take me home."

He did shut up. For about a minute. And then a few blocks later, as we approached the exit of Dara's subdivision, he mumbled loudly enough to be heard over the rain, "I could have out-split that freestyler in my sleep. And you would have out-split the breaststroker by two seconds at least."

"I know," I mumbled. But I also knew that if I had it to do over, I would have done the same thing.

Shafer drove me home first, undoubtedly so he could get Meg alone and try to make some progress. But when he pulled up to my house, Meg's dad's car was there, and Meg said she'd just get out at my house and go home with her dad. Unsurprisingly, Shafer sulked. Surprisingly, I wasn't thrilled. I was running on empty. I needed to be alone. I didn't have the wherewithal to deal with much of anything. Not even Meg.

Especially Meg.

"Hey, how was the meet?" my dad asked as we came in. Our parents were sitting in the living room drinking wine. "You never answered my texts."

The swim meet seemed like days ago. Hard to believe it was only hours. "Sorry. It was good," I said. "I medaled in the hundred breast and had a personal best in the fifty free."

Everyone exclaimed about how great that was. Frankly, it was the last thing on my mind. It felt stupid, trivial.

"You got caught in the rain?" my mom said. She was looking at Meg funny – whether it was concern or something else, I couldn't tell. I thought about what Meg said – about how hard it had been for her and her parents, thinking my mother blamed them – and my stomach undulated. "Otis," my mom said, nodding at Meg, "get Meg a towel and give her something warm to put on. The air conditioner's running – the poor girl will freeze."

"Yeah, sure," I said.

"Thank you," Meg said, so softly I'm not sure my mom even heard her.

Meg followed me upstairs. I took a towel out of the linen closet and handed it to her, then went into my room and pulled my favorite sweatshirt out of a drawer.

"Thanks," she said, taking it. Our eyes met for a silent moment before she stepped out to go change in the bathroom. I took the opportunity to put the wet stuff from my swim bag into my hamper and change into a clean shirt.

When she came back in, she said, "I love this sweatshirt." She draped her damp shirt over the back of my chair. "You might never get it back." She turned and gave me a smile that made me go melty on the edges, then raised it one by adding, "It smells like you."

"Is that good?" I asked nervously.

Holding the sleeve to her face, she closed her eyes and inhaled, nodding.

The rain pinged on the roof as the daylight faded in my room. I just wanted to lie down, to close my eyes and rest under the tap dance of the raindrops. Maybe with Meg lying beside me. Maybe curled up close. Maybe with her head on my chest, her hand on me. I wanted to not talk. I wanted to make the past go away, to live in the universe where Meg never left and Mason never died. I wanted to kiss her, to feel her arms around me, to be able to touch her in all the ways I'd thought of a thousand times. I wanted to be happy. Right now "happy" seemed about as likely a place for me to visit as a beach resort on Neptune.

Meg crossed my room and stood by the window. She rubbed at a spot on the windowpane with her sleeve, just as she'd done last time. "Did you write a poem about the magnolia tree?" she asked, gazing out the window.

My eyes widened. How could she know that? I scanned the room – where had I left that thing? "Why?"

She turned around. "That night at Dara's party, after you left, Kiera asked me if I had a magnolia tree in my yard. She said you wrote a poem about it for English."

Damn that raven-haired, quick-eyed, poetry-loving witch.

"I did," I said casually. "When it was in bloom. It was pretty inspiring."

"Did you know the magnolia tree is associated with beauty and perseverance?"

Well, that was perfect. *You be the beauty and I'll be the perseverance.*

"Could I read it?"

I picked up a gum wrapper off the floor and tossed it into the trash in an effort to conceal my alarm at the question. "Can I read *your* poetry?" I asked.

"I don't have any poetry. I only have a journal." She slid the window up and a breeze blew into the room, scattering papers across my desk. I gathered them together and set a mug of pencils on top of them.

"Okay," I said, sitting in my desk chair and clasping my hands behind my head. "I'll trade you that poem for a page from your journal." I was wildly tempted at the idea of reading her journal, but I was gambling that she'd never agree to the deal; no way was I letting her read that sonnet.

"I can't," she said, turning her hands palms up.

"Oh yeah? Why?"

She ran her fingertips under the neck of her sweatshirt – my sweatshirt. "I'm not supposed to."

"Says who?"

"My therapist."

"You have a therapist?"

She laughed. "Uh, yeah." She glanced up at me. "Did you keep going to therapy?"

"For a while."

She tilted her head. "Did it help?"

I thought about it. "I don't know. I wasn't that good at it. I didn't talk that much."

"Part of my treatment was being able to talk to you without talking to you. Because I needed that distance from you, but I still needed you. You know?" She gave me a sad smile. "I was lost without you."

I laughed bitterly. "Well, that's perfect. Because I sure as hell was lost without you."

Another breeze blew in, and strands of her hair drifted into her face. She brushed them away. "So I had a journal, which was basically just me talking to you. Everything I ever wanted to say to you, and some things I never would have said to you."

"Like what?"

She moved away from the window and sat on my bed, one leg folded under her. "I just talked to you. The way I always did. I told you stuff that happened, stupid things I thought about, movies I saw, songs I liked…" She hesitated. "Dreams I had…"

I wished I could read it. Maybe it would help bridge this epic, impossible gap between us.

I sat down next to her on the bed. "What kind of dreams?"

She shook her head. "I knew you'd ask that."

"Dreams about us?"

"Maybe."

"Anything…" I raised my eyebrows a few times to finish the question.

She laughed, bumping me with her shoulder. "You're bad."

"Come on," I said, bumping her back. "Tell me." I hoped she didn't turn the question back at me. I'd either have to plead the fifth, lie, or reveal way more than she probably wanted to know.

"Maybe someday," she said in a way that clearly meant *don't count on it.* "Magnolia poem?" She gave me a winning smile.

"Maybe someday."

Stalemate.

"Anyway, I already have a poem from you," she said with a sly grin.

I squinted at her. "You do not."

She laughed, a real laugh. To me, it sounded like music. "I swear! I have it memorized." She cleared her throat, tossed her hair back, and recited:

> *Hair of gold, eyes like the sea*
> *To my heart she holds the key*
> *Skin so soft, hair so fine*
> *Someday I will make her mine.*

I covered my face. "Oh God. Oh my God, how awful."
Seriously. It gave me physical pain. I hurt. I stood and went over to the wall, banging my forehead on it.

"Do you remember it?"

"Kind of," I said into the wall. "God. Shoot me."

"Stop that!" she exclaimed. "It was beautiful! Jeez, Otis, you were twelve! What'd you expect? Shakespeare?"

Her tone was teasing, acknowledging my nickname, but it did nothing to dissipate my horror over the abomination I had penned. I turned around, shaking my head.

She laughed. "Your face is red!"

"I know." I could feel the burn in my cheeks. I mustered a smile for her.

And then our eyes met and didn't let go.

She stepped closer, and my pulse instantly sped up. But she just gently laid her head on my shoulder, resting one hand against my chest. I didn't dare move. I wondered if she could feel my heart pounding under her hand.

"God, I miss you," she said.

"Missed? Or miss?"

"Miss."

"But I'm right here," I said into her hair.

"I miss you anyway."

14

MEG AND HER DAD LEFT A SHORT WHILE later. He had made dinner plans for them in the city with work friends, and when Meg waffled about going, I had mixed feelings. I wanted her close, always, but I also felt like I needed a break. I needed time to digest that she had left me on purpose, with intention. And that it was, at least in part, because of me.

I didn't know what the fuck I was doing after Mason died; just getting through a day felt like an achievement. It almost felt unfair that I should be responsible for any of it, for my failings and blind spots. But I guess I was. Whether I could have done better or not, I was still responsible, right? I wondered if I should try therapy again. It occurred to me that I mostly got nowhere on my own – I just sort of spun around in the dark. I could maybe use some help. If

I was going to do better, I would have to learn how to see things I didn't want to see. Hear things I didn't want to hear. Basically, Reality 101.

From my bedroom window, I watched their car pull out of the driveway, wipers clearing the rain that continued to fall. Meg was behind the wheel, and I had never seen a slower backing-up process in all my life. She crept to the end of the driveway and came to a complete stop, right next to the magnolia, before backing into the street. The wrong way. And then pulling back into the driveway and backing out the other way. I had my lights off, so I hoped she couldn't see me in the window, laughing at her. She pulled away at about three miles per hour, and I thought how Dara would go out of her fucking mind if she were ever Meg's passenger. She'd probably get out and push.

Later my mom made grilled fish tacos for dinner, with a spicy pineapple salsa. I was sorry Meg missed it – she would have loved it. I sent her a picture of it, and she sent me a return photo of her dinner. *Squid ink pasta with crab, chilies, and mint. You're lucky I have something good or I'd be mad about the tacos.*

We exchanged messages intermittently over the next couple of days, never touching on anything of substance. Maybe not knowing how. I didn't want to set off any land mines, but I also wondered if my silence would lead to her deciding against moving back. I felt like I was damned if I did, damned if I didn't. So I did what I knew how to do: worked and swam and ate and slept.

Dara was quieter than usual, too. I called her Tuesday when she wasn't responding to messages and asked what she'd been doing. Nothing, she said. I asked how her arm was, and she said it was fucked up – that her hand kept opening and closing. Her actual hand, I asked? No. *The hand that was gone.* Also, that it felt like her phantom arm was getting shorter, like her hand was inching closer to her elbow. How the fuck was I supposed to make sense of that? When I asked her if she'd told her doctors, she laughed.

She didn't sound bitter, though, it occurred to me after. She sounded kind of happy, oddly enough.

And then Meg texted on Thursday to tell me that Football Guy had arrived, and they'd see us soon in Michigan. Which sounded kind of like a blow-off to me. *Fine, Meg, okay. You're busy now, I get it.*

I didn't even respond.

I tried not to think about what was going on over at that hotel – I had no idea what the sleeping arrangements might be. I hoped her dad was strict that way. If he wasn't, that meant Football Guy and Meg could potentially have total privacy. Fuck.

I was miserable. Maybe I should have been that valiant guy who accepted defeat with grace and wished the happy couple all the best. But I wasn't. I was dreading seeing them in Michigan on Saturday. I would have one good day, since we were leaving a day before them.

On Thursday night Dara decided to have some people over, and for once I was all in, glad to have a distraction. Heinz and Shafer picked me up.

It was a ridiculous summer night – the kind where the moon hangs low and yellow, everything smells amazing, the crickets are deafening, and the thick velvet air hovers in that narrow place between warm and cool. The idea that Meg and her idiot boyfriend were together in the midst of so much perfection was too much.

We had to park way down the street. There were a lot more people there than last time – at least thirty in the living room alone, and a mounting pile of empty beers. And Dara was nowhere to be seen. I went downstairs to find her, where some beer-soaked Ping-Pong game I couldn't even begin to comprehend was in motion, and then upstairs, thinking maybe she was in her room.

From the top of the stairs, I heard music emanating from her room. I approached and knocked softly on the door, then louder. I tried one more time, then gave the knob a turn. "Dara?"

I stopped in my tracks, my brain trying to make sense of the tangle of bodies, of the lip-lock, of Abby's hand up Dara's shirt. When Dara glanced up and saw me, she jumped about a mile, sitting up and straightening her shirt.

"Sorry," I said weakly, backing away. I closed the door again, my heart pounding. I wasn't halfway back down the stairs before Dara flew out of her room and raced to me, grabbing me by the shirt.

"Don't be mad. I was going to tell you." She stared down at me breathlessly from the step above me, my T-shirt bunched in her hand.

I couldn't find words. My specialty.

"Look." She ran her hand through her hair. "Meet me in the laundry room. I'll be there in a minute. Okay?"

She released my shirt, and I did as she directed, entirely on autopilot. I went down to the laundry room, closed the door, and waited, unable to find anything useful to think about. I tried to blink away the image still stuck in my head, but pushing that out sent me to the only other thing on my mind, which was what Meg might be doing with Jeff – and the whole reason I'd come to this fucking party in the first place was to forget about that. The unhelpful part of my mind kept raising questions like, *Does Meg go down on him? Is she blowing him right now? Has he ever made her come?* And then the rest of my mind tried to shut down and go blank, but too late – the images were ingrained.

Dara came in a minute later, closing the door behind her. She jumped up onto the dryer, another one-armed feat, and patted the washing machine next to her. I sat on it and we turned to face each other. An economy-size box of fabric softener on the shelf near us filled the air with a chemical version of fresh linen.

"So," she said.

I nodded. "So."

"I'm sorry." She took a breath and closed her eyes. "I wanted to tell you."

I stared at her, uncomprehending. "Why didn't you? I mean, how could you not?"

She shrugged and looked away. "I know, I know. Don't be mad."

"I'm not mad. I just…" I picked at a thread on my shorts. "I thought it was the sort of thing you would tell me about."

She touched my knee briefly. "I wanted to! But, I don't know, saying it out loud… It felt like too much."

I looked up at her. "So this wasn't the first time?"

She hesitated, then shook her head.

"So, when? And how did it happen?"

"Well, I told you we held hands in the hospital. And then we had that talk, about my mom and things. And after that, she was, like, *looking* at me. And she asked me if I'd ever kissed a girl."

Holy Moses. "What'd you say?"

"I told her, you know." She gestured with her hand. "No!"

"And?"

"She was leaning so close – my heart was going crazy.

And she said, 'I kind of want to kiss you.'"

"And?"

"I said okay."

"Oh my God." I sat back, stunned. "And you liked it?" I was sure a week ago Dara would have thought that kissing anyone was gross.

"Uh. Yeah."

"You kissed a girl and you liked it?"

She rolled her eyes. "I so fucking knew that was coming. Anyway. And then she leaned back and said she'd wanted to do that for a long time."

"Aw."

The strand of envy that was weaving through me did not take away in the least from my happiness for Dara. If anyone needed some happiness more than I did, it was her.

"And then, Saturday? At my house? After the River Park meet? After you left, Abby sat with me in my room and we were just talking. But I was feeling really gross and I wanted to take a shower…"

"Oh my God!" My mind filled with images of naked, soapy girls.

She kicked me. "Stop it. I went in and showered, and when I came out, she asked if she could take a shower, too, because she hadn't hung around to shower after the meet. So I was lying on my bed, waiting for her to come out…"

"And she came out naked and—"

She smacked me in the leg with the back of her hand. "Will you shut up?"

"Sorry, sorry."

"So she came out – dressed, Mueller. And I asked her if she wanted to watch a movie."

I stared. "A porno?"

"Oh my God." She stared at the ceiling. "This is your last warning."

"Sorry, sorry." I clasped my hands together and tried to behave.

"So we sat on the couch together in the media room and put in a movie. And we were kind of cold – our hair was still wet from the showers and everything – so I grabbed a blanket. And somehow we started holding hands under the blanket. And she was sort of tracing circles over my hand with her other hand. Which – I can't even explain how incredible that felt, because how do you explain how someone touching your hand can feel that fucking good?"

She didn't have to explain it to me. Any time Meg had ever touched me anywhere, I nearly died of the bliss of it.

"And then she asked what my story was. And I said I didn't know. I mean, how can I be sure I'll never like a guy?"

"Well, if you're not attracted to me," I said, remembering Meg's theory, "you've gotta be gayer than a rainbow."

Dara snorted. "Anyway… More things happened. Last night."

"Oh? Like?"

"Like, you know." She wriggled and turned to examine a jug of bleach, spinning it to face her. *"Stuff."*

And I thought *my* communication skills were sad. "Exactly how much stuff?"

She blushed. "A lot." She grinned at her lap. I had never seen Dara so sparkly; it was a whole new side of her. I wanted to go exploring, to find out if she cared about me and the Olympics anymore, but if she was getting to the lesbian sex, it would have been rude to interrupt.

"Abby stayed over," she whispered, glancing up at me.

Then the door flew open, and Dara and I both yelped.

"Jesus!" I said, clutching my heart.

"What are you two doing in here?" Abby asked. "Dara, I thought you should know that people are now playing strip poker in the basement."

"So you want to play, too?" Dara teased. "Is that what you're saying?"

"That is *not* what I'm saying," Abby said, walking over to Dara and touching her leg. The smile they shared made me weak with envy. I might as well have been invisible when they looked at each other. Was that what I'd be witnessing between Meg and Football Guy? Shoot me now.

Abby turned to me. "Where's Meg?"

"With her boyfriend," I said.

"He's in town?"

"Yup. He's coming on vacation with us."

"Huh." Total poker face. She turned back to Dara. "There's also a chick I've never seen before puking in your backyard."

Dara sighed and jumped off the dryer.

"No!" I cried out. "Wait, don't go. Just five more minutes. Okay, two! Please?"

"We'll talk later," Dara told me.

"What were you guys talking about?" Abby asked, giving us a funny look.

I said "swimming" at the same time Dara said "therapy." We exchanged glances and then gave Abby cheesy grins.

She squinted at us. "You were telling him about last night, weren't you?" she said to Dara. "Oh, don't even bother denying it."

"Were there any details you wanted to add?" I asked Abby hopefully.

She raised an eyebrow at me. "I am not going to be part of this sick equation. You two are so weird."

She turned to go and Dara followed her.

"Come on, Mueller," Dara said.

I followed them out to the living room, grumbling.

Music blared from the speakers, the bass thumping from the gleaming mahogany floorboards. The whole room smelled like beer and chlorine and Axe – and also marijuana, the familiar skunky reek reminding me of my stoner lab partner freshman year. Four or five people gathered on the floor around a wooden tray, bouncing a quarter into a cup. One of them was Heinz, my fucking designated driver. Another was Kiera.

"Otis!" she called out. She patted the floor next to her. "Come play!"

"Give it up, Kiera," Heinz told her.

I went ahead and sat by Kiera; what else was I going to do? She smiled at me, flipping her thick, dark hair. She was wearing a red tank top and tight jeans. My lizard brain stamped its approval.

Heinz bounced a quarter neatly into the cup and pointed at Kiera with his elbow. "Down it, baby."

Kiera gulped down the beer, then grinned, the quarter flashing in her front teeth. She took it out and turned to me. "Sure you won't play?" she asked. "Come on, please?" Her lips glistened. They were on the full side, kind of sexy – not unlike her breasts, which I could see all too well in the tank top. Was it just the *proximity* to beer making me go stupid? She was pretty, dammit. And *sexy*. And she smelled sort of exotic and spicy.

With boldness that came from I don't know where, I asked her what perfume she was wearing.

"Poison," she said. "You like?" She leaned forward, moving her neck close to my nose, creating an ocean-deep trail of cleavage before me.

The blood rushed from my head, leaving me dizzy. "Uh-huh."

Heinz said to Kiera, "Hey, your turn. Quit flirting with Shakespeare and play the game."

"I like flirting with Shakespeare," she said, aiming the quarter. She tossed it down, and it bounced off Heinz's forehead and landed about ten feet away.

"I suck," she pointed out. She turned to me again. The intensity of her gaze made me blush. "Did you know," she asked in a low voice, "that you have beautiful lips?"

I do?

She stared at my mouth. "They look sooooo soft."

I swallowed hard. "Well, you know. I am a fan of the mint ChapStick." I cringed inwardly. *Great line, Shakespeare.*

Doink. Splat. Another guy pointed his elbow at Kiera. I know I'm generally the uptight sort, but if the guys were ganging up on the girl to get her drunk, I really didn't think that was cool.

Kiera drained the cup and then bounced another quarter into oblivion.

She leaned over and whispered, "Let's go for a walk."

Oh boy. Not a good idea, a voice in my head said. But then another voice – one that came from a slightly more southerly location – piped up. *Hey, live a little! Meg's probably having wild animal sex with her boyfriend this very minute.*

The thought cut some sort of cord inside me. I stood

and let Kiera guide me away from the group.

I followed her outside and to the backyard. Shit – she was heading for the gazebo, which reminded me of Meg. "Come on," she called back to me, waving her arms and weaving slightly.

"Did you drive tonight?" I couldn't help asking.

"Don't worry, I'll be fine. I live close." She stepped into the gazebo and leaned out, giving me a definite *come hither* look.

"I don't think it's such a good idea for you to drive." I sat beside her on the bench, leaving a quickly calculated six inches or so between us, which I hoped was neither too pushy nor too intimate.

"Don't be such a ret wag. I mean, *ret wag*. I mean—" She burst into giggles.

"Wet rag," I supplied. "Thanks."

"No, no, I didn't mean it," she said, reaching up and laying her hand on my cheek. "I was just kidding. Oh God, you're so cute."

"Kiera? I want you to give me your car keys."

A sexy smile. A very sexy smile. "What'll you do for 'em?"

I took a deep breath, looking out at the sky. If I continued to meet her smoldering gaze, I might burst into flames.

I ran a hand through my hair. "Um, get you home safely?"

"Well, I might give 'em to you ... if you kiss me."

An electric bolt shot to my belly, and then my heart started to pound. Did I want to kiss her? Part of me didn't, and part of me did. Which part was in charge?

"Come on," I coaxed. "Just give me your keys."

She ran her tongue over her plush lips, her eyes firing hot beams into my brain. Okay, I mostly did want to kiss her. Every time I had a flash of Meg making out with Jeff, an image that kept coming to me unbidden, I wanted nothing more than to forget her fast.

"One kiss?" I asked, my voice coming out weaker than intended.

"Sure," she said in a breathy voice. She dug her keys out of her pocket and placed them in my palm.

My heart drummed in my chest. I sat motionless for a moment, trying to decide if this was a mistake. *It's a safety issue,* I told myself. *So she'll give me her keys. A life is at stake!*

Kiera leaned forward and ended my internal arguments. Her soft lips met mine in a kiss that knew what it was doing. The smell of her perfume made my eyes cross, and when her fingers snaked around my neck and pulled me closer, I was lost.

Kissing Kiera was wild and disorienting, like jumping into a seemingly bottomless lake and being unable to find the surface. After a while, her mouth trailed away from mine and she started kissing my neck, and then her tongue was in my ear, giving me goose bumps the size of golf balls. When she found my mouth again, I put my arms around her and pulled her closer. Feeling her breasts pressed against my chest made me stupid with desire.

Her hands, her hands – how many hands did she have? Her fingertips slid up my inner thigh, causing shock waves that radiated straight to my dick. She wandered around the vicinity for a while until I was so turned on, I just wanted to grab her hand and move it straight to the bull's-eye. She took one of my hands and slid it up until it was cupping her breast. I struggled to breathe. I wanted to keep going so bad, I couldn't think straight. At that moment, what would be more bizarre than me pushing her away?

And yet.

"What's the matter?" she asked, reaching for me again.

"Stop," I said. I panted, my hands shaking.

"You kiss so nice," she said, leaning close again.

I pushed away from her, cradling my head in my hands. "I'm so sorry, Kiera."

"You don't like me?" She sounded confused, hurt. "I've liked you for such a long time." She leaned back against the gazebo wall. "I've wanted to kiss you for, like, ever."

"I do like you!" I exclaimed. "It's just…"

"Is there someone else?" She sounded so sad, it made me hate myself.

"Not exactly." I didn't want to admit I was hung up on

271

Meg. "Things are just complicated for me right now."

"Well, fuck."

Yeah. *Fuck.*

"I'm sorry," I told her. "Can I take you home?"

She looked at me like I was nuts. "Are you kidding? I'm not going to walk in while my parents are awake!"

All I wanted to do was leave, but now I felt obliged to drive her home, since I wasn't about to give her car keys back to her. I just hoped her parents weren't night owls.

We walked back to the house together, holding hands for some reason. When we got inside, she headed for a bathroom. Was she going to cry in there? If I made her cry, I might never stop hating myself.

There was no one I wanted to hang out with and no activity I wanted to participate in. Coming to this party was a stupid idea, and now I was stuck. I went upstairs to see if Dara was in her room with the door wide open and all her clothes on. That question was answered when Abby appeared at the top of the stairs.

"I'm going to check on the chaos downstairs," she said, slipping past me. "She's in her room," she called behind her.

Dara's door hung partway open. She lay on her bed, eyes closed, a lazy half smile on her face.

"Hey," I said.

She glanced up and scooted over, patting the bed. "Close the door."

I pushed the door closed and lay down next to her. "Could you please just tell me about the lesbian sex and help me take my mind off my troubles?"

And she did. She curled up next to me and gave me the details of her night with Abby, which was even hotter than I was expecting. Like, all-the-clothes-off hot. Touching-*everywhere* hot. It was awesome, and I was glad she seemed so happy, but ... honestly, it all seemed kind of fast to me.

She rolled onto her back and stared at the ceiling. "You cannot believe how amazing it is when someone else makes you come."

"Don't depress me."

This would have been the time to tell her about Kiera, but I didn't. I didn't want to. And besides, given the things she hadn't been telling me, the omission felt justified.

She glanced at me. "Dude. You look like shit – no offense. Why don't you bail?"

I sighed. "I have to drive Kiera home. And she's not ready to leave yet."

"Why do you have to drive her?" Dara said, getting up and going over to her dresser.

"She's drunk and I took her keys. I can't just strand her here. What time is it, anyway?"

"Eleven." She leaned toward the mirror, fixing her hair with her fingers.

"Could you just kick everyone out?" I asked. "Then

you can have more lesbian sex, and I can go home."

"I'll drive Kiera home for you."

"You will?"

She nodded. "She lives, like, two minutes from here."

"Have you been drinking?"

"Nope!"

That was new. Was this Abby's influence? "Not to push my luck, but do you think you could take me home, too?" I asked. "I'm done."

"Sure. Come on."

I followed her downstairs and sidestepped a drunken wrestling match between an actual wrestler and Heinz, who was pinned seventy ways to Tuesday and laughing his ass off. Dara went to find Abby to tell her she was taking me home. I scanned the room for Kiera, but I didn't see her anywhere. I wished for the umpteenth time I could turn back time. It was a stupid thing to do, making out with her. Kind of mind-bogglingly awesome, but stupid.

"Here," Dara said, handing me the keys to the Stupid-mobile. "You drive."

"Sweet." I handed her Kiera's keys.

Out in the garage, I started her car, admiring the way it purred and, oh God, that new-car smell. "When are you going to sell it?" I asked.

"As soon as possible."

It was criminal. The car was a thing of beauty.

I backed out, carefully avoiding all the cars parked on the street in front of her house. I pulled away, and we drove in silence for a while, windows down. The sky was lavish with stars, and I longed for the days when Meg and I goofed around in the backyard on summer nights, slapping at mosquitoes and trying to aim my telescope to find something interesting, not really caring whether we did or didn't.

"Hey," I said, glancing over at Dara. "Are you happy?"

She leaned back, eyes closed. "I don't think I've ever been happier."

It was such a rush, hearing those words from her. "Well, it's about fucking time."

"Now if only Meg would pull her head out of her ass."

I could have hugged her for understanding, for caring. But the reminder of Meg made my stomach ache. "I get to watch them together in Michigan," I said, flicking off the headlights as I pulled into my driveway. "At least I have one day before they come." I shifted into park and looked out my open window at the stars.

"She loves you, you know."

I turned to her. "How do you know?"

"Because I know."

"How?"

She turned her gaze out her own window. "I don't know. Because of the chicken, I guess."

The chicken? "What?"

"The winter sports banquet."

When I cut up Dara's chicken? What in the world was she talking about? "But – Meg doesn't know about that."

She stared at me like I was a total bonehead. "That doesn't matter."

If ever there comes a day when a woman makes sense to me, it will flat out be a miracle.

"Well, even if she does love me," I said, "there's no guarantee of a happy ending."

She glanced down, then back out her window. "There never is."

15

THE MORNING WAS BLINDING WITH SUN AND smelled of weed spray and tar from the neighbor's freshly paved driveway. "I wish I weren't going," I mumbled, half to myself, as I helped my dad reorganize the car so everything would fit. He heaved a sigh and turned to me.

"I know, I know," I said, holding up my hands, not wanting a lecture. "Forget I said it."

"Otis," he said, adjusting the god-awful fisherman's cap he liked to wear on vacations, "I know it sucks. All you can do is step up and try to make the best of it."

Easy for him to say. Although that's probably exactly what he'd do in my shoes. He'd probably end up best friends with the guy.

On the upside, it was a good three hours to Silver Lake, and I was only six hours short of my stupid fifty to get my license. This trip would do it.

It was an easy drive, once we got through the city traffic and the worst of my mom's panicky backseat driving. At that point she switched over to stressing about the Brandts and how she'd never get to relax because she'd always be playing hostess and what Meg's boyfriend would be like and if things would be awkward and if Jay would have a good time... She went on endlessly. My dad and I didn't have much to contribute, but she didn't seem to notice; she did fine on her own.

Before long we were into Indiana, home of all those fireworks emporiums. I pulled over at one of them, lured by the sign STOP IN AND SEE THE AMAZING TWO-HEADED TURTLE!!! Sure enough, they had a real live freak of nature there for the ogling, and I took a picture of it that I wanted to send to Meg but didn't. The idea of her boyfriend looking at it with her... Yeah, no.

While we were there, we bought some sparklers and smoke bombs to share with the neighbor kids and a few fountains to set off at the end of the pier, like every year.

Back on the road, long stretches of farmland along the highway brought us closer to Silver Lake. After I pulled off on our exit, we passed all the familiar sights: the U-Pick berry farms and roadside fruit stands, the antique shops, the little Michigan wineries that produced wine whose taste my mom compared to paint varnish. As I drove down the smaller, winding roads toward the house, I tried to forget Meg and just enjoy the place I'd always loved so much.

When we got there, tires crunching over the long gravel drive, I parked under the enormous oak and we hauled our stuff inside. The house smelled like always: old and musty, with a hint of mothballs and pine cleaner in the background. It was a good smell, nostalgic.

Once the car was unloaded, I changed into board shorts and headed out. As I walked across the backyard to the lake, the grass warm under my feet, I soaked up the sounds of this place and time: the roar of a speedboat across the lake, the shrieks and laughs of kids in the distance, the gentle knocking of the paddleboat against the pier... I was back in my happy place. For a while.

I walked to the end of the pier, under the weeping willow whose branches Meg and I used to swing from. Sometimes Mason would watch enviously from the pier, his skin thick with white sunscreen, arms clad in inflatable water wings. I would pick him up and swing him around while he held the branches, then dip him in the water when he let go. Remembering his delighted laughter, how happy he was, clouded everything for a moment. There was nothing that wasn't tainted. Even the best memories I could call to mind had a shadow side.

The sun lit the ripples of sand under the water, creating a brilliant pattern of curved lines. A tiny pink flip-flop floated a few yards out, strands of seaweed draped over it. I stepped off the pier into the lake, my feet stirring up the sand and muddying the clean, shallow water, which didn't even come to my knees. The sandbar was a good 150 feet out; you could walk and walk, and the water would still be at waist level. Once you got to a certain point, though, it was like walking off a cliff, it fell off so fast.

Out on the anchored wooden raft, the neighbor kids shouted, shoved, and dived. Tommy Dunham was a year older than me, and his sister, Stephanie, was a year younger. She'd always seemed like a little kid to me, but seeing her now, in her teensy bikini, I realized that was no longer the case. Colin and Mark, the twins, would be seven now. Once, they'd been the same age as Mason. But they kept growing up, whereas Mason would forever be three and a half.

I swam out to join them. When they saw me and hollered out my name, it was almost embarrassing how glad I felt. It was nice to feel liked, to feel wanted. Like being popular, for a moment.

I spent most of the day with them, swimming, playing water Frisbee, and tubing. I figured I might as well pack my fun in before Football Guy arrived and I climbed into a hole. The Dunhams invited us for dinner, which was nice because my mom hadn't been shopping for food yet. With all the Dunham cousins present and accounted for, there were sixteen kids there, and I kind of envied them their big family, despite the chaos. We had burgers and chips and Cokes, and then Tommy took all the older kids to the Sugar Bear for ice cream in his dad's truck. When we got back, we made a bonfire and watched fireworks, which Silver Lake people take very seriously. But somehow they were a disappointment to me. It felt like something was missing. And it was.

It wasn't just Meg, though – I'd had a couple of years to get used to fireworks without her at my side. But now, sitting on the old plaid picnic blanket next to my mom, I remembered a Fourth in Michigan when I was a kid and Mason was a baby – one and a half, I guess he would have been, just weeks after Meg moved to town – when I got annoyed with my mom for not watching the fireworks because she was watching Mason's face instead. Every time there was a particularly great display, I'd look at her, and she'd be gazing at Mason. "You keep missing them!" I'd told her in frustration.

What I didn't understand then was that, for her, watching Mason's face as he saw the fireworks was better than the fireworks themselves. As I looked at her, her sad eyes on the sky, I wished I could turn back time and do it over. I wished I could see Mason's face the first time he saw fireworks. I wanted to tell my mom I was sorry, that I didn't understand then, but I did now. But I couldn't say those things. It would have been too hard, too much.

So I didn't say anything. I just watched the show and felt kind of broken, until finally I reached out and put an arm around her, hoping she wouldn't make a big awkward deal out of it. But the small gesture hit her as hard as I suppose I knew it would, and when her eyes spilled over, tears welled up in mine, too.

I felt a hand touch my arm, and I glanced up to catch my father's surprised glance. He didn't know my arm was already there.

The next morning I got up early, stirred by the sounds of my dad making coffee. When I came out, he gave me a wave and put a finger to his lips to let me know Mom was still sleeping. I fixed myself a cup of coffee and went out onto the back patio.

A mist hovered over the still lake, and the only sounds were the distinctive, eerie calls of loons somewhere on the water and the occasional splash of a fish jumping. I sat and sipped my coffee, wishing I could press the cosmic pause button and things could stay like this all day, before Meg showed up with her boyfriend and ruined everything.

When my mom was up, we headed out to Grandma Sally's for breakfast, where I feasted on malted strawberry waffles and sausages. I texted Dara a picture of my plate with the caption *VACATION!* ☺, and she wrote back: *Guess that means you put in your 6 grand.* Ha, right. Six thousand yards of lake swimming? Doubtful. But then I felt guilty. I did have Senior Champs coming up – I needed to get some yards in.

After breakfast, while my parents shopped for groceries,

I went to the adjacent hardware store to find supplies for making a folding mirror box.

The hardware store smelled of lumber and paint, fertilizer and rubber. A key-cutter screamed in the back. I wandered around for a long time, thinking, shopping, and planning. I wanted to make the box small enough to fit into a swim bag or backpack so Dara could easily take it everywhere. So she'd always be okay, with me or without me.

After a final stop at the berry farm for a ten-pound box of blueberries, we returned to the house. The Brandts weren't there yet, and the lake was so beautiful, I decided to take the rusted old rowboat out.

I rowed out to the west side of the lake, where there was a wonderland of water lilies that would have made Monet wet his pants. They were Meg's favorite – we would pick armloads of them. But they barely survived a few hours out of the water. *Nothing lasts forever*, my mother would say. I hated when she said that. My dreams were of beginnings without endings.

I wished I could bring Meg there, without Football Guy. But since I probably wouldn't be able to bring Meg to the lilies, I decided to bring the lilies to Meg.

I must have spent an hour or more, hauling lilies out of the lake as the noon sun beat down on me. Sometimes five or ten feet of tubular stem came off with the flowers, like slender garden hoses, other times just the blossoms. The bright yellow centers, the long, elegant petals, the sweet smell of them – it all reminded me of summers past with Meg.

My back ached and I grew wet with sweat as I leaned, grabbed, and pulled, over and over, as if enough water lilies could somehow communicate to Meg how sorry I was for everything that had happened, for all the hurt she'd been through, for the ways I'd failed her. I piled them onto the seat of the bow. By the time I finished, they formed a small mountain. An altar, an olive branch, a message, a plea. *I. Am. So. Sorry.*

I imagined how this gesture would strike Football Guy, but I honestly didn't give a fuck. All I cared about was the way Meg's eyes would light up, the happiness it would bring her.

I was rowing back when I saw them. I'd had my eye on the pier and the rear of the house, trying to find my way back (I could hear Meg's navigation lady voice in my head: *at raft, veer left*). He stood chest-deep in the lake, holding Meg in his arms like the cover of a fucking romance novel.

Suddenly, my romantic gesture seemed idiotic, masochistic. I tried to think of a way to avoid running into them with all my stupid lilies, but short of pretending to be blind and deaf and rowing frantically to the opposite side of the lake, I was stuck. And then Meg started waving at me, and I had no choice but to row over to them.

Meg quickly extricated herself from Football Guy's arms and lowered herself into the water. "Hey, Otie!"

"Hey," I said, slowing the boat with the oar.

"Jeff, this is Otis. Otis, Jeff."

His dark blond hair hung in his eyes. His face was chiseled and cocky-looking. He held out his hand. "Nice to meet you, Otis. I've heard a lot about you."

I shook his hand and mumbled something back.

Meg's eyes widened when she saw the lilies. "Otis! What did you do?"

"A birthday present – a few days early."

"Jeez, look at that," Football Guy said.

Meg reached into the boat and took a lily, her eyes stopping my heart with that outside-the-fifth-grade-classroom way that was so ingrained in my memory. What I wouldn't have given for this moment to be happening without her fucking boyfriend there. He smiled, watching her as she held the flower to her nose and closed her eyes.

But when she opened her eyes, it was me Meg was beaming at. It was a smile that contained things her boyfriend knew nothing about. And it flooded sunshine into the cobwebbed corners of my heart.

I rowed the rest of the way in, and they followed along. Jeff climbed onto the pier and helped hook the boat up. He was tan, and he had green eyes. Even I had to admit it: he was good-looking. Fuck.

On the other hand, he did have just a little spare tire around the middle. I definitely had him in the muscles category. Since it was so hot anyway, I pulled off my shirt to play up my advantage. Kind of pathetic. *Gee, Mueller, you're practically even: you have a six-pack, and he has Meg. Close one!*

I sat down on the pier, my feet dangling. Meg stood in the shallow water and gathered up an armful of the water lilies. She buried her face in them.

"Can you put some in a vase?" Jeff asked her.

Meg shook her head. "They're too ephemeral."

Ephemeral. Ten to one Football Guy had no idea what that meant.

I nodded in agreement. "Most evanescent."

Meg grinned. "Nothing lasts forever."

"Except cat pee."

I was rewarded with her laughter. She stood there under the weeping willow, branches draped like strands of sun-lit emeralds, holding that jumble of green-and-white water lilies. She was so beautiful, it hurt to look. Yet I couldn't tear my eyes away.

I sat swishing my feet in the water, and Jeff sat down, too. He reached out with his legs and pulled Meg to him. *Okay, dude, Meg's yours, I get it!*

Meg held out the flowers toward me. "Could you hold these for a sec?" I took them, and she pulled herself up and sat on the pier between Jeff and me.

"Thanks," she said, taking the flowers back and burying her nose in them again. "So were there fireworks last night?"

"Yup."

"Aw." She stroked the petals of a flower between her thumb and forefinger.

"You'll see them tonight."

"I know, but I'm sad I missed them."

I glanced at her and did a double take, laughing to myself. She had managed to transfer a stamp of bright yellow stamen powder to the tip of her nose. I pointed at my nose, hoping she'd get it, but she just gave me a quizzical look.

"You have yellow," I mouthed.

She rubbed her nose with the back of her hand, then checked back with me. I nodded.

We dragged our feet lazily through the water, the sun sparkling on the ripples we made. A Jet Ski roared in the distance, and that familiar lake smell hung in the air, mossy and fishy and green. Minnows flashed under the surface. It was almost – almost – perfect.

Meg bumped me with her shoulder. "So when's lunch?"

"Mary Margaret," I said, shaking my head. "Do you ever stop eating?"

"Mary Margaret?" Jeff said.

She glared at me, then turned back to Jeff. "My full name," she told him grudgingly.

"What? How did I not know that?" he asked. "Mary Margaret," he repeated to himself. "*Mary.* Huh."

She huffed and tried not to smile, but I saw one fighting

for freedom. I was biting back a smile, too. He didn't even know her *name*.

We headed in for lunch. Meg selected a handful of lilies to bring inside, and we gave the rest a burial at sea. Or at lake, as it were.

Inside, my mom fixed sandwiches while the dads made a run for booze and ice. "How's the lake?" she asked, setting the food on the table.

"Oh, it's awesome," Jeff told her. "This place is really great. Thanks so much for including me."

What a suck-up.

My mom slipped her sandals on. "I'll be back in a minute," she told me. "I need to borrow a pitcher from next door." She paused to squeeze my shoulders for the briefest second before she went out the screened sliding door. *Yeah, Mom, I get it. Poor, sad, pathetic Otis.*

"You excited to get your license, Otis?" Jeff asked. He picked tomato slices off his sandwich, which annoyed me. They were nice tomatoes. Ripe.

I shrugged. Of course I was excited, but I wasn't about to share that with that patronizing jackass.

"Maybe I'll get mine before you," Meg said to me with a teasing smile.

"You on the road," Jeff said to Meg, shaking his head. He turned to me. "She drove halfway here. Lucky we made it alive."

"Ha-ha," she said. "At least I have the navigation lady: *In four hundred feet, turn right.*" Damn, she did that voice dead-on.

As we ate our sandwiches, I spotted a bag of Meow Mix on the counter. "Did you bring Jasper?"

Meg nodded, popping a potato chip in her mouth. "Your mom said it was okay. I hope to God he doesn't pee on anything."

"Yeah, well, fingers crossed," I said, finishing my sandwich and standing up.

"Where are you going?" Meg asked. Was it just wishful thinking, or did she look a little disappointed?

"I got some things in town. I want to make a folding mirror box for Dara." I reached for a bit of crust Meg had left on her plate and popped it into my mouth. Jeff noticed, looking less than thrilled, so I took the other piece of crust she'd left, too, just to irritate him. Which was pathetic, because basically it was me taking exactly what was left to me: crumbs.

"But do you have to do it now?" Meg wiped her mouth and set her napkin down. "Come on, Ot – we just got here."

And yet I'd already had plenty.

"Sorry," I said, heading for the hallway past the laundry room, which led to the garage. "I'll catch up with you guys later."

16

IT WAS HARDER THAN I THOUGHT IT WOULD
be, the mirror box. I sweated and toiled in the garage well
into the afternoon, my ass going numb from hours on the
rough wooden bench. I'd long since pulled my shirt off, and
I used it from time to time to wipe my dripping forehead. It
must have been a hundred degrees in there.

I thought about some of the things I'd read online
recently, searching for good news for Dara. One thing
that stood out was that phantom limb pains in many cases
become fewer and further between over time. Optimism
wasn't exactly Dara's specialty, with the single notable excep-
tion of her blind optimism where my swimming career was
concerned. I wanted to give her reason for hope.

The finished box was not exactly fine craftsmanship, but
it did what it needed to do. It folded up into a reasonable-size

package. Smaller would have been better, but I had to base it on the size of the mirror I'd found. Unfolded, it was pretty solid, I thought. I hoped Dara liked it. I hoped it would get her through when I wasn't there.

"Hey, you."

Meg stood in the doorway in her bikini, eating blueberries out of her hand. She'd gotten a lot of sun – she glowed.

"I hope you wore sunscreen this time," I said, stretching. My back ached.

"I did. How's the mirror box coming?"

"Finished," I said, nodding at it.

"Can I see?" Meg walked over and held out a handful of blueberries to me.

"My hands are dirty," I said, holding them up.

"Open your mouth." I did, and she tried to put the blueberries in, but most of them tumbled to the floor, making us laugh.

She slid in next to me on the bench and put her hand in the box, tipping her head to see the mirror better. She moved her hand around, watching. She turned to me. "You're amazing."

I waved her off.

"How does it work?"

I shrugged. "It's an artificial visual feedback system, basically."

"So it fools the brain into thinking the missing limb is there?"

"I guess."

She nodded slowly, her eyebrows furrowed. "Like dreams?"

I squinted at her in confusion. "Dreams?"

She shook her head, embarrassed. "I guess it's dumb. It's just … sometimes I would dream about you, and it was like I was trying to bring you back because I missed you so much."

That resonated instantly. It was what dreaming of Mason felt like.

"God, it's hot in here," she said suddenly. "How can you stand it?"

"Yeah, I'm dying to get in the lake."

Her eyes flicked to my torso. "You're giving Jeff a complex, you know. After seeing you with your shirt off, he said he was taking up swimming."

I kept my smile on the inside.

"Hey," she said, tipping her head. "I never got to hug you hello."

"I'm all sweaty," I warned, but she was already reaching for me.

And instantly things felt distinctly un-platonic. I was shirtless and she was only in a bikini. The apple scent of her damp hair mixed with the smell of the lake was intoxicating, like past and present and what I wanted for the future, jumbled confusingly together. I was too aware of the feel of her hands on my back, and the feel of her back under my hands.

I pulled away and started cleaning up the leftover bits of burlap and cardboard. She helped me gather the scraps.

"Can I tell you something?" she asked, scooping a pile of burlap strands over to join the pile I was gathering. Her sun-warmed arm touched mine.

"Sure."

"It's about something in my journal." She stared at the worktable. "Freshman year, my English class went to a peach orchard for a unit on writing description. So we were supposed to soak up the details, taking notes and thinking about the colors of a peach or the sound of the equipment or whatever." She played with a scrap of burlap, plucking out the threads one by one. "And all of a sudden I was crying."

I craned my head to try to see her face, but she didn't look up.

"Because there were these bushels of ripe peaches – ones that are too ripe to take to market, so they make jam out of them and sell it in the shop at the roadside. And, oh my God, the smell of them…" She shook her head. "It was the most intense, almost-perfumey peach smell – like, peach to the tenth power. I mean, it almost made me weak." She finally looked up, and her gaze sent a jolt through me. "You know what I mean?"

I swallowed and nodded. "Yes."

She looked away. "I wanted you to smell it."

I exhaled, my shoulders going slack. "Meg. That's happened to me, like, ten thousand times. Not being able to share things with you… We went to Paris for spring break freshman year. And we were walking to see the Eiffel Tower. It was night, and we had just left this perfect, warm little bistro where the lighting was all amber and the food was incredible – you would have loved it. And it was cold for spring – it was snowing a little, and the way the snowflakes looked in the light of the streetlamps…" I shook my head, remembering. "It was fucking magic. It should've made me happy, but all I could think about was how much I wanted to share it with you."

Was that doubt on her face? Hope? "Really? Did you really feel that way?"

"Jesus, Meg," I said, staring into her eyes. "All the time. Whenever something happened, my first thought was of you. The first time I won a medal at a swim meet, I was so happy – at first. And then I thought of you, and how I wished you could have been there to see it… It's like it didn't mean as much without you." I leaned against her a little, pressing my arm into her shoulder. "So, yeah. I do understand."

"I wish I'd known," she said softly.

"Would it have made a difference?" I asked. It wasn't a rhetorical question. In fact, it felt kind of crucial.

She paused so long, I didn't think she was going to

answer. "I wish there were an easy answer to that question," she finally said. She shifted, tossing her hair over her shoulder. "Ugh, I can't deal with this heat anymore," she said, wiping the back of her hand across her brow. "Wanna go for a swim?"

"In a minute," I said, wanting to postpone the inevitable third-wheel-ness as long as possible.

"I think your dad's grilling brats for dinner," Meg said, getting up. "Your mom said she's making potato salad. Do you think she'll make the one with the blue cheese and capers?"

"Probably," I said, standing up, too. "I doubt my mom would mess with your potato salad."

She clapped happily. "We always have the best food here!"

I smiled at her – I couldn't not. It made me happy when she was happy.

"That reminds me," I said, tugging gently on a strand of her damp hair. "I brought you something from the Sugar Bear last night. It's in the freezer."

"What flavor?"

"Triple Caramel Vortex."

Her eyes grew wide. She took my face in her hands and kissed me on the cheek, then pulled away, looking into my eyes. "You're the best." Then she turned and ran into the house.

Great – I was the best. For all the good that did me.

I headed inside and put the mirror box in my bedroom, then texted Dara: *I have a surprise for you when I get back.*

She texted back right away: *Blueberries?*

We always brought tons of blueberries back from Michigan – everyone got some.

I texted back: *Okay, two surprises.*

She wrote back: *I like you.* And then she wrote: *My gf likes you, too.*

Dara, with a girlfriend. Wonder of wonders.

I wrote: *So is this classified, you and Abby? Or can I tell Meg?*

She wrote back: *Knock yourself out.*

A rustling sound emitted from nearby. I crouched down and looked under the bed.

"Hey, Jasper," I said.

He came out and rubbed against me.

When I eventually emerged from hiding, Meg was standing at the kitchen counter eating her ice cream from the carton while my mom made the potato salad. Meg had changed into a white sundress that showed off her deepening tan. Jeff was still outside, playing water Frisbee on the lake with Tommy and Stephanie. I sat at the table, petting Jasper, who had found his way to my lap.

"You put yogurt in it?" Meg said to my mom, scraping ice cream from the container and putting the spoon in her mouth upside down.

"Mm-hm, Greek yogurt. I used to use sour cream," my mom said, scooping yogurt into the bowl, "but I discovered I prefer it with yogurt. Gives it a better tang."

"And you'll put in garlic, too, right?" Meg asked, peeking into the bowl over my mom's shoulder.

My mom's mouth curved into a little smile. "Yes, sweetie." She gave Meg a one-armed hug. "Lots of garlic." She kissed Meg on the cheek, then reached for the celery.

And I might have been okay. I might have been fine if Meg hadn't turned to glance at me. But she did, and the fragile expression on her face made my heart split open. I realized how desperately she needed just that little bit of warmth from my mom. I wanted to hug both of them – my mom, who had been working harder than I would probably ever know to accept that what had happened hadn't been anyone's fault, and Meg, who had never done anything wrong but who had gotten such a raw deal. We all had.

When I looked over at my mom, her hands were resting on the counter and her head was lowered. She lifted a hand and wiped her cheek on the back of her wrist. She turned back toward Meg, then spoke in a strangled voice. "Forgive me, Meg."

Meg's face crumpled, and my mom reached for her, wrapping her in a hug.

I willed my eyes not to spill over. But the awful sound of my mom's crying was more than I could take, more than

I ever could take, and I turned my head to wipe my eyes on my T-shirt sleeve. When I looked up, Meg's eyes were on me, bright and teary like the day she drove out of Willow Grove and out of my life. She and my mom clung to each other, the late afternoon sun pouring in on us through the sliding-glass doors.

Eventually, Meg and I left my mom to finish with dinner preparations. We wandered outside and down to the pier, barefoot. I dangled my feet in the water, but Meg held back. "Could you check for ducks?" she asked.

I sighed.

"Those things are vicious," she insisted.

I rolled my eyes. We had been feeding some ducks, right here on this pier, feet hanging over the water, and an impatient duck had reached up and nibbled Meg's toe. She had sprinted off, shrieking, as if she had narrowly escaped death.

She was just my total fucking undoing. I leaned over to check under the pier. "You're safe."

"Thanks." She settled in next to me, her knees tan against the white of her dress. "Otis?"

"Yeah?"

"I miss Mason."

I couldn't respond. I was overwhelmed with the unexpectedness of it, how much it made me feel.

"I can still see him here, everywhere. In his booster seat

at the table inside. In his little arm-floaty things right here." She nodded at the water in front of us. "Eating s'mores and getting them all over his face."

The ache in my throat grew.

"I'm sorry," she whispered. "Talking about him is so hard. But I don't want you to think I've forgotten him."

I wished I had words for what it meant to me, that she said that. I knew she hadn't erased Mason from her memory, and I knew how hard it was for her. That she was trying … it was everything.

She leaned her head on my shoulder, and for a moment it was like we were thirteen again, sitting on the pier and totally isolated from the world around us, in our own private little bubble. I leaned into her, briefly letting my head rest on hers.

The sound of a motorboat broke our reverie. Jeff was out on the boat with the Dunhams. Meg was right. He was fun. Everybody loved him. He and Stephanie jumped off the boat into the lake. We watched as they grabbed on to the tube and Tommy spun the boat into motion. I wondered if Meg felt like I did, which was kind of astounded that there were people who could play and have fun, people who could just have light times. They seemed so damn *carefree*. Sometimes I wondered if I'd ever feel that way again.

"Some people have all the fun," I tried.

"I was just thinking that." She stared down into the

water at our feet. "We're the walking wounded, aren't we?"

"Yeah." I leaned on her again. "We are." I desperately wanted to put an arm around her, but I had no idea if Jeff could see us. The boat was circling back around for Stephanie, who had been thrown from the tube.

Meg turned to me. "Let's go swimming. Let's be the people who have all the fun."

"I already showered," I protested. "I'm all de-lake-ified." As if I'd really say no to her.

"Last one in a swimsuit's a rotten egg," she said, jumping up and bolting for the house.

I was right on her heels.

I was already waiting on the patio, towels in hand, when she came out. She stopped short when she saw me and sighed in defeat. "I'm a rotten egg."

"The rottenest." We walked back out to the pier, and I stepped into the water. "No ducks," I said. "Jump! You can do it!"

She laughed. "Like Amanda."

She jumped down, then did a perfect impression of Amanda. "Did you see that? Did you see that?"

We walked in the direction of the pier. The Dunhams' boat zoomed across the water in the distance, Jeff and Stephanie flying behind.

"Stephanie's really grown up, huh?" I asked. The water was past our waists now.

"I can't even believe that's her."

"Tell me about it."

She looked at me, squinting into the setting sun. "Do you – do you like her?"

I shrugged. "Sure."

"You mean, you *like* like her?" She stopped walking and stood across from me, running her hands over the surface of the water.

"I don't know. I never thought about it."

"Well, we're not here for long." Meg scooped handfuls of water. It fell through her fingers, catching the sun. "Anyway. Bet Kiera wouldn't like that." Meg lowered herself into the water and started to doggie paddle toward the raft.

I shook my head and smiled. "Doggie paddle…"

"It's my specialty stroke!" she said, lifting her chin to keep her mouth above the water. "You breaststroke, I doggie paddle."

"It'll take days to get to the raft that way. Can't you swim?"

"This is how I swim!"

I did a slow sidestroke, staying with her. "Meg Brandt, Olympic hopeful in the ten-yard doggie paddle with a top time of four hours, twenty-six minutes—"

"That's it," she said, reaching for me. She grabbed my shoulders and tried to push me down, but the water was still shallow enough that I could stand with my head above water. She tried to stand, too, but the water was too deep. She spluttered and reached for my shoulders.

I couldn't think of a decent place to put my hands to help hold her up, so I just let her hold my shoulders as she coughed. "Can you make it there?" I asked.

"Of course I can make it," she said, returning to her doggie paddling. The sun lit her legs, pale under the water's surface.

I sidestroked leisurely beside her until we reached the raft, which she grabbed on to. "We're really going to have to work on your swimming skills," I told her.

"I'll sign up for lessons." She grinned. "Can I ride you afterward?" Her eyes widened and she clapped a hand over her mouth.

"Sure!" I said enthusiastically, and she whacked me on the arm.

"Go on up," I said, gesturing toward the ladder.

But instead she inched her way around to the west side of the raft, the obscured side, the side with a history. My pulse quickened as I followed her.

"Remember the last time we were here?" Meg said, holding on to the raft with one arm and treading.

"Well, yes." I stared into the water and nodded. "Yes, I do."

"The hanky-panky?"

I moved over and held on to the raft with one arm, facing her. "I remember." I looked into her eyes. In the sun, in the water, their color was insane. Nobody had eyes like hers.

She tilted her head. "I think that was the happiest I ever was in my whole life."

My stomach suddenly felt as wavy as the water. I remembered how she had held on to me in this very spot. I could still summon the feeling of her mouth on mine, the taste of warm lake water on our lips, the joy of knowing that an evening lay ahead and then a night after that and then a day after that and then the rest of the summer and the rest of our lives...

A motorboat roared somewhere on the other side of the raft.

"That's probably Jeff," I said.

"Right."

We climbed onto the raft and lay down, riding the gentle waves the motorboat sent our way. The sinking sun warmed our skin. It was impossible not to look at her, lying there in a bikini, drops of water glistening on her golden skin...

"What are you thinking about?" she asked after a while.

I closed my eyes. "I am thinking ... of the way sunlight looks at dawn when it filters through the mist over the lake."

"Mmm... You *are* a poet," Meg murmured. "So what poets do you like?"

"Lots," I said, my eyes still closed. "Yeats. Wordsworth. Frost. Rūmī..."

"Hmph. All men."

"Um, Emily Dickinson, Elizabeth Barrett Browning…"

She smiled and, without opening her eyes, reached out a hand to pat me. She landed on my stomach, just under my rib cage. It felt stupidly good, embarrassingly good. I was sad when she withdrew her hand.

We lay there listening to the sounds of the motorboat zooming back and forth across the lake, and I didn't want it to end. I didn't want Michigan to end, and I didn't want Willow Grove to end. I only wanted Jeff to end.

"Meg?"

"Mm-hm?"

"What about Jasper? If you don't move back. Won't you miss him?"

"Of course I'll miss him. But even if I stay in California, I'll still visit my dad." She turned to me. "So we'll see each other again. Either way."

We lay there in silence for a while as I processed the idea of her going back to California to stay. It had always been a possibility, of course – maybe even a likelihood. But I hadn't wanted to see it, hadn't wanted to let myself believe that I would lose her again. That these next few days might actually be our last together for who knew how long. And now that she was flying back with Jeff, I might not even have the opportunity to say goodbye privately. Instead, it'd be another of those awkward public hugs. My chest ached at the thought. I wished I knew how to convince her to stay.

The sound of splashing bumped me out of my thoughts. I opened my eyes, and there was Jeff, swimming over to us.

"Hey. What are you guys doing?" he asked, treading water.

And even though I wanted to hate him, damned if I didn't feel sorry for him. He flew halfway across the country to be with Meg, and she kept ditching him for me. He was trying to be upbeat, but any idiot could see he felt left out.

"Nothing, just hanging," Meg said.

"It's probably almost dinnertime," I said, getting up. "We should head in."

I dived off the raft, then waited as Meg climbed down the ladder and started her doggie paddling.

Jeff swam on her other side. "All right, you little mermaid, move it along…"

It stung, hearing how patient and affectionate he was with her. I couldn't watch. I took off, sprinting freestyle to the pier.

I toweled off and walked up to the house. My mom had set out a huge platter of sliced watermelon and berries on the picnic table on the patio, and my dad manned the grill.

"How you doin', buddy?" He arranged the coals with long tongs, glancing up at me. "You all right?"

"I'm fine," I said, my tone a little prickly. My parents' concern irritated me. It just reminded me what a loser I was.

Meg's dad came out with a platter of brats. "Hey, Otis, how's the water?"

"Great, you should go in." I smiled.

"Ha." He called over to my dad, "That's a real smart-ass you've got there, Scott."

"My best work," my dad said. He kissed his bicep.

Meg appeared, wrapped in a towel, with Jeff right behind. Jeff made small talk about how great the lake was while Meg picked up a slice of watermelon from the table. Jeff hooked her around the waist and pulled her down into a patio chair with him, right into his lap.

I got up, mumbling an excuse, and went inside before I had to see anything more.

17

I SHOWERED OFF, CHANGED INTO SOME
fresh shorts, and pulled *The Great Gatsby* off the shelf in
my bedroom. I lay down on the bed, propped myself up
on floppy, dusty pillows, and was quickly whisked away
into the gaiety of the 1920s, which sort of made me wish
that I dressed sharp and drank cocktails and knew how to
dance.

A while later Meg knocked on my door. "Ot? Can I
come in?"

"Sure," I said.

She stepped in and closed the door behind her. She was
still in her bikini, her hair drying in a tangle of waves that
skimmed her breasts. I averted my gaze quickly. She seemed
oblivious of the effect she had on me.

I put my book down and put my hands behind my head.

She ducked her head, looking a little embarrassed. "You have nice armpits."

Nice *armpits*? Was that an actual thing? I craned my head around, trying to see what the big deal was. It was an armpit. Not super hairy or anything – not like Shafer's simian pits. Pretty standard, if you asked me.

"Hey, I love that book." She came over and sat on the bed. That's when I discovered that, on a bed, a girl in a bikini looks even more naked. My throat went dry.

"You remind me of Daisy," I said without thinking.

"What? Shallow and self-absorbed?" She pulled her legs up and sat crisscross, which made my brain short-circuit.

"No! Because you're—" I stopped myself. Now I was stuck.

"Because I'm what?" Her breasts. Her stomach. Her legs. There was no safe place to look.

"Unforgettable."

Her eyes met mine, but I couldn't hold her gaze. "Where's Jeff?" I asked.

"He's playing softball with the Dunhams." She picked up my book and examined the back cover. "He's not much for sitting still. And they're more fun than I am." She shrugged.

"I think you're plenty fun," I said. The box fan that kept me from melting at night chugged away, lifting strands of hair off her shoulders. "What bedroom are you sleeping in?" I asked.

"The usual."

"The one next door?"

Meg nodded. "My dad stuck Jeff in the upstairs room."

Good move, Jay.

"I think he figures putting me next to you will keep me safe," she said.

"From?"

She gave me a pointed look.

"Oh! So it's my job to keep you two from having sex, is that what you're saying? Is this a paying position?"

"Ha-ha." She tossed the book down.

"Hey," I said, changing the subject. "I have news for you. Only it's not news, because you already guessed."

"What?"

"Dara and Abby are … sort of a thing."

Her mouth fell open. "I knew Dara was gay! You just found out?"

I shook my head. "It's no longer classified."

She blinked, then glanced down, her smile falling. "You're her secret-keeper, huh?" She picked up the book again and flipped the edges of the pages against her thumb. "Seems like you're everything to her."

"Not a potential sex partner," I pointed out. The irony was that I *would* have been Dara's first sex partner, if I'd acquiesced. In hindsight, I could see that my ego might not have survived it. I'd make a poor lesbian.

"Are you a virgin?"

She caught me off guard. I blinked and scrambled to figure out how to handle it. How would it strike her if I was? Or if I wasn't? It didn't matter. It's not as if I was going to lie about it. So I nodded.

She sat back a little and covered her eyes with her hand. "I shouldn't have asked you that. I'm sorry."

Was I supposed to reciprocate the question? I didn't even want to know.

"I don't know how you've stayed so chaste," she teased. "I know certain girls would jump at the chance to deflower you."

The remark made me blush, so I turned the spotlight back on her. "Who says 'deflower'? You're like an old school-marm trapped in the body of a Greek goddess."

She smiled, recognizing the joke, but continued her line of thinking. "Kiera's a sure thing," she pointed out, still fiddling with the book.

I didn't know what to say. It was hard to deny.

"Maybe she'll be the one." She glanced up. "Do you like her?

"Sure." I shrugged. "She's a lot of fun," I couldn't resist adding.

"I guess. If you like that sort of thing." She unfolded her legs and stood up.

"Seeing you and Jeff together makes me think having a

girlfriend would be really nice. I don't know what I've been waiting for."

Unless I'd lost all ability to read that amazing face I used to know so well, my remark stung. And how fucked up was this? I was happy to see she looked hurt? Yes. But I was also flinching inside, because I had wielded the knife.

Noise trickled in from the kitchen – voices, drawers opening and closing, utensils clanging. My mom called to us that dinner was ready.

As we headed outside to eat, I tried to tamp down the irrational hope that filled me. Meg clearly seemed jealous about the possibility of other girls. But being jealous wasn't the same thing as wanting me, as choosing me. She had made her choice. And her choice was running up to the patio to join us.

"That was a blast – you should have played," he said to Meg. I averted my eyes as he kissed her. I just wanted it to be done – all of it. This vacation. Meg's visit. It seemed clear that she was going to go back to California to stay, and I hated that I'd spent all this time thinking that maybe she'd come back. To Willow Grove. To me.

I tried not to let them kill my appetite. The grilling brats and onions smelled so good. My mom brought out the potato salad and a platter of grilled corn on the cob. I sat down close to her at the picnic table, feeling a childish inclination to stay near my protector. She buttered and salted my corn for me and set it on my plate, as if I were little. She gave me three brats and passed me the kind of mustard I prefer, all without a word. It was comforting. It made me wish Meg hadn't come, hadn't even been invited. Maybe I would have been happier, who knows. For me, happiness seemed to be as elusive as a shadow at night.

I astounded Football Guy by putting away four brats to his two, plus three ears of corn and a heap of potato salad – which he passed on, because he didn't like blue cheese. Didn't he drive Meg nuts with his picky eating?

As I was finishing eating, my parents wandered over to talk to the neighbors. Jeff wiped his mouth with a paper towel and said, "You know what would be fun? Watching the fireworks from the raft."

"I don't know," Meg said, looking toward the lake, a forkful of potato salad suspended in front of her. "Might get too cold."

"I'll keep you warm," he said softly, putting his arms around her and snuggling her neck.

I jumped up.

"Where are you going?" Meg asked me, pulling away from Jeff.

"I need to check something," I said in desperation. What the hell would I be checking? A cake I had in the oven?

As I whirled to go into the house, my foot got caught in the leg of the picnic table. Unable to catch myself in time, I went crashing down on my knee. Hard.

"Otis!" Meg cried, running over. "Are you okay?"

So. Fucking. Humiliating.

"I'm fine! Jesus. It was nothing." I untangled myself, got up, and went into the house, trying not to limp.

I went straight to the bathroom, yanked on the pull-chain light, closed the door, and lifted my foot up onto the toilet. Shit. My knee was scraped and red. It would probably swell. This vacation sucked. I would rather have been home with Dara, eating gritty seaweed bars and swimming eight thousand yards a day and lifting.

When I hobbled back into the kitchen, I found Meg there, packing ice into a Ziploc bag.

"I know that hurt," she said, her expression daring me to challenge her. "Put your leg up."

"Will you forget it?" I said, embarrassed and pissed off in equal measure. "Jesus, this guy follows you across the country, and you're stuck to me like glue!"

She stood there, holding the ice pack, looking like she'd been slapped.

It was an idiot thing to say, especially because I loved it when she stuck to me like glue. I sat and put my leg up on a chair. She knelt beside me and held the ice pack on my knee, not meeting my eyes. I opened my mouth to apologize, but then the sliding door opened and there was Mr. Wonderful.

"Let me see," he said, coming over to us.

"There's nothing to see," I said through clenched teeth.

But Meg moved the ice, and he sucked air in through his teeth. "You're gonna be spending some quality time on the bench, son," he said.

He so did *not* just call me "son."

"Don't be ridiculous," I said. "It's just a bruise. It's no big deal."

"You think?" he asked, looking amused. "Race you around the block in the morning."

"Jeff," Meg chastised him, getting up and leaving the ice balancing on my knee.

"There are no blocks," I said. "Have you looked around?"

He rolled his eyes. "Okay, fine, I'll race you up and down the verdant country roads. Better?"

I ignored him. I was sort of bummed he knew a word like "verdant."

"What are you doing?" I called to Meg. She stood at the sliding-glass doors, rubbing at a spot with a towel as if the survival of the planet depended on it.

Jeff heaved a sigh and walked over to her. He came up behind her, taking her arms gently in his hands, and whispered in her ear. She handed him the towel and snapped the rubber band on her wrist.

What the fuck?

My mom slid open the door, and Jeff and Meg stepped aside. "What happened, Otis?" She hurried over to me. "I heard you took a spill."

"Jesus, it's nothing!"

She gave me a look and picked up the ice to look underneath.

"I'll get the arnica," she said, turning and heading for the bathroom.

"I'll find something to prop up your foot," Meg said, and disappeared into the living room before I could protest.

Thankfully, my mom was back with a tube of arnica cream before Jeff and I had to make small talk. I tried not to wince as she rubbed the ointment into my knee. She winced for both of us.

Meg brought a throw pillow from the living room and lifted my foot to set it under. Then she knelt by my side, one hand on the ice pack.

"You really don't have to —" I began, but she cut me off.

"I don't mind."

Jeff watched her for a minute and then wandered outside.

My mom gave me a Motrin and told me to sit still with the ice for a while, then she joined the others outside.

Meg didn't talk – she just stayed. I felt like crap for being such a dick to her. "Hey," I said. "I'm sorry. I shouldn't have said that, about sticking to me —"

She shook her head. "You're right. I need to get my head on straight, I know that." She sighed. "This is just a weird place to be with Jeff. I mean, this is…" Her eyes met mine. "It's our place. You know? And I go back to California in a

few days. This was supposed to be our chance to talk and…"
She gave a quick shrug. "I had a whole plan for this trip, for these three weeks. A list of things I needed to try to do. But it didn't go so well."

I took off the ice and stood up, because if she was working up to telling me she had made her decision and she wasn't moving back, I kind of wanted to skip it. I could just see myself starting to cry, and then Football Guy walking in and seeing.

Meg rushed to put my arm around her so she could support me. "Let me help you," she said. "Where are we going?"

"To take a leak."

"Ah." She smiled. "Hm."

"I'm fine on my own," I said, moving away from her.

"I should probably get out there, anyway." She glanced outside. "The fireworks and everything…"

"Right. Well, don't let me stop you." I hobbled away quickly, wondering if she'd recognize the words she had flung at me that night at Dara's party.

When I came back from the bathroom, I sat with my back to the windows and played games on my phone, ignoring the whistles of bottle rockets and the shouts of the kids next door. After a while, I got up and poked around in the freezer, finding an unmolested container of brownie fudge ice cream. Chocolate, good. I grabbed a spoon and limped outside.

It was almost dark now. The moonlight shimmered on the now-still lake. Mosquitoes buzzed around the yellow patio light by the door, and firecrackers popped in the distance like gunshots, their smoky sulfur smell hanging in the night air.

"Hey, Ot," my dad said. He scrubbed the grill with a crumpled ball of aluminum foil. "How's the knee?"

"Fine. Where is everyone?"

"Down by the pier. Waiting for the fireworks."

I scraped a layer of ice cream onto my spoon and licked it off.

"You going?" my dad asked. "I think the Dunhams are doing a bonfire. Mom bought stuff for s'mores."

I certainly didn't want to sit there during the fireworks while Jeff and Meg made fireworks of their own. I wondered if he ate chocolate, or if he avoided it for Meg. I hoped he was addicted to the stuff. Suddenly I didn't want the ice cream; now I just wanted to brush my teeth and gargle. "I think I'll call it a night," I said.

"Well, there'll be plenty more fireworks over the next couple nights. You know how it goes here." He came over and gave me a one-armed hug and, weirdly, a kiss on my head.

I limped back inside, tossed the container of ice cream back in the freezer, and went to get ready for bed. Maybe I'd try to sleep through the next two days. And then we'd go back home and then Meg would go back to California and then…

I didn't know what then. I'd start over, I supposed. Again.

I sent Dara a message just to say hi, but I didn't hear back, probably because of the lesbian sex, and then pulled out *Gatsby*. After reading for a while, I stared to doze, and it felt so good that I set down my book and went with it. But then the fireworks started in earnest, and there was no sleeping through that racket, especially with the Dunhams' terrier barking back at it. So I lay there, tortured by thoughts of Meg kissing Football Guy during the fireworks, and waited for it all to be over. Finally, sometime after midnight, I fell asleep.

I was awakened by noises. From upstairs. *His* room.

My heart started to pound. *Please, don't let me hear them. Anything but that.* But even over the rattling whir of the box fan by my bed, I heard them. I pulled my pillow over my head, but the noises were just echoing in my head now, and I was sure I was hearing Meg's moans, headboards banging, all kinds of things. I considered getting up and going outside, putting as much distance between me and them as I could. But when I moved, my knee howled. *Fuck.*

I grabbed the nearest thing to me – it happened to be an old alarm clock – and hurled it at the ceiling. It exploded, louder than I'd dreamed possible, breaking into pieces.

Silence. Total, utter silence.

A minute passed. My mom called softly from outside my door, "Otis?"

Shit.

She opened the door a crack. "Otis?" she asked again.

"I'm fine. It was nothing."

"What was the noise?"

"I broke the clock."

"What? How? Why?"

"I was having a bad dream and – I guess I threw it."

She was quiet. For too long. Finally she said, "This is not passing my sniff test, Otis."

"Well, I don't know what to tell you."

"Are you alone in there?"

"Desperately. Come see."

She sighed. "Okay. Good night. Love you."

I lay there, wide awake, until after what felt like forever, my door creaked open again.

This time, it was Meg.

18

"OTIS?" SHE WHISPERED.

What the hell could she want with me? If she was coming to tell me that the spectacular fuck upstairs had clinched the decision to return to California, frankly I thought that could wait until morning.

"Otis? Can I come in?"

"No," I said. I didn't want her anywhere near me, especially if she was all covered in eau de Jeff and whatnot.

"No?" she repeated, like it had never occurred to her I would actually say that. Maybe because I'd never said no to her in all the years I'd known her. "I just – I really need to talk to you."

"Well," I whispered, "there's broken glass in here and you're barefoot, so…"

"How do you know I'm barefoot?"

"Because you're always barefoot!"

She padded away, and I could hear the door next to mine creak open. I shifted in bed, trying to get comfortable again, but pain radiated from my knee. There was no way I'd be involved in any footraces with Football Guy. Fuck.

There was another tap. "I'm coming in," Meg whispered. I hear the soft smacking of flip-flops across the floor, then the crunching of glass.

"What do you want, Meg?" I said. "It's kind of late for a chat."

"What time is it, anyway?"

"I don't know – you're walking over the pieces of the clock right now."

"Is that what that racket was? What happened?"

"Bad dream," I muttered. More like a nightmare.

"God, it's pitch-dark." She shuffled her way to the bed. "Can I sit? I don't know where you are."

I moved to the other side of the bed, heaving a mighty sigh. "Go ahead."

I felt her sink onto the bed. A hand brushed my arm. "Where are you?" she asked.

"I'm right here, obviously," I said, scooting away from her.

"Why are you being so mean?"

"I'm not being mean. I just don't know why this is your first stop after fucking your boyfriend."

"What?" She sounded confused – and a little indignant.

"I know you're no spatial genius, but I'm right below his room."

"We weren't… God, Otis."

"I have ears, Meg."

"Well, I don't know what you think you were hearing, but it wasn't … *that*."

Silence. Then, sniffling.

"Are you crying?"

"No," she said, in the most tear-soaked voice I'd ever heard.

"Hey," I said, reaching out for her. My hand made contact with some soft fabric, and I patted it reassuringly. "I'm sorry," I said. "I just assumed…"

She sniffled again, then scooted closer and lay down next to me. I could feel the heat coming off her body, only inches away from mine.

"Otis?" she whispered.

"Yeah?"

"You smell like chlorine. How is that possible?"

I shrugged. "It's in my pores."

More silence, then:

"Are you naked?"

"What if I am?" The smell of her hair combined with her speaking the word "naked" was not the thing I needed just then.

"Seriously, what are you wearing?"

"Boxers."

"That's it? Just boxers?"

"It's like a thousand degrees in here. And I wasn't expecting company."

Her hand slid down my arm and found my hand, nestling inside. I was glad it was pitch-dark, because the idiot pig was starting to poke out of the barn, so to speak, and I didn't even have a sheet over me.

We lay that way for a while, neither of us talking. Finally I whispered, "What if your dad checked on you and didn't find you in your room, so he went looking for you in Jeff's room... Imagine."

"I know. But he won't check on me. He has no idea how to do this."

"Do what?"

"Parent. Without my mom."

I thought about that. "Yeah, I can see that. I mean, even with my own dad, my mom is in charge of discipline."

"Ha, as if you require disciplining."

"You'd be surprised. I really piss her off sometimes." After a moment I asked, "Was that part of the draw of Willow Grove? Less discipline? Easier with your dad?"

"Nothing would be easy. Anywhere."

At this point I realized I wished she would just say it. That she wasn't coming back. I wished she'd just fucking say it.

"So? What's going on?" I asked.

"There was no sex, Otis."

"I heard stuff…"

"It wasn't sex. In fact, for the record, I've never had sex with Jeff."

Before I could even begin to soar on this happiest of news, she let go of my hand and shifted. I figured I'd blown it, but she lifted my arm and laid her head on my shoulder, leaving my arm with really nowhere to go but around her.

"Why does this shoulder feel like the safest place in the world?" she whispered.

"Why do people think I'm so safe?" I grumbled.

She settled her head a little lower onto my chest.

This had to have been the most nearly perfect moment of my life. I was so completely nearly happy. And yet. "Meg? Are you going to tell me what's going on?"

She exhaled. "We broke up."

I started to sit up, but of course her head was on me, so I lay back down. "What?"

"That's what you were hearing. Arguing. Not sex. Jesus. Is that how you have sex?"

I smiled a little. "I don't have sex, remember?"

"Well, maybe that's a good thing, if that's how you'd do it."

I could hear the smile in her voice, despite everything. "What happened? And what's going to happen tomorrow? Is he going to stay?"

I felt her shake her head. "Give me a minute. Okay?"

"Okay."

"And I don't know about tomorrow. This sucks. There are no airports around here. We're kind of stuck. He really shouldn't have come – we weren't in the greatest place anyway. I told him I wanted to be friends, but – I don't even know. This isn't fair to him. But it wasn't fair to me, either."

We lay there for a while in silence, and I started wondering if she would ever say anything, or if maybe she was falling asleep. It was so surreal to have her there with me. It was surreal that the boyfriend upstairs was apparently history. It was surreal that we were in bed together. Or *on* a bed, anyway. Technically.

But most surreal of all was the fact that we'd spent three whole years apart, living entirely separate lives, having all these experiences that the other person knew nothing about.

"I don't understand it," I said, as though I'd been thinking aloud this whole time. "I don't understand how there can be three years where I didn't know you."

"Well, you didn't know me before. I mean, before I was nine."

"That's different. You didn't exist for me yet. Everything changed after that. There was life before you, and then life with you. There wasn't supposed to be life after you."

She squeezed my hand. "I know."

"I always wondered what you were doing. All that time."

She lay perfectly still. Then: "They weren't my best years, Otis."

"Well, sure. I mean, I can imagine."

"I could tell you about it. But you won't like it."

I felt the chill of dread, the familiar urge to turn away to protect myself from something I didn't want to hear. But that was the very thing that had cost me Meg in the first place. If I wanted to convince her to stay, to show her we could be okay, this was my chance.

"Tell me."

"Okay..." She took a deep breath. "After we moved, I wanted, I don't know ... I wanted to start over, I guess. I wanted to separate myself from you. From everything that happened. But no matter what I did, I still felt you there. None of it went away. I did so many stupid things, trying to get away from everything, from you... There was this one thing. I've never told anyone." She hesitated. "I want to tell you. I think I need to."

"Okay." I squeezed her hand, although I didn't know which of us I was trying to reassure.

"So when I started at my new school, I went straight to the wrong crowd. Drinking. Smoking pot."

"In *junior high*?"

"I know. It's awful. I actually dyed my hair black that year."

"What?" I tried to envision Meg with black hair. I couldn't.

"My parents weren't doing so great, either. My mom was falling apart because of..."

"Because of what happened."

"Yes, but... Not just that, Otis. Your mom cut my mom off. And it just about killed her."

It occurred to me I didn't know what the hell my mom was doing at that time. She stayed in bed a lot. She cried all the time. And she "if only'd" constantly: *If only I hadn't said he could have his nap at the Brandts... If only we'd used the monitor... If only the Brandts had never moved here...* She pushed both my dad and me to our very limits. Losing Mason was hard enough. But living in the vortex of her grief every day, while she continually replayed what had happened – it was too much. But I knew now that as awful as she'd made it for everyone else, it was probably nothing compared to the hell she herself was living through.

"You okay?" Meg asked quietly.

I realized I'd been quiet for a while. "Yeah, sorry," I said. "It's all just..."

"I know," she whispered.

"Anyway, you were saying...?" I prompted.

"Right, yeah. So, by the time I started high school, my parents and I were fighting all the time. I'd come home drunk, get grounded, act horrible. One night I sneaked out and went to this party. And..." She paused for a moment. "I'm just going to say it: I ended up having sex with someone there. Someone I didn't even know."

Her words filled me with anger, jealousy, confusion – and, yes, disappointment. I fought the urge to pull my hand from hers.

"And it was awful. I didn't like the way he kissed. I didn't like the way he touched me. I didn't like any of it. And I went kind of numb, and then it was like I was watching myself. Part of me was thinking, *I shouldn't do this, this is going to be a horrible mistake…* But part of me was, like, cheering me on. *Wanting* me to do it."

I did pull my hand away then. "Why?"

"Well. I could say it's because I was drunk. And maybe that helped. But it wasn't just that. I think part of me wanted it. Part of me wanted to change myself so I wouldn't be the same person, wouldn't still be mired in everything that happened in Willow Grove. It's like I was walking around as this broken, fucked-up version of that person. And I wanted to be someone else, I wanted out. My therapist says the act was like a burial for my old self. I think he's right. I don't know if I can explain it any better than that."

I wasn't sure I understood it. I mean, I was broken, too, but I didn't try to fix myself by having sex with strangers.

"Afterward I thought, *Well, now I can forget about Otis. He would never want me now.*"

"Because you had sex?" I mean, no, I didn't like it, but it wouldn't stop me from wanting her.

"No, not exactly. It was more because it wasn't sex that meant something. It was kind of trashy, right? And you would never go out with a trashy girl. So, I thought, *It's over.* And I *wanted* it to be over so I could move on – from you, from Mason, from all of it. But I still couldn't stop thinking about you. And I hated myself for what I did. And I thought you'd hate me, too."

"I could never hate you." I found her hand again. "Were you...?"

"He used a condom."

"No, I mean ... I don't know. Are you okay?"

She laughed bitterly. "What's 'okay'?"

"I've never really known."

It was quiet for a while. Then she said, "There was this night – it was the night I met Jeff, actually. I was still kind of a wreck. I was at a party, and I was hanging out in the living room with some people, and suddenly I noticed that there were pictures of this little boy scattered around the room. He looked so much like Mason, Otis. And I just started to freak. My friends tried to calm me down, but I couldn't stand being there for one more second. I ran out the door – and right into Jeff, literally. And he was so nice to me, so caring. And he made me laugh."

I sulked in silence.

"He was really good to me. And I'm not easy. I have a lot of hang-ups, a lot of weird triggers from the PTSD."

"Post-traumatic stress disorder? Like war vets? You have that?"

"Yeah." She shifted, and I heard a quiet *snap*. "You've probably noticed the rubber band? It's part of my therapy. I'm supposed to snap it whenever something sets me off. It's supposed to ground me in the present."

"Does it work?"

A sigh. "It helps. I have things I say to myself, too. Like my name and my address – things like that. Just to remind me where I am."

I couldn't believe how damaged she was by what had happened. How could I never have had a clue? All I knew was that those days of ignorance were gone. It was time to hear all the answers to the questions I'd never dared ask – answers I'd never wanted to know. "Tell me, Meg. Tell me what happened."

She was quiet for a moment. "I've thought about telling you a thousand times," she said. "And you know what? I don't think I can." She found my hand again. "You and I were so close. When Mason died … I felt your pain like it was my own. Because you were part of me."

She was excavating the raw wound inside of me, all my losses bundled up into one tender spot, and it burned and ached.

"You need to, Meg. I need you to."

She was silent for a while, then finally she said, "Okay.

I'll tell you." She took a breath. "It was my Easter candy. I still had it in my room in that basket on my shelf. There were chocolate-covered marshmallow eggs in it – probably stale by then. I found the wrappers."

Breathe.

I remembered that woven pink-and-green basket, remembered exactly where it was on her shelf. Mason would have had to climb for it. He would have been so thrilled at the discovery of the candy inside.

She started sobbing then, her mouth pressed into my shoulder to stifle the noise. "I'm so sorry, Otis!" she wailed. "I wish I hadn't left candy in there! I wish I'd thought of the monitor! I wish I'd—"

"It wasn't your fault." The words were automatic, but of course my mind was already playing the same game: If only she hadn't left candy in there. If only she'd thought of the monitor. *If only if only if only.*

But I knew from watching my mom that this was a game with no winners. And so I shut out the *if only*s – which left only the pain.

Time passed. It was impossible to say how long. Finally, rational thought returned, and I asked, "Is that why you don't eat chocolate anymore?"

I felt her nod in the dark, heard the movement of her head against the sheets. "It's a trigger. I can't stand the sight of it, or even the smell."

Sort of like me with *SpongeBob*, although I knew her things must be ten thousand times worse. I thought for a moment. "What about screaming? That seems to be another trigger, but … if he was…"

If he was choking, how could he scream?

"Not Mason." Her voice was a whisper. "Your mom."

My gut twisted. My mom – God, my mom. "And the windows?" I asked, my voice tight in my throat. "I've seen you rubbing at spots on windows. Is that a Mason thing, too?"

"Yes. Because of the…" She paused, then continued in a shaky voice, "Because of the handprints."

"What handprints?"

"Oh God. I don't want to tell you!"

"Tell me."

"He must have tried to get out, Otis. The sliding-glass doors – you know how they would get stuck… There was chocolate on them, handprints…"

The images – it was unbearable. And poor Meg. The things she had seen…

"We were all in the backyard when it happened. Mr. Esposito was mowing his lawn – if it hadn't been for that, we might have heard Mason banging on the glass."

As Meg wept, I tried to block the images. Mason panicking, unable to draw a breath, banging at the glass… My mom, right there through the door.

Mom. I went weak at the realization of all the things my

mother had been living with. Mason could *see* her through the glass. He tried to get to her, tried to get her to see him, to help him… But she didn't see him! The idea of her knowing that, living with that, split my heart wide open.

"Who found him first?" I asked, pressing my hands into my eyes.

Her muffled cries answered my question.

She turned to me, reached out for me, and I cried uncontrollably. She touched my face with gentle fingers. Said my name. Held me.

And together we grieved.

Later – much, much later, when we were both spent of tears – I propped myself on my side, facing Meg, even though I could see nothing in the dark. I found her hand and held it. "Meg? I'm sorry I wasn't there for you after – after what happened."

"Oh, Otis—"

"No. Let me finish. I'm sorry I couldn't see what was happening to you. I'm sorry I didn't want to listen." I exhaled. "It's so fucked up. All I ever wanted was to be whatever you needed. *Everything* you needed."

It was so silent, she must have been holding her breath. I squeezed her hand. "I never would have knowingly hurt you."

"I know that." She let go of my hand and touched my face. "Otis, it's not your fault. I know how much you were hurting. I know you were doing your best."

She pulled me into a hug. Again we clung to each other, and in those moments, we were in a bubble that nothing could have penetrated. There was only Meg and me.

After a while, she said, "My therapist helped me understand that I needed to find some closure, to face all this again, to face you. Especially with my dad coming back and ... the problems with my mom. So ... he's really been there for me. I'm sorry I had to take his calls. Sometimes I needed to talk to him..."

"Wait, what? When you took those calls? I thought you were talking to Jeff."

"No! That was Dave returning my calls."

I recalled how she dropped everything to answer the phone that first night, and then again after the incident at the pool. So that was her therapist. Not her boyfriend.

"This summer I've been trying to figure out if I could do this. If I could come back. Dave helped me come up with a list of places to visit while I'm here, places that remind me of Mason, to gradually try to become okay, or something closer to okay. I did a few of them – Dairy Queen, Chuck E. Cheese's, stuff like that – but it was hard. And then it turned out ... I couldn't do them all." She let out a long breath. "I don't want to go the rest of my life without you in it, but I don't think I can spend the rest of my life being reminded of Mason."

"I don't want to go the rest of my life without you in it,

either," I told her. "But I can't forget Mason for you."

"I know that. And I'd never want you to."

Was that what we were left with? A no-win situation?

There seemed to be nothing left to say.

We held each other in companionable hopelessness. I listened to her breathing, felt her hand resting on my chest. I didn't know how much time passed, but I started thinking at some point she was going to have to go back to her own room, before the parents woke up and determined that maybe I wasn't as "safe" as everyone assumed. Even if I actually was.

So I savored the last moments with her. I knew that this closeness we'd carved out here tonight was temporary. Because what had we resolved, really? Nothing. The damage wasn't repaired – just illuminated.

She shifted, and her hand moved on my chest – just the tiniest bit, her fingertips skimming my skin. And it felt amazingly good. Also alarmingly good. I whispered, "It's really late. Or early. We'd better get you out of here."

"I guess you're right." She raised her head, her hair tickling my chest. "Good night, Ot." She shifted again, and I could sense how near she was, could feel the warmth of her breath on my face. She leaned in to place a kiss on my cheek, but she missed – or did she? – and her lips grazed mine.

And it flipped me over a hundred and eighty degrees. Did she do it on purpose? Was it an accident?

I hugged her to me, terrified she'd pull away – terrified she *wouldn't*. I heard her inhale sharply, and we hovered there, our lips a millimeter apart.

And then, I don't know who initiated it or how it happened, but it just did, like the pull of the moon. And the moment our lips met, it already wasn't enough. A thousand years of kissing wouldn't have been enough. But I pulled back, needing confirmation that it wasn't just me, that I wasn't misreading her, taking advantage. She pulled me back to her, and with a gentleness that just about cracked me in half, she held my face in her hands and kissed me slowly, softly – like she thought I might break.

And I kissed her back. Every cell of my being wanted to pull her closer, to bury myself inside her, to meld with her. To show her what it could feel like when someone loved you. Hell, to show myself that, too. But I held back, held back everything other than kisses so slow and soft, they were both barely there and more seismic than anything I'd ever known.

I ran my fingers over her hair and down her back, pulling her closer, closer, but she was never close enough. She whispered my name against my mouth as we kissed, which was an indescribable turn-on. She took my hand and slid it under her shirt, onto her back. Her skin was so soft, so hot under my fingers, and the sounds she made as I touched her sent me through the stratosphere.

She ran her hands over my back, my chest, and then her

fingers wandered down, down, brushing over my stomach, nerve endings exploding like supernovas, my heart pounding. I touched her back, her side, hesitating, wanting to touch more of her. She took my hand, tentatively guiding. The room spun as she moved my hand from her rib cage upward. She gasped as I skimmed my fingers over her breast – I pulled away briefly with a smile to *shhh* her – and then resumed, kissing her, touching her, feeling her respond to me in ways that eclipsed every fantasy I'd ever had.

A voice in my head – a very small, faint voice – was suggesting to me that I put an end to this now, as there were few directions left with regard to outcome. I tried to pull away, but Meg pulled me back. "Don't stop," she whispered breathlessly. "Please."

"Oh God. Please don't say please, Meg."

"Please."

And just as my lips started to melt against hers again, my phone rang. I tried to ignore it, but it was such an odd time to get a call…

"Otis, no," Meg whispered when I pulled away.

"Sorry," I whispered. I rolled over and scrabbled to reach my phone on the nightstand, my knee protesting as loudly as other parts of me were.

I checked the screen. It was Abby. "Hello?"

"I'm so glad you answered!" Abby said. "Listen. It's Dara. We had – sort of a fight."

"What happened?" I asked, sitting up, wincing as pain shot through my knee.

"She just started saying all these bizarre things. She wants to move with me to Colorado! I mean, I really like her and everything, Otis, but I'm going to college! I'm not ready to move in together or anything. She said she *loves* me! I mean, we've been going out, what, a couple *weeks*?"

"What did you say to her?" I asked, trying not to sound accusing. I tried to ignore the sound of Meg's rapid breathing, which was distracting.

"I just told her that things were moving too fast, and it wasn't the right time in my life to get that serious, and we should maybe take a step back."

My heart dropped, imagining what it must have been like for Dara to put herself out there like that, only to be shut down. And it kind of pissed me off, that Abby had moved so fast if this was so fucking casual to her. Dara had never let anyone near her before Abby – had never even been *kissed* before Abby.

"What'd she say," I asked, "when you … when you broke up with her?"

"She just went off! And then she started drinking – she has vodka in her dresser drawers, did you know that? And she just got more and more upset until finally she kicked me out."

"When was this?"

"Maybe an hour ago? I've tried calling her, but she won't answer. I thought maybe she'd talk to you."

I rubbed my forehead. "I'll try."

"Call me back!"

I hung up.

"What's going on?" Meg asked, sitting up beside me.

I gave her the rundown.

"Poor Dara," Meg said. Then, tentatively: "But ... isn't this the sort of thing she tends to do? Create drama and wait for you to come to the rescue?"

Although it might look that way to Meg, one thing Dara was *not* was a drama queen. I dialed Dara. To my surprise, she answered.

"Are you okay?" I asked.

"Yeah, why?" She sounded totally calm.

I was baffled. "Abby called me. She said you had a big fight, and you weren't answering the phone."

"I'm fine. I've told you not to worry about me."

I processed that for a second. "Aren't you upset?"

"I'm okay now. It's all good. But I have to go – I have some stuff to do."

"What stuff?" I said. "It's the middle of the night."

"So I keep odd hours. Go to sleep, Mueller. And stop worrying about me. Okay?"

"You sure you're okay?"

"Yeah."

We hung up, but the uneasy feeling stayed with me. "Something's wrong," I said to Meg.

"I thought she said she was okay?" Meg said, reaching out and stroking my arm.

"I know, but…" I thought about it, then shook my head. I was already reaching for my phone.

Meg sighed.

This time Dara didn't answer.

There were a lot of reasons she might not answer. She might not hear the phone. She might be busy. She might be annoyed that I was calling again. But I couldn't rest. I called her again and again, growing increasingly uneasy.

And then she sent a text:

I told you not to worry about me.

And then she sent another:

I'm sorry I never told you I love you.

I paused for about a second. And then I flew into motion.

19

"WHAT ARE YOU GOING TO DO, STEAL YOUR
parents' car and drive there without a license?"

"Yes." Remembering the glass on the floor, I slipped my
shoes on as fast as I could, ignoring my screaming knee, then
went to find the light switch.

"Otis, come on. You're not being rational."

I flicked the switch, and we both squinted in the sudden brightness. I pulled on some clothes and limped to
the bathroom, downing a couple of Motrin while I was in
there. When I came out, Meg was waiting for me in the
hall. "At least wake up your parents and have one of them
drive you," she whispered. "You'll be breaking the law!
What if you get pulled over?"

"My parents will just want to call the cops." I sighed.
"I'm sorry. I know this seems insane to you. But you don't

understand Dara." Maybe she never would. Maybe the only two people in all the world who could understand me and Dara were me and Dara.

"I have to go," I said simply.

She watched me for a moment, then slipped out of my grasp.

And I knew that in Meg's eyes, I'd made my choice: I'd chosen Dara over her. But I couldn't do anything about that; the tug to Dara was too strong. The fact was, my life was with Dara now – it had been for years. Whether Meg came back or not, Dara would be a part of my life. If she was okay.

I couldn't think about any of that, though. I hobbled back to my bedroom and grabbed the mirror box, then took my dad's keys from the hook by the door and headed out.

Our car was in the driveway, fortunately behind Meg's dad's. I eased onto the road and set the navigation lady for home.

As soon as I was on the highway, though, the certainty that had filled me just moments before started draining away. Was I being totally irrational? Meg was right – Dara had acted out before, and eventually she calmed down and things returned to normal. And what if Dara really *was* planning to hurt herself? How could I be sure she'd hold off long enough for me to stop it? Maybe I should call the police after all. But say what? "Dara Svetcova said she loved me. RUN!" I couldn't be sure my gut was right.

Maybe I was just overreacting. And Dara would kill me if I sent the cops to her house and she was fine.

Instead, I latched on to what she'd said about stuff she needed to do. That was pretty common for people who planned to kill themselves, right? To take some time to get their affairs in order? Leave a note or whatever? My stomach twisted at the thought, but I just hoped and prayed that whatever Dara needed to do, it took her at least three hours to do it.

Night morphed into dawn – a time of day that reminded me of Dara like none other. I had seen dawn with almost no one but her, and with her hundreds of times. All those mornings I'd groused and complained about crack-of-dawn practices with her... Right now I'd do anything to make sure they'd continue.

I drove at exactly the speed limit – if I got stopped for speeding on top of driving without a license, I'd never get to her – and took deep breaths to fight down the nausea that rose up in me. I shook all over. And I was so thirsty I drank from a half-full bottle of warm water that had been sitting in the car for weeks.

I argued with myself about whether I should stop to text her and tell her I was on my way. If she knew I was coming, she might wait for me. Or she might see it as a deadline.

No. I was being ridiculous. This was just a bad day. A terrible day. I wasn't there for her. She was alone and upset.

She'd gotten her hopes up – this thing with Abby had given her a new lease on life, and now it was gone and everything looked bleak. I couldn't imagine Dara dying – impossible. She was too huge, too powerful, to just disappear.

But I kept thinking back to her car wreck. It was never entirely clear to me if that crash was an accident. I hadn't pushed very hard for an answer. With a sinking feeling, I realized it was because I didn't want to know.

Hard to ignore where that life strategy had gotten me.

I stepped on the gas a little.

My phone rang an hour into the trip. It was my dad. I didn't answer. My parents continued to ring every few minutes. Abby called, too. I ignored my phone.

Instead I concentrated on the scenery that the rising sun illuminated, the barns and silos and road signs I had seen from the opposite direction a few days before.

But three hours was a long time not to think about Meg, especially with that damn navigation lady reminding me of her every time she piped up with directions. I thought about the kissing, the touching, the things we were doing just hours before. I thought about all that had transpired between us, all the years. Why had I never gotten over her? We had a history – a comfort and a familiarity that I couldn't imagine ever having with someone else. But it was more than that. On some level, I recognized it was about Mason – because Meg was a living link to him. I had never wanted to think about being with someone who'd never known Mason; it seemed an insurmountable gap to bridge. But it occurred to me that it wasn't a good enough reason to cling to Meg – especially because, as it turned out, it was not something we could share. Meg needed to put Mason behind her. And I needed to keep him close. We were at an impasse. I'd spent three years thinking Mason was the bonding point. I never dreamed he was the breaking point.

It was time for me to learn how to let go – and maybe Meg was just another example of that, of my reluctance to move on in life. She had built a new life somewhere else. She'd formed new relationships. She still had a lot of baggage where I was concerned, obviously. Maybe coming back *would* have been a bad idea – maybe it would have been just too much. For both of us.

I tried to sort through it as I made my way back to Chicago. The nearer I got, the more my stomach hurt. My mouth tasted like tin – probably a combination of the stale water and fear. I finally made my way through the city, where I hit some patches of maddening traffic, and up north to Willow Grove.

As I guided the car down Dara's street, all was quiet. No police or ambulance, no signs of trouble.

I jumped out of the car and ran up to the house, ignoring

the pain in my knee. I rang the bell and pounded on the door, rang and pounded.

I called Dara, but she didn't pick up. I texted her to let her know I was at her front door. Nothing.

Four-seven-six-three, a voice in my head said. I punched in the code, opened the door, and went inside.

I ran up the stairs, which was agony on my knee, and to the end of the hall. I pounded on her bedroom door. "Open the door, Dara. It's me."

Nothing.

I tried the knob. It was unlocked. I pushed the door open, my heart in my throat.

She wasn't there.

The rush of relief made me weak. I realized I'd been afraid of what I might find. But where was she?

And what was different? Things looked tidier somehow. My eye was drawn to a place on the floor that seemed oddly empty. And then it hit me: That's where all her swim medals and trophies had sat, heaped in a cardboard box. What had she done with them?

"What are you doing here?"

I jumped. Dara stood in the doorway.

"Jesus!" I clutched my heart. "You scared me." I glanced down. She held three bottles of pills in her hand. "What are you doing?" I asked, my voice weak.

I expected her to yell at me for disobeying orders not to

worry about her. Instead, she closed her eyes. "Why did you have to come?" she whispered.

"Dara?" I walked over to her, and she collapsed into me, limp. I pulled her to the bed and cradled her in my arms, my heart starting to pound. She reeked of booze. Gently, I pulled the bottles out of her hand.

"Dara?" I asked. "Did you take any of these?" I shook her a little. "Dara! Did you take pills?"

"I always take pills," she mumbled back.

"How many?" When she didn't answer, I asked again, louder. *"How many pills, Dara?"*

"I'm tired, Mueller. Let me sleep."

What to do? Call 911 or a suicide hotline? Take her to the ER? I was in way over my head. I scrabbled about in my mind, trying to figure out what someone with a clue would do.

And then I remembered she had a shrink. Surely her shrink would know what to do!

I spotted her purse near the door. As I eased Dara off me and laid her head on her pillow, I noticed that something else was missing. The picture of her mom still sat on her bedside table, but the prayer beads were gone. Where were they? What had she done with her stuff?

I picked up the bottles of pills and hurried into the hall, taking Dara's purse with me. I found her phone in it, with a long stream of worried texts from Abby, and I felt uncomfortable seeing them – they were so personal. I scrolled through her contacts and found a Dr. Singh. The name rang a bell. I dialed, my heart pounding.

Dr. Singh answered. She heard me out and asked a few questions. She sounded calm and competent and in control. Basically everything I wasn't. She said if Dara was suicidal, she had to be admitted to the hospital. "You need to call nine-one-one," she told me. "I'll meet you at the hospital. Don't leave her alone."

I wouldn't.

While I waited for the ambulance, I packed a bag of stuff for Dara to take to the hospital – clothes and her toothbrush and a hairbrush. I tried to find plain shirts, figuring her message tees—"You must be mistaking me for someone who gives a shit" and "Sorry for what happens later" and the like – might not go over well on a psych ward. I wasn't sure what else she needed; it would have to get worked out later.

But there was one thing I knew she might need. I slipped the folding mirror box into her bag, hoping when she found it, she would realize there was someone out there rooting for her, someone who was on her side. Someone who loved her.

I sat on the edge of her bed, checking to make sure she was still breathing, just like the night of her accident. She looked small, fragile. The hair around her scar was growing in, short and choppy. The scar, raised and still red, curved from her forehead into her hairline. More permanent damage. I thought of Meg's words: *the walking wounded*. Yes. That was us. That was all of us.

I tried to prepare myself for what was coming, but when I heard the sirens, a jolt of terror ran through me. I hoped I was doing the right thing. I scooped Dara up in my arms to carry her downstairs so I wouldn't have to leave her alone to answer the door.

"You're gonna be okay," I whispered as I carried her out, my knee screaming at me. "You have to be okay. Please be okay."

"What's happening?" she asked as I hobbled down the stairs. Her voice was groggy. She blinked, as if waking up from a dream and trying to remember where she was. "Why are you crying?"

I turned my face away and pressed my cheek to her head. "I wouldn't know where to start."

When I got home, it was of course to an empty house. It was eerily silent, especially with the central air turned off to save energy during our vacation. I went to the thermostat on the living-room wall and switched it on, then went into the kitchen to get some ice for my poor knee. Then I turned on my phone. It was time to face the music.

I called my parents and gave them the short version of the last five hours of my life. My mother's reaction was something I had coming; I had been unable to let myself contemplate how frantic she must have been, how frightened. She shrieked at me, totally out of control, and I cringed at the thought of the others at the house, hearing everything. Especially Meg. The last thing she should ever have to hear again was the sound of my mother's hysteria.

I hung up and called Abby, who sounded nearly as frantic as my mom had. I hated having to tell her the truth, to put that burden on her, but I knew she'd find out anyway. And I couldn't answer her many questions about what Dara actually did, whether she was okay, whether she could have visitors, whether she would want to see Abby…

"I don't know," I kept saying. And I didn't – I didn't know anything anymore.

I thought about reaching out to Meg. My parents had probably filled her in by now. What could I add? *Sorry for putting Dara before you again? Sorry you're stuck there with my shrieking mother and your ex-boyfriend? Sorry "Operation Willow Grove" was a fail? Sorry you're leaving so soon?*

And what would she even say back? *No worries, maybe I'll see you at Christmas when I come visit my dad?*

Fuck that.

So I did nothing. I didn't have room inside me for any more pain.

As it turned out, though, I was wrong about that. When I limped up the stairs and to my room, I stopped short in the doorway. In the middle of my bedroom floor stood a box.

I tossed the ice pack on my bed and went to investigate. It dawned on me that I'd seen the box before; I recognized the brand of vodka printed on the side. I bent over and pulled the weathered flaps back. When I saw the contents, my heart cracked wide open.

Dara.

I tumbled to the floor, ignoring my screaming knee, and pulled out one of the medals.

CENTRAL ZONE AGE GROUP CHAMPIONSHIPS 13–14 200IM CHAMPION.

ZONE CHAMPION. Jesus. That must have been right before the accident. I held the medal, aching inside. Everything that had ever mattered to Dara was inside this box.

Almost everything. When I pulled myself up into bed to sleep, I found the prayer beads.

They were draped over my picture of Mason.

My parents came home that afternoon in a rental car. I was still sleeping when they came in. I awakened to my mom kneeling by my bed, her hand on my head. I couldn't read her face – it could have been anger, relief, love... Maybe all those things.

"Not now," I said. A plea.

She nodded. "I love you, Otis." She kissed me and left.

I slept until dinnertime. When I woke up, I had messages on my phone. None from Dara; they had taken away her cell phone. She would be permitted to call me at designated times, if she chose to.

There were a bunch of messages from Abby.

And I had a message from Meg: *I hope Dara will be okay. I hope we all will be someday. Whatever "okay" is… I'm headed back to California today. I'll be thinking of you. I'm sorry we didn't get to say a proper goodbye.*

Maybe it wasn't a proper goodbye, but it was a goodbye all the same. I stared at her message a long time before finally texting back, *I'll be thinking of you, too. I always am.*

It would still take some time to process what I should have figured out long ago: that Meg and I weren't bullet-proof after all.

And that maybe our best futures were ones without each other.

To my parents' credit, I never got any harassment about my illegal road trip. They also didn't bring up Meg, and I didn't, either. I didn't know how much they knew – though clearly they knew enough not to raise the subject.

My dad took me to get my license on July 7, the day before Meg's birthday. As much as I'd been looking forward to that event, it was kind of astonishingly anticlimactic.

The next day I sent Meg a brief *happy birthday* message. I couldn't ignore her birthday, but I also wasn't ready to talk, not that I imagined she'd want to. But she replied.

Otis. My birthday is kind of terrible. All I can do is reflect on my failings, especially in Willow Grove. I had a list of things I meant to accomplish, some of which I managed, and some of which proved too hard. This was going to be my redemption trip, my chance to reclaim WG and maybe even reclaim you in some way. But I failed. And maybe it's best, because you deserve better. You told me recently that you had always wanted to be everything to me. I wanted to be that to you, too. But you deserve a girl who can see a smudge on a window and not freak out. A girl who can visit the cemetery with you and listen while you talk about the brother you will always love. A girl who isn't broken.

I will always wish the best for you, Otis.

I read it several times. And I could have written back, *You're not broken,* but to what end? What point was there to a dialogue? I had no interest in doing a postmortem with her. So I left it alone. Even though I could think about little else but her.

She was an unabating ache. Out of nowhere I'd find myself thinking about the things that had happened to her: Finding Mason, too late. Seeing those wrappers. Sitting with me at his grave all those times, trying to bear her grief and my grief, all the while feeling responsible for what had happened. The awful loss of her virginity. The awful loss, in some ways, of her own mother. How alone she had been.

But there was another kind of ache, too: The feeling of being the center of the universe when she tilted her head at me. The incomprehensible splendor of kissing her. The way she took care of Dara the day of the River Park meet.

That bushel of peaches.

I didn't know how I'd ever extricate her from myself. It would take somewhere between a long time and never. And really, if her dad was going to live here and she was going to visit, it leaned more toward never.

She might always be my phantom limb. She might always hurt.

20

THAT PIERCING TWO-FINGER WHISTLE – IT still made me cringe. A metal whistle hung around Dara's neck now, but she preferred to go old-school.

"Out of the pool!" she yelled. "Clearly we need to go over a few things."

I leaned against the wall and smiled as fourteen little swimmers clambered out of the pool and gathered around Dara. She called them the little monkeys.

They called her Coach.

I stood near the door of the high school pool, now reopened after the renovations. I had just finished my own practice, and I was going to run out of time to get some lunch before work if I didn't get out of there soon. But seeing Dara with those kids was something else.

She was doing okay. She was working with a new

neurologist on the phantom limb pain. She was in therapy. Some days were harder than others, but she was trying.

She carried my mirror box in her bag.

She said I saved her life, and maybe that was true. But she saved mine first. It was hard to imagine what would have become of me if she hadn't showed up in my life when Meg left. She picked me up, dusted me off, and kicked my ass. Maybe we all need that from time to time. If we're lucky, there's someone there who cares enough to do it.

"Mueller!" She waved me over.

I sighed and walked toward her.

Dara spoke to the kids. "You guys are looking at our club's record holder in the hundred breast."

A couple of them actually gasped. I blushed, even though it was just a bunch of kids. But I shouldn't have been surprised, because there was no mistaking how pleased Dara was about my swim at Senior Champs. It had been good. The whole meet had been good.

"Mueller," she said. "Show us what arms should be doing in breaststroke."

I demonstrated while Dara pointed out the details of the stroke. "You have to *finish* the stroke, *scoop* that water. You guys try it." She watched as her swimmers imitated my stroke. "Much better! Remember that frog kick. And where do our eyes look when our head is in the water?"

"Down!" a few of them called out.

"That's right, down. Now go kick some ass – I mean, butt." They giggled and scurried back to the pool, some of them practicing the arm motions as they went.

"Any Olympic material here?" I asked Dara.

She squinted. "I have my eye on that Hannah Swanson kid. She's a fast learner, and she's wicked tough."

"Tough is good."

"Tough is important."

Dara had finally let go of her Olympic dreams for me. We modified my goals to qualifying for State in the hundred breast as well as the medley relay. I was happy with that. And Dara – well, she might not have been *happy* about it, but she accepted it. That was all the victory I could ask for. I knew better than anyone that sometimes just letting something go can be a victory in itself.

"Look at her." She pointed to the head bobbing down the lane, yards ahead of the others. "See that? She could be a winner."

We stood watching for a while. Dara was right: that Hannah kid was a different breed from the rest.

"Hey," she said, after a moment.

I glanced at her.

"I got a card from Meg."

That was about the last thing I expected to hear. And yet there was nothing surprising about it.

"Have you talked to her?"

I shook my head.

She watched me for a moment. "Mueller. Don't you think it's—?"

"Leave it," I said quietly.

She left it. We watched the kids for a minute. Then she asked, "How's your therapy going?"

"It's okay," I said. "She wants me to keep a journal." Basically, I guess I was still trying to learn how to talk. I didn't mind the journaling, actually. Even though it made me think of Meg and her journal, which somehow only seemed to emphasize the distance between us.

Dara nodded, not taking her eyes from the pool. "My therapist wants my dad and me to have dinner together three nights a week. So get this: my dad hired a personal chef. We have a dinner date at home on Mondays, Wednesdays, and Fridays. He's supposed to stop traveling so much."

Yikes. "Well, that's nice," I tried.

She turned to me and grabbed a fistful of my T-shirt. "You have to come to dinner tonight. You *have* to."

I shook my head, smiling gently. "You're on your own this time." I shrugged. "Maybe it won't be so bad."

She gave me an *Are you kidding me?* look. "Otis. *Please.* Just for this first time."

"I can't."

"Oh, come on. You're not doing anything and we both know it."

I glanced down at my feet. "Today's the anniversary of Mason's death. I'm going to the cemetery after work."

Dara let go of my shirt and smoothed the wrinkles out. She chewed her lip for a second, then stepped over to the pool and did her two-finger whistle. When all the heads had popped up, she yelled, "Who wants to come to my house for dinner tonight?"

This was met with a loud chorus of *meeee*s and a flurry of hands frantically waving in the air.

Dara gave me a sidelong look, a smug smile working its way to the surface.

I laughed and headed out.

It was after five by the time I'd finished with lessons and showered off. My parents had gone to the cemetery first thing in the morning, as they always did. Because of swim practice and my work schedule, we decided to go separately.

Dara had finally traded in the Stupidmobile – for two rusted clunkers and a sizable wad of cash. The money she donated to the Wounded Warrior Project, which seemed just right to me. One of the cars was for her, to replace her beloved old Corolla.

The other was for me.

Mine was a fifteen-year-old Maxima – gray where it wasn't rusted, with a dent in the driver's-side door. Dara had positively beamed as she showed me its dubious virtues.

It was a stick shift, of course. The stereo system had been upgraded with an amp and a subwoofer. And the engine had been tweaked so it had some good muscle – a stamp of approval from my unlikely driving mentor, although she acknowledged it would be wasted on my "pussy driving."

I drove to the cemetery with the windows down, the warm summer breeze streaming through my damp hair. The sun was starting its descent earlier now. Soon school would start. Dara wouldn't be there. Meg wouldn't be there. And I could only hope that it wouldn't always be as painful as it was now.

I pulled into the landscaped entrance, all low pink and white flowers and taller stalky purple things. On the lawn to the right, some men were moving one of those casket-lowering devices, and I choked under a sudden flash of memory: Mason's casket. So small; so terribly, bizarrely, wrongly small. The tears sprang up, fierce and surprising; it was maybe the first time I had remembered the casket with such clarity. There was so much I had pushed away, for so long. Despite my therapist's confidence, I wasn't sure I was up to the task of remembering. If something is unbearable, then how do you bear it? It's an oxymoron.

And yet I was here, wasn't I? Somehow I was bearing it.

I parked the car and headed up the familiar, winding lane, trying to breathe through the ache in my chest.

The cemetery was oddly beautiful in all seasons. At this time of year, it was as green as hope itself. In a few months, reds and yellows would color the trees and blanket the grass. Later, when I came back for Mason's birthday, all would be bare and still, with or without a coating of snow.

I made my way past the familiar rows of tombstones, pausing as I often did at ESTHER B. CROMWELL, 1899–2002. Esther had survived to see three different centuries, and my brother was barely a blip in one.

From a distance I could see a large bouquet of flowers at Mason's grave, evidence of my parents' earlier visit. White flowers, the flowers of the dead... Mason probably would have preferred a little color.

And then a flash of yellow caught my eye – something small and bright, nestled in the grass against his headstone. I squinted as I approached, trying to make it out. I squatted down, and as I reached for it, my breath caught.

A dump truck.

Warmth surged through me.

She'd been here. She'd come. She'd come *back*. Why did she? As part of her own healing? Or was she stretching herself beyond her limits, as she had done years before, out of love for me? Was there a message in this gesture, or was this just my wishful thinking at work?

It only could have come from her. My parents left only white flowers, never toys. A dump truck – *dumb fuck*... That could only be Meg. I scanned the cemetery, in case she was still there, but I saw no sign of her.

I turned to Mason's headstone, reading it through blurred eyes, my heart aching with all the love and sorrow contained in those seven words: MASON LUKE MUELLER. FOREVER IN OUR HEARTS.

I lowered myself to the ground and sat in the grass. Not being much for talking to God, I talked to Mason instead.

Mason, it's four years now that you've been gone. If you were here, you'd be seven. Seven! You'd be starting second grade this fall. I try to imagine what you'd look like, what you'd sound like, but I can't. I'll always wonder what you'd be like if you were still here. When I graduate high school, when I get married, when I have kids, when Mom and Dad get old... I'll always be thinking of you, wishing for you. It's never going to stop hurting; I know that now. But even though it hurts, I will carry you with me. I hope that, wherever you are, you carry me with you, too.

My closed eyes heightened my sense of surroundings: The sun dappling my face. The sweet, green smell of deep summer. The distant hum of highway traffic and, closer, the unmistakable coo of a mourning dove. The feel of the toy truck, smooth and slightly warm from the sun.

When I opened my eyes, I turned the truck over in my hands and realized there was something underneath the dump bed, taped to the base of the truck. I lifted the bed and discovered paper, tightly folded. I carefully removed the tape and opened it, my heart pounding.

There were two pages, both in Meg's handwriting, round and small.

I read the top one first. Its ragged edges suggested it came from some kind of notebook. It was dated over a year ago:

> *Your card came today. I wish I could tell you how much it means to me. I keep staring at that familiar handwriting, so small and boyish but so weirdly neat. I will keep it with the other notes you gave me. I've saved them all.*
>
> *Cassie was a good ol' girl, you're right. When you said you missed her, it made my heart ache, but when you said you missed me, too? It was almost too much.*
>
> *I miss you, too, Otis. Every day. But you probably wouldn't even want the "me" I am now. Some days it feels like there is nothing I haven't ruined, especially myself. I'm trying to move on, but mostly what I wish is that I could turn back time. If I could do just one thing different, we'd still have Mason, and you'd still have me, and I'd still have you. And everything would be better if I still had you.*
>
> *Love, Meg*

My eyes stung. I couldn't stand to think of her hurting so badly, all that time. It was tempting to think, *if only* she'd reached out to me sooner, *if only* I'd noticed how much pain she'd been in. But I knew better than anyone the futility of *if onlys*. We can't turn back time. But we can try to see things how they were, how they are. And we can try to learn from them, to make the tomorrows better.

I flipped to the second piece of paper.

> Dear Otis,
>
> If you are reading this, it means I achieved the final item on my list: the cemetery.
>
> It means I visited Mason and left him this dumb fuck.
>
> It means I sat at his grave and told him how amazing his big brother turned out to be, and how much I miss both of you.
>
> When my dad and I got back to our hotel room after Michigan, I found your magnolia poem slipped under the door, with a note scrawled at the bottom: "DO NOT FUCK THIS UP." Dara, I presume. And since we had a deal about that poem, I've left you a page from my journal. I hope it helps you see that even when we were far apart, I was always thinking of you.
>
> The thing about not coming back to Willow Grove is that staying away does not resolve the Mason problem. He is in my thoughts, my memories, my triggers, my dreams. He's forever in my heart, like his headstone says. That doesn't change, whether I'm in Willow Grove or somewhere else. And when it comes down to it, I would rather face the pain of Mason than face the pain of losing you – again.

I love you, Otis. There was never a time when I didn't.

New hope illuminates days dimmed by grief;
You are and e'er shall be my heart's relief.

*Is that really how you feel? Because it is very much how
I feel. And if you still feel that way, and if you wouldn't
mind having me around, I would very much like to come
back to Willow Grove. To stay.*

*So if you have any interest in seeing a girl who loves
you, I am here – back at the Extended Stay, room 118.
Shaking like beef. Wanting to not fuck this up. Hoping
there's a chance your navigation lady is still set to me.*

Yours with so much love,
Meg

I folded up the note and set the dump truck against
Mason's headstone, then sat there, overwhelmed. When I
could stand, I got up and made my way down the path to
my car.

I imagined our first unspoken compromise taking shape.
*You will come to the cemetery if I really want you to, but I mostly
will go on my own. When I come home, you will hold me. And you
will remember Mason with me, but I won't stew in the past because
I know that our life is right here, right now. I will try harder to
listen, and when I try to talk, no matter how inept the effort, you
will tilt your head at me and make me feel important and loved.*

I will do the driving. You will decide how much sriracha sauce to put on our food. And I will always, always check for ducks for you.

I yanked the car door open, which took some force because of the dent. I suspected this was one of the things Dara liked about the car: the damage. But damaged doesn't necessarily mean broken.

I closed the door and sat, staring at Meg's note. How had this even happened? How? I thought about the sonnet, trying to figure out how Dara had done that. And then I remembered: I'd put that sonnet in my swim bag. I'd left my swim bag in Dara's car. A + B = this. All this.

I started up the car and put all the windows down, thinking about my last conversation with Dara, right before I tore out of Michigan. I guess my house wasn't her only errand on what was meant to be her final to-do list.

It was a lot, realizing how she had wanted to set things right. How she had wanted to give me in death what she couldn't in life: Freedom. Happiness. A glimpse of how much she loved me. I had underestimated her so many times, in so many ways. It hurt. But I knew her better now. She was a wonder. And she broke my fucking heart. Which was already broken a million ways to Tuesday, but ... hearts can break a lot. That is a thing I know.

But broken doesn't necessarily mean damaged.

As I put the car into gear, a crescendo of chirps filled the air. I turned my head to the sound, and a million little birds launched skyward from the hedges in a flurry of bright yellow. I watched them disappear into the sky, then eased out of the lot and made my way to Highway 43, headed straight for the Extended Stay. My navigation lady was *always* set to Meg.

There were no guarantees for Meg and me. I knew that. But I was hopeful. Hopeful we'd endure. Hopeful that next May, when the magnolia bloomed again, it would find us together. But even that couldn't be the perfect, sepia-toned image I'd always held in my mind. Because *we* weren't the same. We were battered and dinged, both well past the weight limit in personal baggage. And, like the rest of humanity, it would be our destiny to be tossed and torn by events unseen and unplanned.

But that didn't stop me from hoping we could somehow navigate it together.

Long odds, I realized. But holding on always was my strong suit.

Enjoyed *Phantom Limbs*?
We'd love to hear your thoughts.

#PhantomLimbs @paulajgarner
🐦 @WalkerBooksUK @WalkerBooksYA

📷 @WalkerBooksYA

ACKNOWLEDGEMENTS

There are so many people who made their mark on this book, and I owe them more thanks and recognition than I can even begin to express.

Zach. My swimmer, my eater, my brilliant boy. It is thanks to you more than anyone else that this novel made it to this day. Your unflagging love, devotion, and encouragement over the years kept me from ever giving up. No matter how many times I had doubts, you never did. Thank you for your steadfast support and love – and for all the ways you made sure I wasn't screwing up the swimming parts too badly. You are a phenomenal person, and I am so glad you're mine.

Gabe, my other sweet and brilliant son. Thank you for enduring the years I told you that you weren't old enough for this book – and then for loving it when I finally let you read it. Since then you have helped me make countless decisions and have lent your own particular brand of savvy to everything, and I am kind of glad in the end that this process took long enough that both you and Zach were a part of it. I adore you, but who doesn't? Go clean your room.

Thanks also are due to the lovely Mia Drelich for quick and helpful answers when I messaged with a question during writing. Mia, you are the ultimate teen consultant – bright and funny and sweet – and you never let me down. Thank you for your cheerful and reliable willingness to help.

A great debt of gratitude goes to Noah, my husband, for his limitless support and patience during all the years I've worked on novel writing. Thank you for never once suggesting I maybe get a paying job, and thank you for not complaining about a lot of pizza delivery for dinner when I was in the thick of things. Your belief in me made everything possible, and I will always be grateful for it.

Endless thanks go to Audrey Coulthurst, my unfathomably amazing critique partner, my all-things-bitter disciple, my salmiak sister, my dolty and devoted friend. Aud, you are the greatest CP a writer could ever hope for; I would never want to do any of this without you. Thank you for reading my work so carefully, for keeping me sane and calm, for doing confusing tech things for me, and for making sure

I don't screw things up (and fixing them when I do). From tracking my novel timelines to helping me problem-solve to keeping me from getting fired on forums, you have been impossibly generous and wonderful to me, and being your CP for your gorgeous novel has been a privilege. Plus, your deranged sense of humor is the source of boundless hilarity – you are ridiculously fun and you make me laugh like no one else. TL;DR: I'm keeping you.

Enormous gratitude goes to Rafe Posey, my incomparable critique partner, my twin anachronism, my museum of favorite things, and the person who understands without explanation everything I think/say/feel/do. Pet, you are a wonder and a treasure, and I wouldn't trade you for anything. Thank you for all the grand adventures, for all the places and nouns, for all the things you have shown me and taught me – things I always wanted to know and things I never knew I wanted to know. Your nerdy and pedantic proclivities have come to the rescue time and time again in my work, and your love for this novel was a constant source of reassurance. It is an honor to be your critique partner, and reading your beautiful writing is one of my greatest joys. You amaze me every day. NOW GO DO SOME WORK OMG SO POKEY.

To Kaylan, my wise, devoted, insightful editor: I wish every writer could at least once have an experience like the one I've had with you. The level of thoughtfulness and care you brought to this book completely blew me away. This process with you was such a privilege, and I am so pleased with the ways you helped me shape this book into what it is today. You knew when to defer and when to push, when to make suggestions and when to leave me to it, and you were always, always there to answer questions or offer help. Your contribution meant everything to me, and I am so grateful to have you in my corner.

Thanks also to the incredible team at Candlewick – Matt Roeser, Nathan Pyritz, Maggie Deslaurier, Erin DeWitt, Susan Batcheller, Tracy Miracle, Elise Supovitz, and many others whose names I may not know. I am honored by your support and your thoughtful and beautiful work on this book.

Many thanks to my agent, Molly Jaffa. You are my favorite study in contrasts: sweet yet fierce, hilarious yet serious, encouraging yet ass-kicking. Your belief in this novel and your sure hand with decisions along the way were always reassuring and calming. I wouldn't trade your knowledge, guidance, and hand-holding on this journey for anything.

Thanks go to Bonnie Blackburn and Leofranc Holford-Strevens for ongoing thoughtfulness and generosity in fielding questions no one else I know could possibly have answered.

To my many amazing beta readers and writer friends,

thank you endlessly for your help, support, and friendship. There are too many to name you all, but I would be remiss not to mention Marieke Nijkamp, Helen Wiley, Susan Bickford, Rachel Solomon, Jessica Bayliss, and Brian Katcher, whose thoughtful reading and feedback were enormously helpful in guiding this process.

A big thank-you to Tena Russ, my beautiful ogre, for the high bar you set (and for the pleasure of reading your lovely pages).

Much appreciation goes to Jessica Golub, who fielded questions along the way and always offered helpful insights and suggestions. (Thank you also to Lauren, who was gloriously impatient to read this book. Finally, right?)

For a variety of reasons, special thanks go to: Elissa Whiteman, Harriet Heifetz, Adelle Katz, Sybil Ward, Lindsey Sprague, Brenda Drake, Katie Locke, Dahlia Adler, Rachel Simon, and Mark O'Brien.

Special thanks to Ashley Herring Blake, Karen Hattrup, Emily Henry, Kerry Kletter, Kali Wallace, and Jeff Zentner for your early reads and overwhelming responses. Your generosity means the world to me.

To all my fellow Sweet Sixteeners and 2k16ers, thank you for the pleasure of your company and friendship on this ride. It has been a privilege to feel your support and to cheer you on in return.

And finally, a sheepish thank-you to Otis Heymann.

I stole your name for this book in 2008 when I first saw you at a swim meet and there were girls fawning over how cute you were. I hope you don't mind.

PAULA GARNER lives in Chicago with her family and their psychotic cat. *Phantom Limbs* is her first novel.

Lennie Walker, seventeen, Wuthering Heights
obsessed, clarinet player, band geek. Also hopeless
romantic, prone to scattering poems all over town
and, as of four weeks ago, sisterless...

A heart-breaking, heart-lifting, utterly
compelling and completely unforgettable
novel about first love and first loss.

"Heartwarming." *The Independent*

Jude and her twin Noah are close until a tragedy
drives them apart. Now they are barely speaking –
and both falling for boys they can't have.
Love's complicated.

**"This is the big one – the BLAZING story
of once inseparable twins whose lives are
torn apart by tragedy."** *Entertainment Weekly*

New York Times bestseller

That year she found the power
to be extraordinary

That year she found the power to be extraordinary

With a grandmother from China and another from Ghana,
fifteen-year-old Wing Jones is often caught between worlds. When
tragedy strikes, she discovers an extraordinary talent she never
knew she had. Wing's running could bring her family everything
it needs. It could also keep Wing from the one thing she truly wants.

"I loved Wing Jones. And it makes you
want to pull on your shoes and start running."
Katherine Rundell

"In her darkest time, Wing finds her own strength.
I fell in love with Wing Jones and you will too."
Laini Taylor

A POWERFUL AND BRAVE NOVEL ABOUT WHAT PREJUDICE LOOKS LIKE

Sixteen-year-old Starr lives in two worlds: the poor neighbourhood where she was born and raised and her posh high school in the suburbs. The uneasy balance between them is shattered when Starr is the only witness to the fatal shooting of her unarmed best friend, Khalil, by a police officer. Now what Starr says could destroy her community. It could also get her killed.

"Angie Thomas has written a stunning, brilliant, gut-wrenching novel that will be remembered as a classic of our time." JOHN GREEN

Lina is spending the summer in Tuscany, fulfilling her
mother's dying wish that she should get to know her father.
With the help of her mother's journal, Lina uncovers a
magical world of secret romance, art and hidden bakeries.
People come to Italy for love and gelato, someone tells her,
but sometimes they discover much more.

*"The reader will
find it difficult to put this book down."*
VOYA (starred review)

*"A sure bet for fans of romance fiction and
armchair travel."*
Kirkus